------The Jewele

THE JEWELER'S DAUGHTER

BY

JANICE WILLIAMS

------The Jeweler's Daughter------

Author: Janice Williams

Title: The Jeweler's Daughter

First edition July15, 2020 without

ISBN: 9798574999455

First and foremost, I thank God for the imagination I was blessed with.

Thank you to my husband, Rick, who encouraged me to pursue my passion for writing.

Many thanks to my sister, Linda, my niece Madison and nephew Jack, who were *captive* listeners on road trips during development.

Thank you to my sister, Debbie, who stayed up into the wee hours of the mornings reviewing chapters.

To my sister in-law, Melodee, thanks for all the help with my first draft.

****

------The Jeweler's Daughter------

TABLE OF CONTENTS

CHAPTER ONE

Anna stood next to Papa, taking in the sight of the beautiful gemstones. She loved it when he poured the gems out of their little bags onto the black velvet. She took one of the bags, opened its drawstring, and gently poured the shimmering stones through her fingers, letting them cascade onto the velvet like a rainbow waterfall.

"Be very careful, Anna," admonished Papa. "They're our livelihood and must be handled with extreme care." Still, she let them gently flow through her fingers, watching the different hues create colorful prisms under Papa's work lamp. Little did Anna realize that one day, all that glitter was going to pay for her survival.

Joseph separated the stones, found the ones he wanted to include in a piece he was working on, then put the remaining gems back in their bags, placing them in the safe. Normally, he worked long days, but the Nazi hatred of Jews was driving him out of business. Dusseldorf had once been beautiful, but now, Nazi troop occupation and Jewish hate graffiti covered the once pristine city, making Joseph fume to himself. He thought Anna was somewhat oblivious to their situation, but little did he know, her naivety was only in his mind. Anna's parents were unaware that, each night, she crouched down on her bedroom floor and listened to their desperation through the crack under the door.

Everything packed away for the moment, Joseph grabbed Anna, giving her a big hug.

"How about a short hike today, my little gem?" he asked, squeezing her a little tighter.

"You bet, Papa! Let me grab my sweater first." The outdoors was a passion they both shared. Anna was glad he had more time these days. He always had ideas to make a normal day seem like an adventure. Even though she was seventeen, well into her "difficult" teens, she loved to spend time with her parents.

"I'm ready!"

Joseph threw a small pack over his shoulder, as they strolled out the back door and into the woods.

"Why do you love the woods so much, Papa?"

"I suppose for the solitude, the sound of peace from the city. There's nothing ugly out here," he muttered, more under his breath than aloud. "Sitting in one spot working with small stones all day is tense. I need to get out and stretch sometimes. Besides, I get to spend time with my favorite gem, you," he said with a smile.

Anna smiled back at him. She loved it when he called her his favorite little gem.

"Papa?" Somewhere in their conversation, she had lost his attention. "Papa?"

Joseph broke from his trance. "Anna, the world's gotten ugly. I need to talk to you about staying safe." Sitting on a fallen log, he motioned for her to sit next to him. "I don't know if I will always be able to protect you from what's happening. Germans hate us, and this war scares me."

"Not all German's hate us, Papa. Peter and Mr. Reinhold don't. They'd never turn on us."

"Hmm… probably true, but you need to be prepared, and you shouldn't trust *anyone*."

It didn't seem like war to Anna. At most, she thought it was a momentary lapse in the government's judgment.

Papa took Anna's hands, gently caressing the tops of them. "It's time you understand what's really happening in the world. I have important things that I need to teach you. I pray you'll never need them, but you will be prepared." He was scaring her!

She could feel the hairs stand up on the back of her neck, goose bumps prickling her skin. She pulled her hands away, not wanting to listen.

"Papa, I'm not ten anymore. I know what's going on. I think the hate splattered over our windows and being forced to wear a yellow star, says a lot."

"It's not just graffiti, yellow stars and outright hatred anymore. Things are changing."

Anna knew things were, but she tried to ignore it.

"You're lucky. You don't have the Jewish features. Your great grandfather was a dark blond-haired German boy with hazel eyes. You resemble him. It's a blessing, Anna."

Mama and Papa always said she didn't look very Jewish, and it had always bothered her. She wanted to look like them, not some long-lost relative she didn't even know. Perhaps he was right, though; maybe there was a reason for her unconventional looks.

That day, indoctrination into "living invisible," without being seen or heard, began. Anna's life was going into stealth mode.

"Anna, you should always have a place to hide. Only you, Mama, and I should know where it is. You need to learn how to live out of sight, where no one will look for you."

"But why? Can't I just go to the Reinholds'?"

"No!", he shouted angrily, shaking his head violently. He had never raised his voice to her like that before, and she started to cry. "I'm sorry, my little gem," he said softly, pulling her into a hug. "I'm scared for you. The world's turning ugly, and this is the only way I know how to help you."

"But you and Mama will be with me." Her lip was quivering uncontrollably now.

His shoulders drooped in defeat. "We may or may not be. We can't be sure, so I want to prepare you for the worst. Okay?"

All she could do was nod her head. She understood that the boycotts the Nazis had instigated against the Jews was hurting their business. She was thankful Papa was a jeweler. Even though Germans weren't supposed to give patronage to their store, they did anyway, except they only paid a tenth what each piece was worth.

"Will we lose our home?" she asked, scared of what he might say.

"We have a home for now, but harder times are coming, and if we have to move, we'll cross that bridge when it comes."

Papa looked sad, and for the first time, old. She'd never thought of him like that. He had always been quick to laugh and positive about everything. If anyone could find a silver lining in something, it was him.

"I don't want to move," she said angrily, crossing her arms in defiance. Her eyes were burning, trying to hold back the tears. "My friends are here. This is my home!" The tears won, spilling down her cheeks. "Why do people hate us just because we're Jewish?"

Papa lifted her chin and gently wiped her tears away. "Oh, my little gem, Mama and I want to stay in our home too, but we don't always get what we want."

After that, Anna started really listening to her so-called friends. She knew they had been distant, but now she understood what her parents had been saying. It's amazing what you hear when you *really* listen. The words "dirty Jew" and other expletives were extremely common.

Her parents had always allowed her to stay naive, encouraged it even, but those days were over. She was growing up faster than a speeding train now. There was no choice.

The neighbor girls would no longer hang out with her. She was "diseased," and they would chant as much in unison, noses in the air, laughing as they all went off together. She was stunned, but mainly hurt. Even her best friend, Margaret, would no longer talk to her. They had been best friends since they were five. Many times, she'd sneak up to her room without Mama seeing her, crawl under the bedcovers, and cry.

The only person who still talked to her was Peter, who lived next door. He was almost nineteen, two years older than her. All the girls had a crush on him. He was tall, with broad shoulders, sandy-blond hair, crystal-blue eyes, and a big smile that showed off two huge dimples. There was no denying, Peter was handsome.

Peter's mother had died when he was ten, so Mama had helped fill the void. There were times when Peter would come over after he and his father had a disagreement. Mama would hug him, fill him with milk and cookies, and just love him. He would eventually saunter home to make up with his father. Peter was a huge part of the Feiner family, and Anna was glad. She liked Peter, not like other girls, but like the brother she wished she had. Not that she hadn't noticed how his T-shirt stretched tight across his chest when he was baking, or how his biceps popped out when he hefted bags of flour. Peter made her feel safe.

Peter's father owned the local bakery shop next door. They lived on the top floor of their business like the Feiners. Peter worked there after school and most weekends, so they had happily grown up together. Occasionally, on a slow day, Peter's father, Mr. Reinhold, would let Peter grab his bike, and they'd go riding for hours in the park. Mr. Reinhold was a gentle man, always ready with a smile and kind word. He was rather rotund from working in the bakery and sampling his own goodies.

"Anna," he would say, when she came into the bakery, "taste this. Isn't it delicious?"

Everything was delicious to him. She'd pop a piece of pastry into her mouth, nodding her head in agreement that he was justified in his assessment of delicious. She loved the bakery. Most days she could smell the aroma of warm, fresh-baked bread waft over to their windows, making her mouth water.

Things began to change now when Anna went to the bakery. Mr. Reinhold just nodded, smiled, but never said much anymore. At most, he would say hello, and then busy himself at the ovens.

"Peter, is your father mad at us now too, like everyone else?"

"No!   It's not you. We've been told not to associate with anyone who's Jewish. The Government's watching us, and so are the neighbors. If we're too friendly, we can lose our business and be considered traitors to the Führer.   It's not you, Anna, or your family. We don't agree with what's happening, but my father has to protect our livelihood, and he's afraid for your family too." Peter hadn't looked her in the eyes, ashamed with the choices being made. He loved Anna and her family.

****

CHAPTER TWO

L ife used to feel like it was moving in slow-motion, but now it was speeding to a destiny that scared Anna. The atmosphere that had once been filled with laughter around the dinner table had been replaced with fear that someone in a German uniform would come pounding on their door. Neighbors were prone to tell the Nazis lies about Jewish neighbors, causing the Gestapo to break into their homes.

The table was always set with beautiful dishes and the best silver, but it felt like everything could come crashing down in an instant! Dinner was no longer a full course meal, but consisted of what little meat they could find, canned vegetables, and bread the Reinhold's still secretly sold them.

It was hard trying to live a normal life. Jews had curfews, could only shop in designated places, had fewer rations than Germans, could no longer use the transportation system, and a multitude of other stifling laws froze them from a regular life.

A few days had passed since Papa had first spoken to her about learning to live invisibly. The conversation was always about German troop activities, what new law was stifling the Jewish community, and last, survival, survival, survival! It felt like she was sitting at the movie theater waiting to see what the end would be, only now, she just wanted to rewind to when life was good.

Anna was so tired of listening to Papa talk about what gear they had to procure for her to live in secret, invisible to the world. She didn't want to be invisible, she wanted everyone to *see* Anna Feiner.

"Anna, you need to be prepared to live on your own, to not have to depend on us," he said during dinner one night. She froze, her fork inches from her mouth. Mama slowly put her fork down and started to cry.

Turning to Mama, his voice came out soft but firm. "It's time, Miriam. If we don't prepare her for the worst now, then we've failed her."

Mama nodded her head, acknowledging he was right, but the tears kept rolling down her cheeks. Papa reached over and pulled her hand into his, caressing the top of it.

"It'll be okay," he whispered. He continued to stroke her hand until she quit sobbing. Anna smiled at Mama, trying to pretend it would be okay.

"I know you're thinking of what's best for her," she sighed. "I'm just worried."

Papa's head bobbed up and down, showing that he understood, and then he turned his attention to Anna.

"You're to go on your own tomorrow and look for a hiding place. You need to learn to be resourceful without us."

He set the parameters for her; close to a creek or river for water, close to the woods for escape, yet close to a town in case she needed to scavenge for food.

"You're not to be seen," he reiterated. "It must be a place that you can get to fairly quickly."

The next morning, Anna headed out the back door to start her search. Heading into the tree line, she flinched as someone yelled at her. Looking back, she saw Peter waving, running to catch up to her.

"Hey!" yelled Peter. "Wait up!"

Anna felt the panic rise. "No," she groaned. Of all the days for him to see her! There was no way he could come with her. Papa would have a fit.

"Where are you going? If you wait until I get my work done, I'll come with you," he said, puffing hard from running to catch up. She didn't want to hurt his feelings, but he was not part of the plan.

"I'm just heading out to look for mushrooms," she lied, shrugging her shoulders. "Mama wants me to hurry so I can't wait, but maybe we could go together in the next couple days." Peter looked dejected, but he still remembered how mothers could be when they wanted you to do something and get it done.

"Okay," he said, obviously disappointed.

Anna smiled and said, "maybe next time." She was thinking what she wouldn't do to have Peter along now. Turning back toward the hills, Anna hiked into the trees and disappeared. She felt guilty not letting him in on her secret. They shared everything, but Papa insisted they couldn't trust anyone, not even Peter, and if she told him, then she put him in danger.

She had a full day to look for a hiding place. The creek gurgled below as she wound through the trees. Mama wasn't fond of the outdoors, other than picnics, but Anna had gone on many walks and had also been camping with Papa in the surrounding woods. She was familiar with the area which was essential to staying safe. *Well, one part accomplished,* she thought, making a mental check off the list. Water. Papa would be happy.

Anna was tired, fighting the brush and tree limbs, and the day was heading to high noon. She could tell because the sun was high in the sky, and her stomach was fairly good telling time. She had nothing to eat and thought of heading back, but she knew Papa would be upset that she'd given in so quickly and had left unprepared. She should have brought something to eat but hadn't thought about it. Her first day, and she was already failing! This was something Papa would have thought of. He probably knew she'd left without food but would let her learn a lesson.

Anna marched on, stopping only for a cold drink of water from the creek to quench her thirst. No one was in sight, and the only sound was the water rushing over the rocks and slight wind rustling through the treetops. Occasionally, a squirrel would scurry about, but other than that, she was alone, which felt scary. The forest was always a little dark during the day, and pitch black at night. She looked for hours for somewhere to hide, a hollow tree, a rock enclave, but nothing stood out. She was disappointed she was going home empty-handed but also elated, as she had no intention of living on her own.

Anna trudged home, knowing Papa was hoping for good news. If she was truthful, she would admit to him that she hadn't tried that hard. She wouldn't need to live in the woods, so why go to all the effort?

Dusk was setting in as she came into the house. Both Mama and Papa were there, sitting at the kitchen table, talking.

"Hi Mama, Papa," she greeted, hoping they wouldn't ask any questions. Of course, Papa wanted to know how it went.

"I looked, but I didn't see anything worthy of living in." Her eyes couldn't meet his, because she knew she hadn't tried hard.

He just nodded. "Another day," he said. "It's only been your first day and finding a good hiding place can take time." There was no judgment or disappointment, just a nod to try again.

It was the same routine for the next month, sent out to look for a hiding place on her own. Each time, she came back tired and with no news. Anna thought that, over time, he would give up and just let things be, but she was strongly mistaken.

Every day more Nazi troops scattered the city, and the town became more hostile. They were called filthy names, spit on, and had rocks thrown at them.

It wasn't hard to know who was Jewish because the mandatory yellow star worn by all Jews, branded them the Führer's enemies. Those not complying were dragged off to work camps or certain death. Jewish owned businesses were branded as well. Huge Star of David symbols were painted boldly across their doors and windows, warning true Nazi followers not to patronage those stores, the Feiners' included. This made Papa more determined for Anna to hunt for a place to hide.

Anna was so tired of searching, but Papa sent her out day after day. Life was becoming more unstable, and he was relentless in forcing her to explore for someplace to hide.

Avoiding Peter was wearing on her. Seeing the look of rejection on his face each day made life seems unbearable. She could tell he thought something was wrong between them, and it bothered her. He was her confidant, and now she wasn't allowed to tell him anything.

Today, Anna was determined to go beyond her comfort zone, past the places she'd been before. Packing up a rucksack for a long day, she slung it on her back and headed into the woods. Hiking deep into the forest for a good two hours, she searched every nook and cranny, hoping to find a space that could be considered livable. She was covered in dirt and grime, but she kept at it.

Finally, coming to the edge of the forest, she spied an open field that had been plowed up into multiple piles of huge berms, tree trunks and branches layered on top of each other, intertwined into huge piles. Anna tucked herself safely into the bushes at the edge of the field, taking in the surroundings. A farmhouse sat well beyond the fields, what looked to be a good seven to eight acres away.

The field had been plowed up but left unplanted except closer to the house, where corn sprouted in neat rows, stretching skyward. The wood berms had been pushed toward the forest's edge, making room for as much planting as possible. Most of the land still lay unplanted, though, obviously stopped by the Führer's need to feed his army with men rather than food for his people.

Most men had been called to duty, leaving the women and young children to tend to daily farm chores, resulting in a large percentage of farmland void of crops.

Off in the distance, the farmhouse blew smoke from its chimney. The house was close enough to see, but far enough away for comfort. Staying hidden behind the trees, Anna walked along the edge of the field. She knew the fields had been left stagnant because weeds grew where crops should have sprouted. The berm piles lay within ten to fifteen feet beyond the forest edge and acres of open dirt and weeds beyond them.

Slowly, Anna snuck over to the nearest pile, inspecting it closely. It held nothing but a heap of limbs and tree trunks tightly twisting into each other, reaching about eight feet high and six feet wide.

Crouching low, she made her way to the next one, its mass a good ten feet tall and eight feet wide. The limbs knitted together, holding tightly onto its many layers, but a small hole toward the bottom held promise.

Poking her head inside, a small opening greeted her. The inside was about two feet deep and two feet across. Not much but something.

The last berm, which was the largest, had a small opening, but it had little room, with only a foot and half wide and two feet in height.

Anna felt a thrill surge through her! This was it; she could feel it in her bones! This was her hiding place. Even though these two openings were full of rocks, field grass, and tree limbs, they were the first places that held potential. Excitement ran through her, anticipating how Papa would react. Making a detailed mental picture of everything, she headed home.

It was now late afternoon, and there were miles to go before she'd get home. Picking up to a trot, she hoped to make it back before dark, and before her parents started to worry. Her worst fear was running into German soldiers who now strolled the outskirts of the woods. Just thinking about it made her shudder. It was common knowledge what they would do to an unaccompanied Jewish girl.

Reaching home, Anna entered the backdoor, where Mama stopped her in her tracks, staring at the dirty, messy girl before her.

"Good Lord! Don't even think about walking in here, young lady! Don't take one step! You strip those muddy clothes off and head straight to the bathtub!" Mama threw her a towel, and Anna quickly stripped down.

The water looked so inviting, hot steam spiraling upward. Slowly, she slipped into the tub, adjusting to the heat, and then immersed her whole body below the surface, reveling in its warmth.

"Aw..." she sighed. Her muscles, tense from the long day's hike, relaxed.

"Set the table," called Mama. "You're going to be an old prune if you don't get out of that tub."

She wasn't ready yet, but Anna forced herself from the now-grayish water, toweled dry, and pulled on clean clothes. Her hands and toes were wrinkled from lying in the tub so long, but the luxury had been worth it. Pulling her wet hair up and clipping it off her neck, she quickly slipped into the dining room, pulled the china from the hutch and began to set the table for dinner.

"How did your day go?" asked Papa. "From the looks of it, you had quite the experience."

She knew he had expected her to come home empty-handed, as she had every other day, but not today. "I headed north, almost three hours from here. I found a farmer's field with some wood berms that may hold promise." Anna continued to give all the details about the mounds of cleared forest that had been plowed up, shoving the trunks and branches into large berms with small, cave-like entrances. She hadn't meant to sound so excited, but she had to admit, today, she felt immensely proud of herself.

"I'll go with you tomorrow and inspect it," Papa said, his own excitement showing. "I'm proud of you!" he beamed at her.

Mama wasn't happy, made apparent by her face. Her brow was furrowed, and her arms crossed. She never said much, but Anna knew how she felt. No, she wasn't happy. Anna was happy yet sad, wondering if she'd ever have to use her new-found shelter. In her mind, she wasn't planning on it.

The next day rose to the sun beaming into Anna's bedroom window. A small breeze was blowing, making the treetops sway slightly. She lay in bed watching the branches sway back and forth as if dancing to a slow waltz. A perfect, late August day. Anna stretched her slender arms and legs, and then promptly curled back up, pulling her pink flowered comforter over her head.

"Get up!" called Mama. "Rise and shine, young lady. " Anna ignored her.

Mama gave her fifteen minutes, then came into her room and pulled the covers back.

"Anna, it's time to get up," she said.

"I don't want to," she groaned, reaching for the comforter.

"I know, but you have to go with Papa today and show him your hiding place. This is hard for me too, you know. You're my daughter, and I'm afraid for you to do what he asks but I'm also afraid if you don't. The things your father has been talking about are coming true, and we're finding it hard to get out of Germany. Please, for me, get up and make your Papa happy."

"Okay." Anna reluctantly pushed the comforter the rest of the way off and stood up. Mama hugged her and told her to make sure she wore her hiking clothes.

"Good morning," said Papa as he pulled her into a hug. "How's my little gem today?"

"I'm good," said Anna, forcing a smile. She wasn't happy, but she wouldn't let him know. She was going to spend the day with him in the woods and didn't want him to be sad in a place he had always found peaceful.

Mama had packed some cheese, bread and a piece of fruit to share. It was getting harder and harder to keep a proper supply of food because the Jews were only allowed to buy from certain stores in certain areas. The Reinhold's bought groceries for the Feiners and snuck them to their back door inside a small tin bucket.

It took a massive load off Joseph, but they couldn't always rely on it. The Reinholds never spoke about it when they left groceries. They were quiet as a mouse. Papa would leave money under the bucket, and Mr. Reinhold or Peter would buy what they could with it.

"We must be careful not to waste," Mama would say. "We should be thankful we still have places to buy food and especially for the Reinhold's. Your father was smart in turning some of our gems and diamonds into money before the Germans were told not to buy from us."

"Yes, Mama, I know." Anna was thankful, but some days were harder than others. She had no control, but she knew from watching and listening, that her parents didn't either.

Papa handed Anna a small pack and she put the lunch inside. Pulling the water canteen over her shoulder, Anna was ready for what would probably be a long, grueling day. Papa's pack was much bigger and heavier. He had a small hand shovel, burlap bags, a tin pail hanging off it, along with other items. She was glad she didn't have to carry it.

It was seven in the morning when they left, and almost ten when they finally wove their way through the hills to her secret spot. The sun was hot, but at least the forest had provided cool shade most of the way. Still, both Anna and Papa had beads of sweat dripping off their foreheads. Sneaking up to the edge of the field, they took cover behind the trees and thick brush. The farmers' house was blowing smoke from his chimney which told them someone was home, but it was far enough away that they couldn't be seen. The outside of the wood berms stretched before them.

"The middle one has the most room," said Anna. "They're both small, but I figured you could make more room."

"Size isn't always the deciding factor. The inside and how they're knitted together will determine if we can make them livable." Papa moved from the brush and closely looked at the dirt next to the mounds. Moving even closer he inspected the ground in front of the berm piles.

"What are you looking for?" asked Anna.

"I'm looking for footprints," he replied, still concentrating on the ground. "We need to know if anyone comes out here. I don't see any signs, but we need to be extra cautious."

Anna hadn't even thought about that. She was gaining new respect for his skills.

Sneaking up to the middle berm he popped his head inside. All Anna could see were his legs protruding out. An hour later, he appeared, dirty from head to toe, with a bundle of broken branches and clods of dirt shoved into one of the burlap bags, a satisfied half grin on his face.

"This is possible, Anna. I don't think anyone would think to look in here, especially if we make a door of branches that blends into the opening. We'll have to adjust the inside for more room, but the structure has so many big branches and stumps holding it together, I think this is good. You can pull wood from the extra pile, so you don't have to forage in the woods all the time. I'm so proud of you."

Anna had to admit she was extremely pleased with herself, a smile bursting across her face. She still didn't want to live in it, but she was appeasing Papa and would make the effort to be interested, considering it an adventure.

Once again, part of Papa disappeared into the last mound, which was smaller than the previous one, coming out even dirtier, mud caking his clothes. "This will work for extra supplies. First, we'll make more room in the larger one and turn it into a livable space. We'll work on it for a while today, and come back tomorrow. We'll have to watch the farmer's routine, so we know when and if he comes out this far."

Anna stood guard by the bushes while he crawled back into the main berm and started shoveling dirt and breaking branches into small sticks, shoving them into the burlap bags. A few hours later, he had two of the bags filled to within inches of the top, just enough to roll the top and have room to grab and carry them.

"Let's eat our lunch down by the creek and then we can discard the dirt and sticks along the way," he said. "You must never leave a trail that someone has been here. You must not leave a footprint or any evidence."

Anna just nodded, noting how serious he was. She didn't want to argue that she wasn't planning on living here and all this was a waste of time.

The bags aside, Papa took out a small hand broom and gently brushed over their footprints, then stepped back into the forest brush.

With his backpack on and each hand gripping a bag, they proceeded to the banks of the creek. Making their way through the brush, Papa discarded small amounts from the bag's contents along the way.

"No trace," he reiterated. "It's best to leave a little here and there than one big pile."

They stopped by the creek and ate their lunch. In between bites, Papa told Anna some of the stories about when he was growing up, and how his father had taught him survival skills.

"Your grandfather taught me hunting, tracking and survival skills, not out of necessity, but out of fun. As a young boy, it was always an adventure. The difference, Anna, is your life will depend on it." Lunch eaten, they headed home. About a mile from the house, they heard voices. Papa yanked Anna into the bushes.

"Shhh!" he whispered, putting his finger to his lips.

Two boys in their late teens passed within inches of them, talking to each other.

"I can hardly wait to join the army," said the tall one with dark hair. "My father says he can get me into the SS like him. He said they're extinguishing the Jews, cleaning up our race."

"It's about time! I hate those filthy Jews. We'll help get every one of them, Stephen." Pretending to have a noose around his neck, he pulled the fake rope into the air, and they both doubled over in laughter. "Hey, maybe your Father can get me in too," he said, slapping his friend on the back, letting him know how lucky he was. "I mean, after all, we are best friends!"

"Yah, it would be great to join together!"

Anna gasped in horror and Papa threw his hand over her mouth.

After some time had passed, Papa pulled Anna from the bushes. Her legs were numb from squatting so long, but she made them move because she couldn't get home fast enough. They hurried the rest of the way, arriving just as dusk was setting. Rushing in the back door, Anna slumped into a chair and burst into tears.

Mama stood frozen.

"What happened, Joseph?" She rushed forward, wrapping her arms around her distraught daughter.

"We had to hide from some German boys. One of their fathers is SS and the boy was saying his father was going to help get rid of the Jews." Joseph kept the word "extermination" to himself. "There are bad things coming Miriam, I know it."

"Oh, Anna," she cried, as she pulled her into her arms, squeezing her tight. "I'm sorry you had to hear those things. Let this be a lesson—*we must be extra careful*." Mama looked at Papa, worry written on her face.

Dinner was eaten mainly in silence, as no one felt like talking. Finally, Papa spoke.

"Anna, you'll stay home tomorrow with your mother and help her with errands. I'll go back to the farmer's field and do some work."

She just nodded. For once, she had nothing to say. After helping Mama with the dishes, she went to her room. All she wanted to do was curl up in bed. Sitting, knees tucked under her chin, she couldn't help but think of how scared she had been today. She could hear her parents talking. They were whispering, but she could hear through the crack under her door.

"Joseph, this isn't good for her. She's scared, and she's barely seventeen. Would we take away her innocence so early in life?"

"Miriam, don't you see, this is protecting her. You can't spare her the ugliness of our situation. We must prepare her and ourselves for what may come. I've tried to get us out of Germany, but it's not happening. And now, even if I could find someone to help us, we don't have enough money."

She could hear Mama's stifled sobs.

"Miriam, Miriam," Joseph said softly. "I wish it weren't this way, but it is what it is. Two people can't change the way the Nazis think. Tomorrow, you'll take Anna and buy items on my list. Just do the best you can."

"But who will open the shop?"

"It'll stay closed. It won't matter. Hardly anyone comes now anyway."

Anna could hear her parents walk to their bedroom, the floorboards groaning out their familiar squeaks, then shut the door.

Papa left early in the morning, so early, the sun hadn't even come up and Anna still slept for hours. Mama finally came in, slipping under the covers with her, pulling her tight against her, hugging her and cradling her in her arms like when she was a toddler. Anna snuggled up to her, melting into the moment.

"Time to get up. We have things to do today, and I want to head to the market before it gets too crowded." Mama slipped out of the bed, giving Anna the look that spoke clearly, there would be no excuses for dallying.

Anna came out to the kitchen and settled herself up to the table. Two eggs, over easy, and a piece of toast loaded with homemade strawberry preserves filled her plate. She hadn't had two eggs in forever. She slurped them down, enjoying each slippery piece, using her last bite of toast to soak up any leftover yolk before popping it into her mouth.

"Thank you, Mama," Anna smiled. Her smile disappeared when she saw Mama's plate had only a piece of toast. Smiling a big smile, Anna got up and hugged her, but now the eggs felt like they were sticking in her throat. She hadn't thought about where the extra egg came from, but from now on, she would.

"What's on Papa's list?"

"There's quite a bit, and I don't think we'll be able to find all of it or afford it if we do, but, like Papa said, we'll do the best we can. He wants us to get you leggings, socks, wool blankets, boys' pants, boots, and a dark wool coat."

"Girls don't wear pants! I'll look hideous! I won't wear them!"

Mama's voice came out sharp and made her jump back. "You'll wear pants if Papa thinks you need to wear them! Now, come, let's get going, so we can get back as soon as possible." She felt hurt at Mama's tone but stayed silent.

They had just made their way down the stairs to the front of the store and opened the door when a well-dressed man and woman started to come in.

"I'm sorry," said Mama, "we're closed today."

"What do you mean, you're closed! Do you know who we are? You'll just have to be open until we're done!" snarled the man. He had pulled off his fedora, waving it around in anger, almost hitting Anna and her mother in the face with it. His face was turning bright red, his bald head perspiring, sweat glistening on it.

"You ungrateful Jew trash," he muttered. "You need to let us in right now!"

Anna wanted to scream at him, they hadn't done anything wrong and these trespassers were the rotten ones. She was fuming.

The woman looked around to make sure no one was near, giving them a disgusted look. "You should feel lucky we even want to buy your garbage! Maybe the Gestapo needs to teach you a lesson!"

Mama froze, her knuckles turning white from gripping the doorknob. Anna was holding her hand tight and could feel her trembling. Anna squeezed her hand, trying to give her mental courage. Somehow Mama gathered her wits.

"I'm sorry, sir. My husband is not at home, but he'll be happy to help you tomorrow." Her voice came out calm, but Anna could feel her body trembling. She quickly closed the door, locked it and swiftly pulled Anna away with her. Both Mama and Anna scurried away before the couple could say anything else.

They were both worried that the couple had mentioned the Gestapo, which was a sure death sentence. Neither spoke a word the whole time they were walking to the market. The silence was deafening.

Making it to the used clothing store, Mama started going through the boys clothing. She picked out a pair of khaki work pants, holding them up to Anna. "I think these will fit your brother Jacob quite well," she said and winked. "He's just about your size, but is growing so fast!"

She knew Mama didn't want anyone to know they were for her and she didn't either. Papa had been specific about not letting anyone know their plans, and for them not to leave any evidence. Besides, Anna would have been horrified if anyone knew she was even thinking about wearing pants.

"Oh, yes." She smiled at Mama. "Jacob will like those and as quickly as he's growing, he'll be in them in no time," she grinned. "I think that wool shirt will work well too." She pointed to a brown and green plaid wool shirt.

Mama chuckled softly. "Oh, Anna, your brother will surely appreciate your fine taste to make sure his clothes match. You know how he likes everything to be color coordinated."

They both burst into laughter but quickly calmed down, noticing people were staring at them. Anna knew Mama was making fun of her. She liked her clothes to coordinate with each other and not be mis-matched. It drove her crazy!

After picking out another pair of deep brown wool pants, a sweater, and a pair of hiking boots one size too big, they headed home.

The market had been uneventful, except haggling over prices. The cost for used clothes was like buying new. Mama said it was because of the dislike for Jewish people, and hopefully it would pass. Anna just nodded and hoped it would. She felt German like everyone else, so why was everyone angry with them?

As they approached their street, Anna could see the anxiety on Mama's face grow. She didn't think Mama could take another encounter with an angry customer.

"It's okay, Mama," Anna whispered.

They detoured toward the back of the building and slipped in the back door. Papa wasn't home but it was getting toward dinnertime, and Mama started supper using the few groceries she had picked up. She had managed to haggle for some chicken legs and potatoes. Everything went into a large pot to make soup which you could stretch much farther. The Reinhold's had given them bread the day before which was an added blessing.

Anna's stomach growled, reminding her she hadn't eaten since breakfast. All the restrictions on the Jewish community made it necessary for them to conserve. Instead of three full meals a day, it was two small ones at best. Two minutes later, a large growl came from Mama.

"Well this certainly isn't how I planned on losing a little weight," She chuckled at her own announcement.

Anna laughed, but Mama's thin frame worried her.

"Set the table, dear," said Mama.

Even though food was harder to come by, they still set the table with Grandmother's dishes, trying to maintain a normal life. Anna loved the beautiful pink flowers and green foliage on them.

"Anna, if you can't spoil yourself, you might as well not own it," Grandmother would say. "One day they'll be yours dear." She remembered the moment her Grandmother had told her that.

The screen door hinges creaked and slammed shut, announcing Papa was home.

"Oh my!" exclaimed Mama. "Joseph, you're covered in dirt from head to toe! Go, go outside and shake yourself off," she admonished, her hands on her hips. Papa knew better than to cross her when it came to messing up the house. The screen door creaked again, slammed, and then you could hear him brushing off his clothes.

"Sorry," he said. "I got so caught up with getting home from working on the hiding place that I forgot I was full of dirt. It did my soul good to be outside today," he said. "Ah, if only we could just put on some backpacks and head into the woods forever, leave this ugly bitterness against the Jews behind." Mama went up to Papa and kissed him, careful not to get dirty.

"Yes, that would be great for you, Joseph," She chuckled, a smile on her face. "You love the outdoors. I, on the other hand would make a terrible outdoors woman." They both started laughing because they knew it was true. It made Anna feel good to hear them laugh like they used to. For a slight moment, everything felt normal.

"I'm starving," said Papa as he pulled a piece of bread off the loaf. Mama lovingly slapped his hand.

"Joseph, you're filthy. At least wash your hands first!"

Dinner was full of conversation as Mama told Papa about the rude man and woman who came to the store that morning. Mama was still shaken. You could see her hands tremble as she passed the soup, telling Papa all the details.

"I'm sorry," he said, and you could see the anger shoot from his eyes. "I wish I would have been here. He won't contact the Gestapo," he said, shaking his head. "He'd have to admit he was trying to buy from a Jewish establishment in order to do that, and it's forbidden. I think this is only the beginning of things to come, though," he fumed. It was apparent Papa was angry, his hands balled into fists.

"I'm glad I worked on the hiding place and I'm almost finished. Early tomorrow, we'll all take some of the things we need to hide out there. We don't want to be seen carrying a bunch of stuff, so we need to head out before the sun starts coming up."

Softening his tone, he smiled at Mama. "How did you do with the list I gave you, Miriam?"

"Oh, Jacob will be very well dressed," Anna piped in and both she and Mama started laughing hysterically.

"Jacob? Who is Jacob?" he asked, confused.

Mama and Anna laughed even louder. "Why, my brother," Anna said. "Why else would we buy boy clothes? You told us to be discreet and not draw attention to what we were buying, so we made up a brother for me. He's going to be growing, you know. We bought him a size a little larger than mine." She smiled.

"Yes," said Mama, "and Anna made sure Jacob was going to *at least* be color coordinated, even though she didn't like the clothes." All three burst into laughter now and it felt so good.

"I washed them, and they're hanging in the bathroom drying," said Anna. "We thought we better not hang them outside, or the nosy neighbors would suspect something."

"Smart thinking." Papa smiled warmly at the two people he loved the most in this world.

The next morning came early. Papa and Mama had put together backpacks and a smaller one for Anna. Papa had the heaviest pack. It had a couple small pots, a foldup cot, canned food, a sleeping bag, and other items stuffed tightly in every available space.

Mama's backpack was lighter and held clothes they had purchased at the market yesterday, along with some of Anna's regular clothes, a jumper, a winter coat,

41

hat and mittens and lots of extra socks. Anna's sack had underclothes, some canned meats and foods, matches and candles. It was heavy, but she couldn't complain after seeing what her parents were lugging.

"I think we have everything," said Papa, looking around to see if he had forgotten anything.

They headed out the back door, snugly shutting and locking the door. Anna saw Peter from the corner of her eye, but she knew Papa wouldn't want her to draw attention to them. Peter waved and smiled. She drew her hand up to her waist and did a slight wave, then turned away and headed off with her parents. Anna turned around once just as they approached the wooded area. Peter was still standing there, his head cocked to one side, watching them fade into the forest.

The day was tiring, but no one complained. Papa was doing most of the work and packing. They had made it to the hiding spot and laid their packs under some brush. Both Mama and Anna snuck up to the berm openings and peered inside.

"Oh my," exclaimed Mama. "It's so deceiving. From the looks of the outside you, wouldn't know you had so much room. It's amazing!"

The main one was like a huge branch hut with branches weaving in and out of each other, creating a secure, livable space. One at a time, Papa took each pack and unloaded them into the berms. It was a little after noon time when he had finished.

The packs were now empty, except for the light lunch in Mama's. They strapped them on and headed home, winding down along the river.

"How about some lunch?" suggested Papa. "I think we're all a little famished."

"I am," piped up Anna, "and I'm tired."

Anna sat down on a large stump, thankful for the rest. Mama looked frazzled. She was not fond of the outdoors at all. She tried for Papa's sake, but she just never took to it.

"Well, it's not much, but at least it's something." Mama smiled. A half loaf of leftover French bread appeared, along with some thick slices of cheese. Papa cut an apple into slices to share and brought out the canteen filled with water. It wasn't a glamorous lunch, but it was filling and gave everyone extra energy for the journey home.

Days later, Papa and Anna headed to camp. He was adamant that he teach her everything he possibly could. In his mind, it would never be enough.

"Today, Anna, you'll start a small fire and cook over it for our lunch. It's important you can stay warm and dry, but also be able to cook. We have canned meats and other foods packed in the camp, but you still may need to catch squirrels and forage for food."

She shivered, thinking back a couple of weeks ago when Papa made her trap squirrels, pull the guts from their bellies, skin them, and take them home for dinner. Anna hoped survival would not come to that.

She didn't mind eating squirrel, but killing and gutting them was another thing. He'd made her do it numerous times lately. In the past, she'd only had to watch him do the disgusting job, not be a participant.

As they approached the hideout, Papa made Anna go first. She knew the drill. Watch the farmhouse and fields and confirm no one would see them. Papa came up behind her, brushing away the images their boots had pressed into the dirt.

Inside the berm, items were stacked on top of each other, leaving little room for two people to maneuver. Papa pulled out a tiny gardening shovel and handed it to Anna.

"Let's see how you do with starting a fire today. It must be extremely small. You don't want a lot of smoke or huge flames. It should be just big enough to heat your food and to help you stay warm. Keep the pile of dirt ready to smother it just in case. Anna nodded. Make sure to use dry wood, or you'll get too much smoke, "said Papa.

Anna gripped the shovel and dug a small hole about six inches deep and ten inches in diameter. Papa had previously gathered moss and it had been drying for weeks. Putting moss in the bottom of her hole, she then stacked small dry sticks back and forth. Striking the match, a small flame flickered, and Anna gently touched it to the moss. The flame took hold and a small fire came to life.

"Good job." He smiled, nodding his head in satisfaction. "I'm very proud of you. Remember, if you don't have moss, you can always make lint from a blanket; it makes an excellent fire starter. Run your knife over the wool until you get a pile big enough to use. Making the fire is only a small part, Anna. You need to make sure your fire won't draw attention to anyone outside, and that it is small enough that you don't catch anything in here on fire. Always be ready to smother it."

"I understand." She nodded confidently. Slowly, she crawled out the opening, staying low, she moved to the edge of the trees. There was a slight waft of smoke coming from the top of the berm but hardly noticeable. It disappeared in a couple minutes giving no sign a small fire was crackling inside. Crawling back in, careful to cover her footprints, she attached her make-shift door, confirming all was good.

"Let's see how good of a cook you are." He chuckled, handing her a can of meat to open.

"You know what kind of cook I am." She smirked, rolling her eyes. Mama tried to instill a love of cooking, trying new recipes, and baking, but Anna hated it. "It's a chore," she had complained. "All that work, so everyone can gobble it down in twenty minutes and you still have all the dishes to clean!"

"Well, you better think about getting used to it if you're ever going to get married," declared Mama.

"Your husband isn't going to survive on bread and bologna."

Using the metal opener, Anna worked it around the lid, leaving a tiny portion still attached. Pushing the lid back down, she placed four rocks in a square, two inches apart from each other into the small fire that had burned down to almost embers. Balancing the tin on the edge of the rocks, she set the can over the coals. Ten minutes later, the juices in the can started sizzling. Lifting the can off with a pair of pliers, she pulled the lid open.

"Lunch is served," Papa smiled. "I guess your husband will eat more than bread and bologna," he said, then laughed heartedly.

"Papa, I have no doubt my future husband will not starve. Besides, maybe he'll be the cook in the family!" All Anna could think was, *He won't have a weight problem.*

They ate the contents, wrapped the can in a bag and stuffed it in her backpack. Papa had warned her not to leave garbage about. The smell of garbage would draw vermin in that could destroy her hideout and strew garbage alerting passersby to her presence.

"Make sure your fire is out," he warned. "You don't want to leave any embers that could cause it to restart. You'll give away your hiding place and lose all we've prepared."

She nodded, working the coals away from each other and shoving the dirt back on top before she packed it down.

"That's good. You've done a wonderful job, my little gem," he said, hugging her tightly, "and you've taken a lot of worry off my shoulders. I believe you can take care of yourself. Your instincts will kick in when they need to."

****

CHAPTER THREE

S ummer was ending, though the weather was still warm. Anna loved the feel of the sun soaking into her skin. The warmth always made her feel as if she were wrapped in a cozy blanket. Summer had always been a busy time in the store, but now it was pretty much dead. Few people came in, and if they did, they looked around constantly, to see if anyone was watching. Papa sold them jewelry, but it was hard making ends meet. Buying food was expensive, and the locals wouldn't sell to anyone Jewish. The bold yellow star marked them, separating them from the rest of the community.

Mr. Reinhold sold to the Feiners anyway, but Anna and her parents were careful not to enter the bakery when anyone else was there and they always snuck in the back. Mr. Reinhold was afraid for his family, but Anna knew he was scared for hers too.

"Anna, run over to the Reinholds and get a loaf of bread, or we'll only be eating vegetables," Mama called to her.

As she approached the back door and started to enter, Mr. Reinhold looked up and angrily shook his head no. Anna stood frozen. Mr. Reinhold came over and shut the door in her face. She realized he was telling her she couldn't come in because she was

Jewish. Anna's face flushed red as she turned and ran back to their apartment. As she ran in the door and through the kitchen, crying, Mama grabbed her.

"What's wrong?" she asked. "Where is the bread I sent you for?"

She looked up, tears streaming down her face. "Mr. Reinhold wouldn't let me in. He shut the door in my face." Her breath hitched as she sobbed.

Mama hugged her tight, whispering under her breath, "What's the world coming to?"

They ate dinner that night without bread. Even if they would have had it, Anna thought it would stick in her throat. She couldn't believe that even her neighbors, the Reinholds, had turned against them. Papa was right, they couldn't trust anyone.

"You know, Anna," Papa spoke up. "The Reinholds are in a difficult position. If they let us buy from them, the government can take their property and put them in jail, or worse. It's not them you should be angry with. They're only doing what they must, to survive, just like everyone else, just like us. They put their lives on the line every time they sneak us groceries."

Anna just nodded, but she was angry. She trusted the Reinholds, especially Peter.

"I'm exhausted," said Anna, giving a fake yawn. "I think I'll head to bed." Mama hugged her tight, and Papa kissed her on the forehead, but they knew she wasn't tired.

Late into the evening, after the sun had long been down, there was a slight knock at the back door. Papa padded down the hallway in his pajamas and robe, Mama and Anna watching. The door opened and then the screen door. They could hear muffled voices and finally the door closed. Mama and Anna went to the kitchen just as Papa was laying down two long French baguettes on the table.

"Mr. Reinhold," said Papa. "He apologized to you, Anna. He was afraid of what might happen if he let you in. Some of our other neighbors are watching him and complaining he's too nice to the Jews. There were some soldiers in the store at the time you came over, and he was afraid for himself, Peter, and us as well. If they would have seen you, he didn't know what they might've done."

"Did you pay him?" asked Mama.

"He wouldn't take anything for them. I told him I couldn't just take them without paying for them, but he wouldn't hear any more about it. He said he'd no longer take money from us for bread when it cost him hardly anything to make. He said the Nazis could pay for it in what he charged them. He smiled when he said it." Papa chuckled, a smile spreading across his face.

Anna felt the shame creep up her neck for thinking bad things about the Reinhold's and for being mad at Peter for something he couldn't control. She'd have to hold her anger in check from now on. She wasn't the only one suffering.

A few days later, Papa came rushing in the backdoor, out of breath and panting heavily. He grabbed Mama and yelled for Anna to come at once. He looked petrified. He was sweating profusely, and his eyes were wide and frightened.

"What's wrong, Joseph?" cried Mama. "You're scaring us!"

"It's the Nazis! They're gathering up all Jews and sending us to designated places. We have to hurry! Gather our money, jewelry, and valuables, and take them to the hiding place!"

Mama and Anna stood paralyzed.

"Now!" They both jumped at his tone, but he didn't soften. Mama knew Papa wasn't angry with her, just scared, which made her even more terrified.

"But where would they send us? Surely, they won't make us leave our home?" she asked, trembling.

"I don't know, Miriam. I just know what I heard! They're rounding them up a few towns over right now." Frantically, Papa pulled his hands through his hair, clearly distraught. "I suspect they'll be here within the next day or two, if not within a few hours. Now, get everything together, and hurry!" he shouted.

Mama and Anna scurried after him, gathering their valuables. Mama dropped her jewelry into a black velvet bag, and Anna did the same. Even though hers wasn't as intricate as Mama's, the pieces had been made by Papa and Grandfather, so they meant the world to her.

Papa rushed into their bedroom and retrieved the money he had hidden. He took their jewelry bags and put them in a silver tin box, along with the money. He grabbed the matches sitting on the table and a flashlight and told them not to say a word and listen to him carefully.

"Put on warm clothes and your hiking boots. You must be extra quiet when we leave. We don't want the neighbors to see or hear us," he said. The sun had just set, and he knew the neighbors would be eating dinner.

"Shouldn't Anna and I stay here, Joseph? Surely you can make better time on your own to hide everything. We'll slow you down," Mama protested. Papa grabbed her shoulders, shaking his head.

"Miriam, from now on, we stay together. If the Nazis come while one of us is gone, then we could be separated. If they take us to different camps, then what will we do? They don't care if they break up families. No, from now on, we stay together unless I decide otherwise," he said firmly, dropping his grip from Mama's arms.

Anna knew he was right. If they took them at different times, they may not be able to get back together again. She was going to be sticking to her parents like glue.

"Do you really think they'll make us move?" whispered Mama, so low you could barely hear her.

"This is our house. It's been in my family for generations," she said, the panic setting in.

"It doesn't matter to the Nazis," he said, shaking his head no.

"Don't think of things as they were. It will be what *"they"* want it to be, and we have no say. They've already confiscated businesses and homes. They're sending Jews to designated areas in the ghettos."

Mama and Anna gasped, and then Mama started to cry. Anna had heard about the slums before, and she knew she never wanted to go there. We're together, and we'll be all right," Anna whispered. She wasn't sure if she believed her own words, but they made her feel a bit braver.

They grabbed their coats, pulled on their boots, and followed Papa out the back door. He held the door open for them, and then, without a sound, closed the screen door behind them, making sure it didn't slam. Holding onto each other's hands, they disappeared into the dark.

The forest was pitch black, and the one flashlight they had gave little light. Hours later, the hiding place came into view. Papa turned off the flashlight, telling them to let their eyes adjust. It was extremely dark, but he wouldn't turn it back on.

"We can't take a chance that someone will see the light," he whispered. Papa approached the edge of the field and looked for tracks. He didn't see any, but it was so dark, you could hardly see your hand in front of your face. Lights shone from the farmhouse windows, but if the chimney was smoking, you couldn't tell.

Mama and Anna tucked inside the berm, but the space was so small that Anna had to lie on the cot, so Papa could fit. There was a little over four feet in height, about six feet in length and five feet deep. Even though it was a tight area, Anna was amazed at how organized Papa had made it. The lantern and a box of candles were near the front, so she could have light as soon as she entered.

Papa pulled a candle and a box of matches from one of the boxes and put it into what had been Grandmother's and Anna's favorite silver candlestick holder. With the candle lit, Anna saw the .22 pistol and bullets inside the box. She knew how to use it, which was what Papa counted on. He had taught her how to shoot when she was twelve years old. It was something she really enjoyed. Some of her best memories she had were when she, Papa, and Peter went to hit targets. Papa had made Anna go rabbit and squirrel hunting over and over again during the last couple months, even though he knew she didn't like killing animals. Still, he made her gut, prep, and cook them over an open fire. He kept saying she had to have experience and options for a food source.

The cot was laid out against the south wall, since the wind usually blew from the north. Wood slat boxes were neatly tucked under the cot like drawers that contained kitchen supplies, toiletries, garden tools, blankets, and clothes. Against another wall were three boxes filled with canned meat, fruit, vegetables, and Anna's favorite, Mama's famous crispy pickles. Her parents had to have taken all the food in the house to fill the boxes! Papa had done a spectacular job. There was still just enough room to build a small fire to cook and keep warm.

"We won't hide everything here," said Papa. "If they find this hiding spot, at least you'll have another place to get some money and protection. We'll find a place in the woods that you can easily remember that won't be conspicuous to others." He separated the gems and money, putting one half into a small glass jar, fitting the lid on snugly and leaving the other in the tin. He dug a hole in the back part of the berm and buried the tin about six inches deep.

"Remember this area, Anna. You don't want to dig up the whole floor to find it."

"Yes, Papa."

The sun was barely coming up as they made their way through the woods. Papa had left the flashlight in the hiding place for future use, since they had an extra at home.

"You need to remember that you may not always have something to light your way, and a light could put you in more danger. Allow your eyes to adjust."

Making their way along the river, Papa stopped and said they should take a quick rest. There was a huge alder tree that had a long branch bent like the letter "U."

"We need to hide the remainder of our valuables. I think this is a good spot," he declared. "Will you remember this, Anna, or do we need to keep looking?"

Anna looked at the tree, mentally measuring how far from the river it was and made a mental note of her surroundings for future use.

"This is a good spot, Papa. The big bend in the limb is a good marker. I can definitely remember this place." Mama nodded her head in agreement.

Pulling out his pocketknife, he carved a big "AF" into the bark, just in case Anna became confused. Pulling the glass jar and a small shovel from his pack, he dug a hole six to seven inches deep near the base of the tree. He laid the jar in the hole and covered it up. Sweeping the dirt over the area with his hand to make it look like it had not been touched, then scattered some bark and leaves over the top. Stepping back, satisfied, he declared the job done. They all stood there, staring at the spot. It felt like their past had just been covered up and they had no idea what the future held.

Anna's stomach growled, but she didn't say anything. She was sure they were all hungry, considering they'd left the house in a rush. They made their way back out of the woods with a little help from the sunlight shining into areas where the foliage was less dense.

Papa stopped, hesitating. "I think it's time for Anna to leave the house. I can't predict what will happen, and if she doesn't leave now, she may not escape."

"No!" cried Mama and Anna at the same time.

"No, Papa! I'm not ready. Please, I'm not ready. Not yet!" Anna cried. She felt the panic rise, her body starting to tremble.

"Joseph, please," begged Mama, grabbing his arm. "Let's find out what's happening first. If you hear news that they're definitely taking Jews to the ghetto, then she'll have to leave."

Mama looked over at Anna, sadness and fear etching her face. Mama pulled her into a hug, whispering, "it will happen."

Papa hesitated but agreed with the condition, if they heard any bad news, she was to leave immediately. Mama and Anna felt the tension ease and followed Papa home. As they approached the edge of the neighborhood tree line, Papa scouted it out. One of the neighbors was out hanging laundry, so they waited until she had gone back inside, and the coast seemed clear.

Making their way out of the trees and back along the neighbor's tool shed, they hurried to the back of the house. Papa opened the door and they rushed in, but he made sure to quietly close the door behind them. They were exhausted, both mentally and physically.

After cleaning up, Mama made a breakfast for lunch, eggs in a blanket, from the few eggs they had left. Anna had loved eggs in a blanket when she was little and still did, but more for the emotional memory. Mama would make a two-inch round hole in a slice of bread and then lay the bread in a fry pan with butter. After the bread had toasted lightly, she would crack an egg into the bread where the hole was, letting it cook until the yolk was still a little runny, then flip it over to cook a little longer until she slid it onto the plate. The round piece she pulled out would be toasted too, and she would lay it on top of the egg, proclaiming the egg all tucked in, so it didn't get cold. *Someday when I'm a mother*, thought Anna, *I'll do this for my children.*

****

CHAPTER FOUR

A Week had passed since they had hidden the last of their money and family treasures. Papa hadn't heard any more news, and everyone felt the tension and worry start to fade. Maybe things weren't as bad as they thought. Anna had just set the table for lunch when the doorjamb came crashing in, sending splintered wood flying across the room, hitting grandmother's beautiful pink vase. Pieces of porcelain splattered everywhere. Anna jumped back, startled, and then rushed into the kitchen. Papa and Mama grabbed her and pulled her behind them. Soldiers were yelling, pointing their guns at them.

"You have ten minutes to pack and be out front!" one of them yelled. "One suitcase each! *Schnell! Schnell*," he shouted. He put the barrel of his gun to Papa's chest. "Schnell!" He smirked. You could tell he was enjoying himself. They were terrified.

Anna grabbed hold of Papa tighter. The soldier lowered his gun from Papa's chest and looked at her.

"You need to go home," he said, a large frown forming. "You shouldn't be with Jew's! The Führer doesn't like Jew lovers! Go home!"

"They're my parents!" snapped Anna, thrusting her chin out in defiance.

"You're adopted?" he asked, surprised.

"No! I take after my great-grandfather. He had blond hair and hazel eyes. We're German, just like you!" she shouted.

The soldier pulled his gun barrel back up, placing the muzzle under her chin, and laughed hard.

"You don't look Jewish, but you have a mouth like a dirty little Jew."

Anna's eyes spit fire, her fists curled, wanting to punch him. Papa stepped in front of her, trying to calm the situation.

"Get your things!" the soldier barked again.

Anna and Mama quickly followed Papa down the hall. Papa quietly turned to them, telling them to pack only essentials.

"Warm clothes," he said. "Put on extra clothes over the ones you're wearing. We need to take as much as we can, and hurry. They'd much rather kill us than wait for us. Anna, watch yourself. We don't need to make them more hostile."

"Yes, Papa." She knew he was right, but she still fumed inside. Anna hurried into her room and put on a dress over the one she had on. Mama rushed in, wearing two dresses, a sweater, a coat, and with her pockets stuffed full. She pulled Anna's suitcase open and shoved a bunch of clothes in, mainly warm ones.

"Here, put this on over those dresses," she said handing her a wool sweater. "Put these leggings on and this pair over those. Hurry, "she said. Then she pulled her best dark gray wool coat with the fur collar out of the closet and put it on her. Anna could barely bend her arms, but Mama continued to stuff all her pockets with underwear and socks.

"Put your hiking shoes on." She had to help her because Anna couldn't bend over from all the clothes she was wearing. At the last minute, Mama pulled a wool scarf and hat off the closet shelf and stuffed them in the suitcase.

"Schnell!" yelled the soldier. "You have two minutes, or I'll shoot you!"

Papa had stuffed his small valise full of clothes and was wearing a pair of pants over the pair he had on this morning. He had a sweater pulled over his shirt, his coat over that, and his hiking boots on. The soldier had started to come down the hall, pointing his gun at Papa.

"We're coming." shouted Papa, "We're ready!"

Mama pulled Anna from her bedroom as she tried to take one last look at all her personal treasures, like a picture, so she could pull it from her memory and look at it when she wanted to. She doubted she'd ever see it again. Mama pushed her forward toward the front stairs, her arm snugly against her back.

At the last minute, Papa grabbed the loaf of bread, cheese, and apples that had been set on the dining table for lunch and stuffed them in his pockets, handing Mama some to put in hers with what little room she had left. Reaching the stairs, Papa grabbed the candle in the candlestick holder and matches.

The soldiers pushed Joseph and Miriam with the butt of their guns down the stairs and into the streets where other neighbors were, looking as frightened as they were. Papa grabbed Anna's suitcase, and her arms were thankful. The case was stuffed so full it was a wonder it had closed. Mama had sat on it while Anna hooked the latches, both praying silently the locks and hinges wouldn't pop off.

It was late September and Anna was thankful for the light crispness in the air. She was still perspiring from all the layers of clothing but at least it wasn't summer, or she thought she'd faint.

Huge brown transport trucks with canvas tops lined the street, many already crammed with people, all Jews. The soldiers were yelling to get in the trucks.

"Schnell! Schnell! Hurry! Hurry! In the trucks, now!"

On one side of the street stood on-lookers and on the other side were the Jews, each wearing the yellow star. Soldiers lined the street, guns aimed, just wishing they could use the yellow star for target practice.

Mr. Feinstein, the neighbor down the block who owned an accounting firm, stopped in front of one of the soldiers and asked where they were going. The soldier just yelled at him to get in the truck. Mr. Feinstein refused, saying, "we all need to know; we have a right to know." Mr. Feinstein became angry. The soldier turned the butt of his gun up in the air and brought it crashing down with a crack on Mr. Feinstein's head. Blood spurted everywhere as he crumpled to the ground. Blood pooled around his head onto the cobblestones, running a bright red stream down the cobblestone grooves. Poor Mrs. Feinstein was trying to help her husband, but the soldiers grabbed her, shoving her into a truck.

Mama and Papa grabbed Anna and hoisted her into the nearest truck. Papa then pushed Mama up and threw their cases in before he jumped up with them. All Anna could do was stare at Mr. Feinstein lying there, still not moving. She listened to his poor wife stuck in a truck shrieking, crying his name, "Benjamin, Benjamin, my Benjamin!" Mr. Feinstein's suitcase still sat in the street next to his limp body as the trucks pulled away. A German soldier kicked it across the street. All the soldiers laughed as the contents spilled into the street. This was the last time anyone would see Mr. Feinstein.

Sadly, all the neighbors who weren't Jewish were standing by their doors and windows clapping, yelling and cheering the soldiers on. To think they had liked them at one time. The only ones not cheering were Peter and his father. Mr. Reinhold was holding onto Peter tight, afraid he would try to help them.

The truck rumbled down the road, all of them holding onto the wood bench seats and to one another, no one saying a word. Papa pulled her close, whispering so low she could barely hear him.

His lips were almost on her ear, his breath warm, making her ear sweaty. His beard tickled her face.

"We need to watch for landmarks, things that we can remember so we know how to get back home," he said.

Papa looked intensely into her eyes and told her to concentrate because it may prove to save her life. Anna nodded and watched outside the truck, but it was hard to stay focused. She was petrified. She knew what Papa was thinking. He hoped she hadn't missed the opportunity to escape. So did Anna. Anna's back ached from the bumpy ride, but she watched the scenery, glimpsing things she thought would be good landmarks for going home, if she even had the chance.

Once in a while, she'd glance over at her parents. Mama was clutching Papa, and he was patting her hand as if everything would be okay. His other hand was wrapped tightly around his valise handle, his knuckles white from gripping it so tight. Anna was amazed that he could project calm with one hand yet fear with the other, all at the same time.

It was over five hours later when the trucks rolled into what had to be the ghettos. You knew just from the stench. Anna's nostrils burned, and all she wanted to do was plug her nose. Papa told her to grab her case and was lifting her from the truck, holding both her arms.

The soldiers were barking orders and yelling, "Schnell! Schnell!"

Was that the only word they knew? Did they have to be so rude? thought Anna. Grandmother always said you get more with a little sugar.

They watched as soldiers yanked people from the trucks if they were too slow. The poor old people who had trouble moving and walking were shoved to the ground, the soldiers kicking them, yelling at them to hurry. How were they supposed to hurry if they were pushing and kicking them? Women and children were crying. It was all Anna could do not to scream at the top of her lungs and tell everyone to shut up! Just shut up! Papa must have read her mind because he grabbed both her and Mama and whispered to stay silent and hold on to each other.

Papa was gripping Anna's hand so tight, it was going numb, but she didn't care. She had no intention of getting lost in the sea of people clambering out of the trucks and getting in lines before they were beaten. She stood between both her parents as they got in line with everyone else. All three of them were sweating from all the clothes they had on. Finally, they made it to the front of the line.

"Names!" barked a soldier.

"Feiner," said Papa.

"How many in your party? Well," he barked again when Papa didn't answer immediately. "We don't have all day!"

Anna wanted to yell obscenities at the soldier, but she clamped her lips shut. She didn't need to end up like Mr. Feinstein or embarrass her parents. Children were to be seen and not heard. Although that wasn't the rule in their home, it was fitting today. Besides, any bravery Anna felt had long disappeared.

There were multiple soldiers at the entrance, guns ready. Anna brought herself back to reality.

"How many in your party?" barked the soldier.

"Three," said Papa. The soldier looked up to count and noticed Anna.

"Her?" questioned the soldier. "She's Jewish?"

"Yes," said Papa, "our daughter."

"Hmmm," said the soldier, eyeing Anna. "She doesn't look Jewish." He shrugged his shoulders, handed Papa a piece of paper and told them to pass. Anna looked back as they went through the gate and saw that the soldier was staring at her. He smiled at her, blew her a kiss and then winked, bursting into laughter. Anna quickly turned back around; for once she didn't want to be noticed. Her confidence was waning.

As they neared the ghetto housing, a woman approached them and said she was there to help them find an apartment. Papa pulled the paper out from his coat that the soldier had given him and gave it to the woman.

"You're down one street, second building on your right," she said.

"Danke," said Papa.

"Don't expect a lot," she said as they moved down the filthy street.

All Anna could do was stare at everyone. *Didn't anyone take a bath around here, or iron their clothes,* she thought.

"Anna." Mama pulled on her arm. "Stop staring, it's rude. I don't care where we are, mind your manners." Still, she kept staring from under her eyelashes.

"Here," said Papa, "It's right here." They all looked at the building. It was dirty brick; two stories, with a stench that made Anna's eyes water, and what little she had in her stomach rise into her throat. She fought it back, but it was hard to do, the sour acid burning her throat. She lowered her eyes, telling herself not to look and to breathe through her mouth and not her nose.

"Come," said Papa, trying to be lighthearted.

Mama and Anna knew this wasn't going to be good. Filth was everywhere, and current residents were covered in dirt and grime. Everything looked brown and bleak and had a stench that grabbed your nostrils and eyes and didn't let go. They could only hope that inside would be better.

"Here we go," said Papa, as they came into the hallway. "Look, we're on the first floor; we won't have to climb stairs. How lucky."

Mama and Anna just looked at each other but stayed silent. Anna thought, in a way it was lucky, after seeing the stairway that didn't look like it was going to be there much longer. It was filled with garbage and filth too. The paint in the hallways was peeling off the walls. *You would have to use a wild imagination to put this place on the livable list,* thought Anna, trying not to touch anything.

Papa opened the door to the flat. He didn't need a key because nothing had locks on the outside. The floor was littered with dead bugs, a few dead rodents and what looked like a couple of them scurrying away. The floor was covered in brown grime. Mama's shoulders slumped but she didn't say anything. Anna knew she didn't want to make it worse for her and Papa. There was one small wood stained table with four heavily scuffed chairs near the wall by the kitchen. That was it.

Papa reached for the light switch, but nothing happened. "The electricity doesn't work, "he said. "We'll have to let them know in the morning."

Setting their cases down on the dirty floor, even though they didn't want to, Papa shut the door. "Well, we might as well see what we have here," he said a little too lighthearted.

They moved into the tiny kitchen. Pieces of wallpaper hung loose and had been torn off all the walls. Papa opened one of the cupboards only to discover a tiny mouse munching down on what must have been leftover crumbs. Mama screamed and jumped back. Papa wrapped his arms around her and just hugged her.

"It will be okay, Miriam. I'll take care of it." A broom closet held a small coffee can, a broom with bristles worn half off, and a piece of metal that had been shaped into a dustpan.

No one said a word as they worked their way down a short hall to the bathroom. Saying something wasn't going to make it better.

The tub was rust-stained, a black ring running all the way around it. The sink was brown and smelled like someone had peed in it, multiple times. Papa opened the toilet lid; human waste filled it to the brim. All their hands flew to their mouth and nose, gag reflexes taking hold. Wallpaper from the kitchen walls also filled it. Papa quickly dropped the lid. A light clicked on in Anna's brain, a confirmation of why the kitchen walls were missing strips of wallpaper.

Mama's face drained of color as she pushed Anna out the door. Leaning over the sink, she retched what little she had in her stomach into the sink bowl. Papa wrapped his arm around her, trying to soothe her. Mama just heaved over and over. She no longer had anything to retch, but her body kept convulsing.

"Miriam, it's okay. I'll fix everything. It will be okay."

"How can you say that!" shouted Anna. She wanted to scream at the top of her lungs but knew it wouldn't help. She slammed her fists against Papa over and over, tears streaming down her face. He turned around and glared at her, holding her fists back.

"What would you have me do?" he asked. "What? Would you like me to tell the Germans we don't like our living conditions? Well, would you?" he growled, his fists clenched around Anna's. "Would you like me to be more like Mr. Feinstein? Will that make you happy, Anna?"

She pulled her fists free, throwing her hands over her face, covering the tears now coming down like rain, unchecked. She wanted to disappear for the shame she felt. She was sobbing so hard she could barely breathe, gulping for air.

"I'm sorry, Papa. I'm so sorry," she gasped between gulps. "Forgive me."

Papa pulled her close and hugged her until her sobbing subsided.

"Oh, little gem," he whispered, his warm breath against her cheek. "I'm sorry too. None of us wants this or likes it, but we'll have to bear with it until we find a way to fix it." Mama came out and wrapped her arms around them, tears clearly running down her face, her eyes now red.

It took them all a few minutes to calm down before they could explore the only room left, the bedroom. It was small with one dirty mattress lying on the floor, and an old worn chifforobe set in the corner. The only window in the room had been broken and scattered over the floor and mattress. Boards had been nailed over the hole.

"Watch where you're walking," warned Papa. They all had hiking boots on, so Anna wasn't too worried. Papa pulled her and Mama close to himself, wrapping his strong arms around them.

"We'll make the best of our situation because we have no other choice right now." He looked at his daughter. "Anna, you must prepare for leaving this place. I have a feeling; this is not our last stop, but it will be yours. When I tell you to leave, you'll go to your hiding place this time, and there will be no questioning me. Do you understand?" He glanced firmly at Mama too, expecting her to comply.

"Can you find your way back?" he asked.

Anna nodded and then burst out sobbing. "I can't leave you and Mama. Why can't we all go together?" she cried. Tears streaked down her face.

"Yes, you can," he said, hugging her tightly. "You're a strong young woman Anna. You are mentally and physically strong. You can and *will* do it," he said. "There's no way for us to hide three people. At least we know you'll be safe. Do you understand?" She nodded her head yes.

Mama drew her gently into her arms and whispered, "You can do it, Anna. You'll do it for us, so we will know that no matter what happens, you are safe." She held Mama tight.

"Let's take all our extra clothes off," said Mama. "You should probably leave your suitcases packed since there's no dresser." She had gained control of herself and was obviously trying to be strong. Opening the chifforobe, she found four wooden hangers on the clothes bar.

"That's a great idea," agreed Papa. "We each get at least one hanger, and I'll fight you two for the other." He chuckled, trying to lighten the mood.

They all secretly knew he would give the extra hanger to Mama to keep her clothes from looking too wrinkled. Anna now understood why no one in the ghetto was clean or their clothes pressed. She knew she'd better learn not to be so critical since she was now in the same boat.

Mama pulled the wood hangers down one by one and wiped them off with a silk scarf she knew was not going to come in handy here. She handed each of them a hanger and told them to strip down to their first layer of clothes. Papa and Anna did as they were told. Each of them helped hold the clothes they took off, so they wouldn't end up on the dirty floor.

First Anna hung up her two extra dresses, then her sweater over it, and finally her coat. Mama held onto her arms as she pulled her boots off, so she could strip off the extra layer of wool stockings and then put her boots back on. Anna felt her body cool down by fifteen degrees as she discarded all the extra clothes. As she thought, Mama was the one who used the extra hanger and she was glad.

"Mama," whispered Anna, looking panicked. "I have to use the bathroom."

"Oh dear. Well, we're going to have to think of something." She cocked her head to one side in thought, "Get the coffee can from the kitchen and that will have to do for now," she said.

The look of shock and disgust must have registered with her because she told Anna she could use the coffee can or use the toilet, it was her choice. There was no other solution.

"I'll use the coffee can," she mumbled. There was no way she was going to use the toilet. Just thinking of it made her convulse. She took the can from the broom closet and went into the bedroom, shutting the door. There was no way she wanted to step foot in the bathroom, let alone, use the toilet. Anna set the can down, pulled up her dress, stripped her stockings and underwear down and crouched over the can. God answered a prayer because her urine hit the can. It must have been the prayer because she had always been a lousy aim in the woods. Having no toilet paper, she shook herself over the can for a few seconds, and pulled her clothes back into place. Her underwear lay slightly damp, making her feel disgusted. She knew the wallpaper would be used for something more than piddling in a can, just the thought of it making her shudder.

Papa told Mama he was going to fix the toilet but needed to find some tools to use. Mama's face turned green. They both felt sorry for him. It was tough being the man of the house, having to do all the dirty work and things women didn't want to do.

"Change into your worst clothes," said Mama, grabbing Papa's hand, acknowledging she was sorry he had to do it. "We might as well designate a set of clothes for cleaning."

"That's a good idea," he agreed. Anna left the bedroom so he could change his clothes. He soon came out in his khaki pants and a brown shirt, ready to find something he could use to attack the bathroom.

Papa opened the door leading to the outside hall, noting there was no lock on the inside either.

"We'll have to make sure there's always someone here, since there's no lock from the outside. I have a feeling stuff will disappear around here if you don't watch it."

Just as Papa started out the door, what looked like two families appeared on the steps leading up to the second floor. Everyone stopped in their tracks. Anna pulled up to Papa's side, staring at their new neighbors. They were Hasidic Jews. She knew this from the clothes they wore and the long curls the men wore on each side of their heads. They always wore black and white and strictly followed Sabat. The women were wearing the traditional Tichel head scarf to cover their hair, which was required of married women. They had long, plain black skirts on with white blouses. The boys were all mini versions of their fathers.

"Hello," said Papa, reaching out his hand to their new neighbors. "I'm Joseph Feiner and this is my wife Miriam and my daughter, Anna." Anna just nodded.

"Hello," said one of the men, shaking Papa's hand. "I'm Samuel Blumstein. This is my wife Sarah and my sons, Izak and Jacob."

"Aaron Goldhirsch," said the other man as he reached for Papa's hand. "This is my wife Esther and my son, Ezra." Papa shook his hand and they all nodded to each other.

"You're both located at the same flat?" asked Papa, thinking that was strange.

"Yes," said Mr. Goldhirsch. "They're making everyone double and triple up. They don't have enough flats for everyone. At least both our families are of the same sect."

"Oh, dear!" exclaimed Mama. "We're currently not sharing but there's only one bedroom and our flat's extremely small. How can they expect everyone to live together?"

"They don't care," said Papa angrily, curling his hands into fists. "They'll shove us together like cattle just to make us miserable." Everyone knew it was true.

"I hope you find your flat in better condition than ours is," said Papa. "It needs a few full days of cleaning and then I still wouldn't consider it livable."

Papa headed off down the hall to the streets and the new neighbors finished their way up the stairs. Anna was still standing in the doorway when she heard their bags drop and the women start to cry. Just like Papa, their husbands were telling them everything would be okay. Anna couldn't help but think, it wouldn't be. How could it?

Papa was on a mission to fix up the flat and when he set his mind to something, he never gave up. Even when he worked on a piece of jewelry, if there was even a small detail he was less than pleased with, he would start over, even when it was almost done. "Our customers expect and deserve perfection," he would say.

Mama and Anna wiped down two of the chairs and sat waiting for him to come back. Mama kept looking at her watch which just made the time go slower. It was three hours later, and dusk had set, when a soft knocking on the door could be heard.

"Miriam, Miriam, it's me, Joseph." The doorknob turned and in walked Papa. Mama ran to the door, grabbing him into a huge hug. Anna followed, wrapping her arms around his waist, squeezing tight.

"We've been so scared!" they both said in unison.

"Joseph, we were scared you weren't coming back, it's been so long, and we heard gunshots," said Mama, still clinging to him. "We've been sitting in the dark too afraid to go out."

"I'm so sorry," he said. "I didn't think to give you the flashlight I threw in my valise at the last minute." He kept saying he was sorry, over and over again. He went to the bedroom and brought out the flashlight, along with the candles and matches. At least there was some light now.

"I learned there are trucks coming all the time dropping more of us off every day," he said. "I think we can expect to have more than just us living here. They're putting multiple families into one flat. We need to hurry and take over the bedroom as ours. I expect it'll only be days, at most, before we have company."

"But how can they expect more than one family to live here?" exclaimed Miriam. "There isn't enough room!"

"They just do," he said, shrugging his shoulders. He didn't know what else to say. "On a good note, I ran into one of the council members. They have a system here, which is good. They have rules to follow, and jobs for everyone. I'll be meeting with them tomorrow to learn how this place runs. At least it's not utter chaos, so people can't just do whatever they want." He smiled. "I did get some supplies to clean with. One of the council members, Mr. Feld, got me some things from the cleaning room. I'm going to start on the bathroom. On a bad note, there will be no electricity or running water, and the sewers don't work, so the toilet's useless. I still need to clean it up to get rid of the smell."

"What!" Mama's face grew red with anger. "The toilets don't work?" she yelled, throwing her hands up in the air. "What in heaven's name are we supposed to use Joseph, what are we doing here?"

"Calm down, calm down," he said as he wrapped his arms around her, trying to soothe her. "They have a community bathroom facility which is what we'll have to use. Other than that, I'll find a bucket for nighttime. For now, the coffee can will have to suffice. I'm sorry, but I can't do anything about it." He looked haggard.

Anna could see he felt like he'd failed his family but there really wasn't anything he could do. The German soldiers were in charge. Mama looked spent. She had no more emotions left.

"We need to eat," she said, very monotone. "Anna and I are starving, and you must be hungry too."

"I am," he said, unable to look at them.

Mama wiped down a chair for him and laid a handkerchief on the table. They both pulled out the food they had grabbed and set it on the table. Papa pulled the small loaf of bread in half, and then the half into threes. He pulled his pocketknife out of his trouser pocket and cut three big slices of cheese off the hunk. Then he cut one of the apples into slices.

"Dinner is served." He smiled. Anna smiled back just to make him happy, but Mama sat stoic and silent.

"The rest we'll save for tomorrow, since we don't know what to expect yet. I'll learn all I can once the sun comes up," said Papa.

"Thank goodness you grabbed our lunch off the table before we had to leave." Mama sighed. "If I would have known, I would have packed food."

"Miriam, we couldn't have known. We'll figure it all out."

"Maybe we could get to the hiding place and get some canned food from there," suggested Anna.

"No." Papa shook his head. "We can leave the gates, but we have curfew, and Mr. Feld told me, they'll kill you if you try to smuggle food in."

"But why won't they let us go get food?" exclaimed Mama. "Why would they kill us over it?"

"Let's talk of other things we need to do in here," said Papa giving Mama *the look*. Anna always knew when her parents didn't want her to hear or know about something. They had "the look" that passed between them, silently saying, not in front of her. Mama, nodded ever so slightly to Papa, thinking Anna wouldn't notice. She wanted to tell them she'd been noticing since she was eight.

"Eat up," said Papa.

With supper done, Papa trudged off to the dreaded bathroom.

"What's the shovel for?" asked Mama.

"You don't want to know," he called back, shaking his head again.

"Well, maybe I can get the kitchen sink cleaned out," said Mama, not too enthusiastically. "Anna, you get the cupboards and mice," she told her, her body shivering to show how much she hated rodents. *Thanks,* thought Anna.

****

CHAPTER FIVE

Anna watched as the trucks lined up at the gate, Jews pouring out of them. The soldiers were pushing, pulling and shoving them to the front registration. Most of them were wearing a single layer of clothing. Their suitcases were mostly stuffed with family pictures, heirlooms and nonessentials that wouldn't help them here. They would soon find out that clothes were the most valuable thing you could own. A silver candle stick wouldn't keep you warm in the winter. If you were lucky, maybe you could sell it, but not to anyone already in the ghetto and if the soldiers wanted it, they just took it.

It was common to hear gunshots during the day. Those arriving hadn't learned to keep their head down and their mouths shut. Disagree and you found yourself in the dead pile.

The SS soldiers had established Jewish councils to help run the ghettos. The only problem was, they didn't have any authority and were really set up to do the dirty work soldiers didn't want to do. The council members, however, took their jobs seriously, determined to make life the best they could under the circumstances. The exception was those who exploited their positions for self-preservation regardless of the outcome for their fellow Jews.

There were jobs for most everyone. Everyone worked, young and old. Food was your reward, although it wasn't enough to keep most people alive. The usual diet consisted of a watery soup with little nutrition in it and a slice of bread. Papa's job was working in the repair shop. Because he was a jeweler, he got all the projects that required steady hands working with small parts. It didn't take long for his hands that were once soft and impeccable to become calloused and split.

Mama and Anna worked in the kitchen. It was well understood that anyone sneaking or hiding food outside of their usual minor rations would be immediately shot. It had happened more than once that coworkers were found with a piece of bread or a small piece of carrot in their pocket, and then were taken off to never be seen again. Still, even considering those who disappeared, as examples, hunger sometimes made someone feel desperate and bold.

The days were long and tiring. Work began early in the morning and seemed to last forever. Exhaustion was a constant companion.

Time wore on day after day, month after month, and soon two years slipped by in misery, and another winter would soon be here.

Papa, Mama and Anna had all lost weight, their clothes hanging on their gaunt bodies. They all knew, if Anna didn't get out soon, she wouldn't survive. It was now or never. A plan had been put in place.

All Anna could think about was how tired, dirty and hopeless she felt. She knew the time was finally here. It was time to escape. Papa and Mama were right. This wasn't even existing! The gates to the ghetto were closed and the thought of how she was to escape made her shudder. If she had still had any food inside of her, it would not have stayed there long. Bile filled her throat, but she swallowed down what little filled her airways.

Was she capable of pulling it off? So many lives were in danger if she didn't. Instant death would come to those who helped her escape, including herself. She had to keep it together, she must. Still, the thought of lying on the dead cart with bodies of the young, old, friends, and the traitors who had worked with the Germans, made her shiver. Pretending to be dead amongst the real dead would be a challenge. Thinking about it made Anna convulse again. This was when she was thankful her stomach was empty. Starving to death had its benefits.

My last evening, thought Anna. Two years had already gone by. Two years she could have been living in her hideout if she had listened to Papa. But that also would have meant two years less with her parents. She wasn't sorry she had missed her first chance to escape. Now she wondered if she'd ever see her parents again. They all doubted it. They had reconciled the thought as much as they could that this was the last goodbye, the last words to be spoken aloud to each other. Would she be able to remember their voices, their faces?

Mama, Papa, and Anna lay on the mattress together, Anna sandwiched between, just like when she was little. Her parents each held one of her hands. She held the moment in her heart, burying it deep, to reclaim later in time.

"Anna," Papa said softly, "you know we love you. From the day you were born, you became our world, our reason for existence. Why the world's brought this on us, only God knows, and you must trust in Him. Remember that. I'm sorry I can't protect you against all this. I've failed you and your mother," he said, his voice catching. She could feel Papa shaking. He was trying to hold it in, but she and Mama knew he was crying.

"No!" cried Anna. "You saved us, Papa! You've done all that a man can do and more. We would have never survived this far without your skills and willingness to see what others never saw coming. I love you and Mama, and I'm thankful for every day we've had."

"She's right, Joseph." Mama reached over and squeezed Papa's hand. As slender and gaunt as she was, the strength with which she squeezed Papa's hand reached his soul. He could believe they'd thought he had done all he could, but tears still streamed down his face. There was but one thing left to do. They had to get Anna out. They had been here far too long. If she didn't go now, she'd never make it.

"Tomorrow will be a hard and scary day," Papa choked out. "The only way out is the dead cart. It'll take all of your mental and physical strength to endure it until you can climb from the grave."

Mama lay still, not saying anything. Suddenly, she grabbed Anna, wrapped her arms around her and cried. The tears came and came, her body sobbing against her, her bones pushing into Anna's. Mama's now ninety pounds was made up of nothing but protruding bones. Anna stroked her hair and wiped the tears from her sunken face. She had to be the strong one now.

"I love you, Anna," whispered Mama. "I love you so much." Her breath was warm and soft on Anna's ear, taking her back to her childhood in the old house, where she would cuddle with her in bed and whisper, I love you over and over. Anna closed her eyes and melted into the moment and the memory, snapping a mental picture of the three of them together for what would probably be the last time.

Morning arrived with the air cool and crisp. Anna was glad she had her heavy gray wool coat with the fox fur to keep her warm. It was ragged and two sizes too small now, but still warm. She couldn't help but think, her coat would give her a heavy layer away from the dead and decaying corpses. Today was it. She was to be pronounced dead.

Mama's face was streaked with tears, her eyes red and swollen, and so were Papa's. No one had slept, dreading their final goodbyes.

Anna had risen, put on her warmest leggings, another pair over those, two dresses that hung huge on her bony frame, two pairs of socks, and Mama's hiking boots, which she had insisted she take. Anna's feet had grown over the past two years. The rest of her belongings would be left behind, hopefully put to good use by someone who needed them, or perhaps something that her parents could barter with.

Wrapping her scarf around her neck, she pulled her coat off the hanger and came out to the front room. Both Mama and Papa's eyes were almost swollen shut. They sat at the table, holding each other's hands. Papa reached out, caressing Anna's hands in his.

"I'm ready, Papa," she said softly. "I'm ready." She was trying to be brave, but her body was shaking. Mama jumped up and hugged her, pulling her into her chest, the tears streaming down her face. She pulled one of her handkerchiefs from her dress sleeve and gently dabbed her perfume on it, the only personal thing she had brought with her from home.

"Place this over your face while you're on the cart. It'll help you breathe. When you smell it, you'll think of us and not your surroundings. Close your eyes and think of us." Then she grabbed her and kissed her repeatedly on the forehead until Papa pulled her away.

"Miriam, we have to go. They're waiting for us." Papa helped her with her coat, the yellow star missing. She wouldn't need to draw attention to the fact she was Jewish if she managed to escape and was seen. Mama had brushed the coat until almost all evidence that a star had been on it was gone.

It was time. Anna looked back at Mama as she and Papa slipped out the door. "I love you, Mama," she said one last time, choking on the words. "I'll live, I promise." Papa closed the door softly behind them. She could hear Mama crying hard, sobbing uncontrollably, as they moved down the apartment hallway.

Papa and Anna made their way down the dirty streets to the burying detail, a few blocks away. Anyone who died went to the "dead pile," where they were put on the big wooden cart, piled two to three high and three across and taken out of the ghetto walls to the mass gravesite. The grave detail would pile them into the mass grave multiple high, twenty to thirty across and then cover them with dirt. Weeks after the grave was full, it would be completely covered, removing any evidence they had ever existed. Papa had told her that some were getting out by pretending to be dead, but the soldiers were getting smarter. She prayed she would cross dumb soldiers today.

Anna recognized Mr. Feld. He and Papa had become good friends. He was the man in charge of the burial details. Papa had encouraged Mr. Feld to help get Anna out by offering what little money he still had. He had said no, that compensation wasn't needed, but Papa wouldn't take no for an answer. Mr. Feld finally accepted, but only a small payment to make Papa feel better. The rest, Papa had tucked into Anna's coat pocket to find later.

"Hello, Anna," greeted Mr. Feld. "Are you sure you can do this? A lot of people are in great danger if you get caught."

"I'm ready. I can and will do this. I'll live to tell our story, for my parents and all of us. I can do it," she said, holding her head high in defiance of any German soldier who thought she couldn't.

"Good," said Mr. Feld. "I believe you. You're a strong young lady. Your parents and I are proud of you. You'll be on the bottom of the pile. This is to ensure the soldiers don't look too closely, and to help cover any movement you may have from trying to breathe. You must draw slow breaths, so you don't move too much. Remember, shallow breaths. You don't want to shift the bodies on top of you. The bodies will be layered to give you as much room as possible, but they'll be heavy. Place your hand about four inches from your mouth to provide space to breathe. Once the cart's loaded, we'll have to place vomit and body waste on top of the bodies. I know it's repulsive, but the more stench, the less likely the soldiers will look at the cart. They think they have strong stomachs, but they're babies in the stench of death."

Anna shivered and tried not to convulse just thinking about it.

"We'll push the cart out the gates to the grave-site. This will take about an hour. The soldiers will accompany us and wait for us to bury the dead. Remember, you're dead until night comes. Do you understand?" She nodded.

"Good," said Mr. Feld, nodding his head. "We'll lay you into the grave last, so you must be still while you're on the cart and as we pull you off. We'll lay you toward the end, so it'll be closer to crawl over everyone and escape into the woods. A layer of dirt will be shoveled over you, to make it look like we're done. Late into the night, crawl out quickly and run as far into the woods as possible."

She nodded again. Her throat felt too dry to speak.

"Let's begin then." Anna laid down on her stomach in the middle of the cart. She turned her head to the side, so she could breathe. Papa laid Mama's handkerchief over her face, shielding her eyes, nose and mouth. She could smell, almost taste Mama's scent. She put her hand close to her face and closed her eyes as the bodies were laid next to and on top of her, pinning her further into the cart.

"There's a small bit of cheese and potato in your pocket," whispered Papa. "After you get far away, eat so you have energy to move on as fast as you can. Get away Anna." Papa's voice caught and he paused before he continued. "Remember, God is with you no matter what and Mama and I love you. You must live!"

Her mind raced through the plan they'd laid out. She was to escape and make her way back to the hiding place where they'd hidden their valuables and food. What condition she would find it in, no one knew.

"I love you, Papa," she whispered. She didn't know if he could hear her, but she said the words for herself. Anna could smell the body waste, and her throat wanted to heave. She breathed into the handkerchief, focusing on her parents. She tried to think of good times to get her mind off the smell. The cart began to move, and she knew Papa couldn't come, but she wished he could. She wanted him to see the soldiers walk away from the grave and watch her rise in defiance from the dead and be free.

As the cart moved, hair from the person on top of her fell over the handkerchief. She sucked in her breath and opened her eyes. She could see the dark hair lying against the hanky. The hair was long, like hers. Her face had been placed looking away, but she knew it was a woman. She closed her eyes, willing the picture of her to fade away.

Anna was dead. She was going to be reborn only when she got out and free of the ghetto. She knew in her heart she would give it all she had to survive. She had to.

The cart stopped, and the soldiers started barking orders to dump the bodies, so they could get back. One by one, the grave detail pulled the bodies from the cart and laid them into the mass grave. Mr. Feld put his face near Anna's ear and whispered.

"Be still, they're watching."

She stiffened as they grabbed her arms and legs, and then she mentally told herself to relax and let her body go limp, as the dead should be. The gentleness that they used as they set her body in the grave made her want to whisper thank you, but she lay quiet. Mr. Feld had magically placed Mama's hanky back over her face before setting a fine layer of dirt over her.

"God speed, Anna, whispered Mr. Feld.

"Schnell! Schnell! yelled the guards. "They're dead, you don't need to be so gentle. Throw them in and be done unless you want to join them!"

"Yes, yes, we're done," called out Mr. Feld as the burial detail hurried back to the guards.

She could hear the cartwheels rumble over the gravel as they left. Slowly, Anna opened her eyes. Mama's handkerchief shielded her from seeing her dead companions. The sun was barely out, and clouds were moving in. The cold air and night dew were settling to the ground. She could feel the cold bodies underneath her, and the stench of decay of those who had been buried long before. She continued to take shallow breaths, breathing in the scent from the handkerchief.

Anna kept still for a good eight hours, until the darkened sky finally gave her the courage to move.

Slowly, she lifted her head up a few inches, shaking the dirt from Mama's hanky and her face. It was cold and dark, a low layer of fog settling to the ground, the moon slightly hidden by the clouds. *A lucky omen,* thought Anna.

Slowly, she got up, crouching as low as she could. The body next to her was a man. A bright yellow star adorned his coat. His hair was dark, his nose slightly large and his mouth was half-open, dirt lying inside of it. His eyes were closed, and Anna was glad. Even in the dark, she could see him, and it made her shudder.

Anna tucked Mama's hanky in her pocket, feeling the precious morsels of food her parents had selflessly given up. Her stomach growled, but all she could think about was escaping. She pulled herself over the bodies, stepping on the backs, arms, and legs of the deceased.

Climbing out, her foot took hold on the face of a decaying body. Anna's heel slipped, and she felt the person's skin peel away from their bones under her boot, making her stomach churn. She didn't dare look down or she'd lose it. Reaching the edge of the grave, she hoisted herself up, stepping on the bodies to get out. She silently apologized, but she knew down deep, they were probably glad they could be useful in their death and that someone was actually fleeing from the grave.

With one last hoist, she pulled herself up and ran into the woods. She ran and ran, until, despite the coolness of the night, she was sweating profusely. She wasn't even sure which way she had run; she just did what Papa had said. Get away fast, and then get your bearings.

Anna stopped and sat on the ground, crying and trembling. She had made it; she had really made it. Did Papa and Mama know? She wanted them to. She was breathing freedom! She sucked it into her lungs, long and deep and wept some more.

Finally, pulling herself together, she moved. Even though her legs felt like rubber, she kept moving, picking up speed, careful to watch and listen for anyone following her. Her stomach growled loud and long, begging for food. She wasn't far enough away to stop and eat, despite what her stomach was saying. She ignored it, moving through the woods as fast as her legs would let her.

The sun was coming up, along with a crisp wind and what promised to be snowflakes. Anna had to get her bearings quickly. Papa had given her instructions to crawl out of the grave, run to the brush ahead, and deep into the woods. Once into the woods, she was to hang left and keep going until she ran into a road where signs would give her directions.

"Don't be afraid," he'd said. "It'll take some days before you find any signs, but they'll be there. God speed Anna, God speed." She could hear Papa say it now, smiling, but his forehead wrinkled in concern.

Anna moved as quick as her frozen feet would take her. The sun was coming up and she was spent. She scouted out shelter. There was a fallen log with lots of dropped leaves. If she propped some extra branches against the log, there would be plenty of room to hide. In her mind, she could have sworn she heard Papa approve her choice.

Pulling extra branches against the log and scattering leaves on top, Anna crawled inside, pulled the collar of her coat up around her neck as far as she could, pulled her hat down over her face and put her head down on a pillow of leaves. It was wet and cold, but she was exhausted and didn't care. Pulling the potato from her pocket, she ate quickly, leaving the piece of carrot for later. Feeling semi-content, she closed her eyes and fell into a deep slumber. Sleep came swiftly but so did the dreams.

The Germans were cleaning out the ghetto. Anna was gripping her parents, shouting, "Don't go, don't go." No one could see or hear her. The trucks rolled up and everyone got in them. The trucks arrived at the mass grave. One by one, the soldiers pulled the bodies out, soldiers grabbing the arms and legs, swinging them up into the air like they were target practice, shooting them as they came down with a thud on the pile of dead.

"Stop, stop!" screamed Anna, but they kept shooting. They pulled her father off the truck, threw him in the air, bullets piercing his body over and over until he fell to the ground. Next came Mama, Mr. Feld and all the people she had befriended in the ghetto.

Anna woke choking back her tears, her chest heaving. Papa had said they probably wouldn't live. Was this dream an omen that she'd be alone in the world? Anna pulled Mama's hanky from her pocket, holding it to her nose. She pushed the branches off the log and sat up, her back against the fallen tree, soaking in Mama's smell.

****

CHAPTER SIX

Days had passed since Anna had left. The ghetto was swarming with death. Joseph pulled Miriam close. "You must try to go on, dear," he said. "You must. You asked this of our daughter, and now you must ask it of yourself."

"I don't want to go on, Joseph." Miriam sighed. "I know I'm going to die, and you know it. We know Anna got out, and that's enough for me. Mr. Feld said her body was gone when he did his next burial detail. I can be happy in death knowing my precious Anna made it. Look at me, Joseph. Really look at me."

Joseph hugged his wife. She was nothing but skin and bones, and deep down, he knew it was weeks if not only days before she would lie down and not wake up.

"Miriam, I love you. You and Anna are my happiness. My world is empty without you. Don't you want to try and see Anna again?"

"I love you too, Joseph. I always have and always will. You are a good man and I'm proud of you. You must live to find her when this is over, but I know I won't make it. Promise me you'll find her. Promise me," she urged.

Joseph wrapped his arms protectively around her frail body. "I will, Miriam. I promise you, until my last breath, I'll find Anna."

Two days later, Miriam died in her sleep, Joseph lying next to her. They lay that way for hours, Joseph unable to move. He just wanted to soak in her smell, her face, stroke her hair, and not give her up.

Hours later, he covered Miriam up and went to find his friend, Mr. Feld. They came back with the cart, wrapped her in her coat and gently laid her on top of the dead cart.

Anna was walking in the woods when an overwhelming feeling of sadness hit her hard. She got down on her knees and wept for what seemed like hours. She knew Mama was gone. She reached into her pocket and pulled the handkerchief to her nose, sucking in Mama's scent.

"Oh, Mama," Anna wept. Her heart ached but she marched on with more determination than before. "For you, Mama," she told herself. Tears were still streaming down her face, freezing in their tracks, but she didn't care.

During the day, Anna slept, and evening, she marched on to find her hiding place. Moving in the brush at night was difficult, so she switched to the road she had finally found, hugging the ditch in case she had to jump to safety. A road sign said she was about ninety kilometers from Dusseldorf. She had a long way to go, but at least she was headed in the right direction.

Just seeing the name of her hometown on a sign, gave her hope.

In Anna's mind, she knew it had been only days that she had been walking, but it seemed like forever. She was completely exhausted. Her hands and feet were frozen, the feeling in them long gone. She knew if she stopped, she'd never make it. Stopping was death. Her stomach gnawed on itself. The only food she'd had since she escaped was the small amount Papa had slipped in her coat pocket, a few frozen rotted apples along the way and the little number of roots in the woods Papa had shown her were edible. She had to find food. She needed real food.

Dusk had set, making it hard to see in front of herself. A light appeared from behind, quickly getting brighter, and then she heard the engine roar, shouting coming from the vehicle. Anna dove into the wet ditch filled with leaves and muck. She lay still, waiting for them to pass by, but instead, they slowed, the truck's brakes squealing to a stop. She sucked in her breath. Had they found her? Did they know she was there? She lay still, not moving, listening.

Twenty yards ahead, loud, drunk soldiers jumped from the truck. If anymore lined up to relieve themselves, she would be doomed.

"I've had so much beer; I think I could piss a keg" one of them said and laughed. She could hear everything they said, they were so close. She could hear the pee hit the dirt, the smell of urine drifting to her nose. She was scared but even more, disgusted! They were responsible for Mama's death. It was all she could do to stay put and not let her rage take over. It seemed like forever before they all managed to crawl back into the truck. She heard the engine rev, their drunken voices finally fading into the night air.

Anna waited a few minutes and then pulled herself out of the muddy ditch, doing her best to brush herself off. Her hair and clothes were covered in muck. There was no resemblance to the real Anna.

She could still see the steam coming from where they had peed on the side of the road. It rose, the hot meeting the cool air. All Anna could think was, *"Piss on you, Hitler."*

Anna's feet were so cold that she could no longer feel her toes. The morning light was coming up as she slipped into the woods and made a small lean-to, piling leaves on the outside. Slipping her boots off, she pulled her wool hat off and wrapped her left foot in it. Wrapping her scarf around her right foot, she slipped her boots back on as best she could. She could feel the tingling in her feet, tiny needles telling her the feeling was coming back. The pain felt good. Anna crawled into the lean-to hoping she hadn't left any of herself exposed. It didn't take long for slumber to greet her. Good dreams of Mama and Papa swept through her sleep. It felt so good, her body relaxed and melted into euphoria.

Anna woke with a start, not knowing how long she had slept. Daylight was quickly slipping away which meant she could move on. She had learned to make night her daytime and day her night. She heard voices and trucks as she stretched, ready to get up. Barely lifting her head, she saw rows of army vehicles rumbling by, one, two, twelve, eighteen, and more. She quit counting. All of them were filled with soldiers, heading her direction. She shuddered. Was it still smart to head toward home, to her hiding place? Was it even intact? She had no news as to what was going on in Germany, or the world. The volume of trucks and soldiers had finally stopped passing.

Snow started falling, lightly at first but then fast and thick, a blizzard. It was only dusk, but Anna knew staying out in it, she'd die. She got up and headed to the road, hoping she'd hear if anyone was coming before they saw her. She hadn't seen any trucks for a while and hoped there were no stragglers. She walked a few miles and finally saw smoke. A farmhouse about a half a mile in the distance was spiraling smoke from its chimney. She could only hope to sneak into the barn and find some warmth. Anna headed in its direction, snow swirling in every direction, covering the ground. As cold and blinding as the snow was, it helped conceal her, and she was thankful. She moved from tree to tree until she had to move across the open field to get to the barn. The only hope she had was no one would be out in this weather, and the falling snow would cover her tracks.

Anna made a run for it to the edge of the barn. It was old, the paint long peeled from its boards. The grayish color was what was left after years of deterioration. Peeking around to the door, it looked clear. She snuck up to the door and pulled on the iron handle. It opened about two inches, the hinges screeching, making her freeze in her tracks. Pulling again, the hinges groaned as Anna snuck into the barn's darkness. Flattening herself against the cold plank wall, she let her eyes adjust to find a cow staring at her, inches from her face. She almost screamed, pee rushing down her legs, helpless to do anything about it. The cow mooed softly and sauntered away.

Her eyes adjusting to the dark, she looked around and saw a ladder to the loft. She climbed it, hoping to find some place inconspicuous that would be safe. Barn implements, tack, old tools, and an old trunk cluttered the floor along with a huge pile of hay. Anna slipped into the middle of the hay, hugging her feet up to her chest. Warm, it was so warm. Despite her underclothes and stockings being soaking wet, she fell asleep.

Anna woke up and tried to get her bearings. She was so warm. A humming sound floated up to the loft. A woman's voice continued to hum and work down below, talking to the animals, calling them by name, as if they were old family members. The humming became louder and she could hear someone make their way up the ladder. Anna panicked. Now what? The woman was still humming when Anna felt the pitchfork strike her thigh. Anna moaned, and then threw her hand over her mouth.

The humming abruptly stopped, and the pitchfork poked her again. The woman slowly pulled the hay away, until they were both staring at each other. Anna froze, stiff as a statue. The woman just stared. Anna was petrified. She started to rush up, but the woman put the pitchfork up to hold her back. She was caught! The woman looked her up and down and finally spoke.

"What's your name?"

"Anna," she whispered.

"Where are you from, and why are you here, miss?" asked the woman, still holding the pitchfork inches from Anna.

"I'm making my way up north to family. I was cold and needed a warm place and I saw your barn."

"And the rest of your family?" questioned the woman, cocking her head with a resignation that Anna was not telling her the whole truth.

"My parents are dead. I have relatives that I'm trying to get to. I'm alone."

"Hmmm," mumbled the woman. "I expect you're not being truthful about everything, considering you have an outline of a star on your coat."

Anna's body stiffened. The woman knew.

"You don't need to fear me, young lady. I have no animosity to the Jews. I may not agree with what's going on, but I'm unable to say anything. My husband's a German officer, but he's gone, so you're safe. He'd turn you in immediately, or shoot you. As for me, you're safe with me. Like I said, my husband's gone for months, and I'm not expecting company. Come with me. You can't stay long, and after today, I never want to see you again."

Anna nodded, relaxing a bit.

"Well, come on. You look and smell like you need a bath and food. After that, you'll need to leave. Do you understand?"

"Danke." Anna nodded, struggling to hold back the tears at the thought of an actual bath.

"It's best you don't know my name, and as of now, I have forgotten yours. Come on, then. Let's get you something to eat."

The woman guided Anna out of the barn and into the house. Anna was hesitant, but did she really have a choice? The house was nice. A typical farmhouse, nice soft wallpaper adorned the walls, a strong oak table and chairs stood in the kitchen, and a lovely tablecloth with embroidered bluebirds draped the table. Anna soaked in the morning breakfast smell, and her stomach grumbled loudly.

"Just as I thought," said the woman. "Sit, and I'll get you some breakfast." Within minutes, the woman had served Anna eggs, golden brown biscuits with homemade strawberry jam, crispy bacon, and a stack of hotcakes dripping with maple syrup fit for a large man.

Anna dug in, so fast she started to choke. The woman pulled the plate away, scolding her for eating too fast.

"It won't do you any good to eat all that food just to have it all come back up. Slow down," she admonished, sliding the plate back in front of Anna.

"Danke," whispered Anna.

A full glass of milk was set in front of Anna's plate. She took a few gulps and then set the glass back down, remembering to slow down. Her stomach began to feel warm and it was all Anna could do to keep her eyes open.

As Anna tried to finish the food on her plate, she noticed the lovely pattern on the dish. It reminded her of home and Mama. A sadness crept over her and it was all she could do not to burst into tears.

When she had finished eating, the woman told Anna to follow her. She led her to the bathroom where a warm tub of water and a large bar of lavender soap waited for her. "Strip off your clothes so I can wash all but your coat, and you can clean yourself up. You are in dire need of a bath, miss."

Anna was scared. Not to have her clothes on would mean no escape if necessary. Anna didn't move, wrapping her arms around her waist. The woman touched Anna's arm and smiled at her. It was the first time Anna had been touched in days. She burst into tears, letting them stream down her face.

The woman pulled her into a strong hug.

"You're safe, dear, my husband will be away for weeks or even months. You're safe, I promise. You're safe," she reiterated, trying to reassure Anna that she could trust her.

Anna felt she had no choice and she desperately wanted a bath. She stripped down, handing her clothes through the bathroom door that had been left open a few inches, then slowly slipped into the tub.

"Oohhh," Anna moaned as she sank down into the hot water. She hadn't had a real bath since they'd been forced to leave home. Hot water had been a luxury, and now she just let it caress her body. She let the water rise around her, and then she slowly dunked her head below the water, letting her hair float freely. Slowly pulling her face out of the water, she sat up. Dear God, how good it felt. At that moment, Anna didn't care if she got caught. This might just be worth it.

Pulling the bar of soap and washcloth down into the water she scrubbed herself, letting the lavender scent encase her. She scrubbed her hair not once but twice. The water was already a light brownish gray, but Anna kept scrubbing until her skin was bright red. Oh, how wonderful it felt. The water was now the color of dirt and had cooled, letting her know the luxury had come to an end.

The woman came in, startling Anna. She wrapped her arms around her naked body, covering what she could.

"Don't worry miss, you have everything I have," she chuckled. She proceeded to wrap a warmed towel, heated from in front of the fireplace around her and handed her another one for her hair.

"Danke" said Anna. "You've been so kind."

The woman parked Anna in front of the fire. "Make sure you dry your hair good. It won't do you any good to catch pneumonia when you leave." The woman smiled at her, making Anna feel like somebody cared if she lived or died.

Her clothes had been washed and were drying by the fire. They looked nice and clean, considering what wear they had been through in the previous years. Anna pulled the towel from her hair and used the brush the woman had given her. When her clothes were finally dry, she slipped them on. Her worn, thin socks that had multiple holes were gone, and a new thick hand knit wool pair lay in their place. All her clothes were toasty warm which made Anna even more sleepy. Her eyelids felt heavy, and she could no longer fight to keep them open. Minutes later, a gentle snore escaped her lips.

When she awoke, day had slipped into night. Anna shot up from her chair, not remembering where she was.

"It's okay," the woman said, as she gently patted Anna's shoulder.

Recognition hit her, and she collapsed back into the chair. She was still exhausted, but her body had been revived some. Anna was handed a warm cup of tea and a plate with a ham sandwich and some cookies. She sipped the tea, savoring its warmth and flavor. She ate the sandwich and cookies slowly. It would be a long time before she would be spoiled again, if ever. It was all she could do not to break down and cry again. God was surely with her.

"I'm sorry I can't ask you to stay." the woman frowned. "Neither of us can risk it."

Anna understood. Neither of them wanted to think about the consequences if they were caught together. The woman handed Anna a coat that had no outline of a star. It was the woman's own coat. Anna just stared at the coat. No words could express how thankful she was.

"I have another." The woman shrugged. "I'll burn yours. It's funny, you don't really look Jewish."

"I know. My great-grandfather had dark blond hair and hazel eyes. I take after him. I guess I was lucky."

The woman handed Anna her boots. "I waxed and polished them. It should help seal out the snow. I don't have much money, but I slipped a few marks into the coat pocket."

Anna was overwhelmed with how kind the woman had been. She'd never forget her. Anna knew it was time to go, even though she wasn't ready, but her time here had run out. Still, she was thankful.

They both stepped to the back door, and Anna slipped the woman's coat on. It was a little big, but warm, and most importantly, no star. Handing Anna a cloth bag, the woman smiled at her and gave her a hug.

The woman may have been German, but she held onto Anna like a mother. For the first time in days, Anna smiled.

"Thank you for your kindness. I'm sure God led me to you. Just when I thought everyone had turned their backs, here you were."

The woman hugged Anna again, smiled, and opened the door. The frosty night air hit Anna hard, making leaving even more depressing.

"Follow out to the barn and go out the way you came in. The snow's light, but it'll fill your tracks. Up the road is a German camp, so make sure you stay off the road a few miles up. It's dusk, so night should give you some cover." For the first time, the woman spoke Anna's name. "Good luck to you Anna, and God be with you." Anna smiled and slipped out the door.

Making her way through the woods to the road, Anna thought back to her parents. She was sure Mama was gone, but Papa, what about him? He was resilient, but the Germans were persistent in their efforts to destroy them. Anna prayed her father was still alive.

She could hear the trucks out on the road and moved a bit farther into the woods. The snow lit up the area, and the last thing she needed now was to be a silhouette in the night. Drawing near the camp the woman had mentioned, Anna made haste to skirt around it. She could see buildings with the lights on and movement about the compound. She had no intentions of running into soldiers. She shuddered at what they would do to her before they killed her.

The snow continued to fall, and Anna felt the chill, but being clean and well fed made all the difference. How God had blessed her with kindness today. The coating the woman had put on her boots was helping to keep her feet dry, and her mouth watered for the bag, of food the woman had given her when she left. She hadn't eaten any yet, hadn't even wanted to look in the bag, in case it made her even more hungry. No, she would wait until she became famished. She couldn't afford to splurge.

Anna guessed she had walked about fifteen kilometers, and she was bone-tired. Traipsing through the woods instead of the roads was tough going. Daylight was sneaking up on her, so she had to find shelter. A few birds flew overhead cawing hello. Her only companions. *I'm alone again.*

Off to the west, Anna thought she spied a small building. She cautiously drew closer. It was a dilapidated wood building, ready to fall down. The door was half off its hinges, the wood rotted and gray from the weather. It must have been an old hunter blind, she thought. It was just small enough for two people to crouch inside, and it had small open windows on three sides. It was filled with snow, but it looked like no one had been there in years. She'd take the chance.

Using her boots, Anna scraped the snow off the floor and out the door. She pulled herself inside, yanking the door closed as best she could, and pulled the wood window blinders down. At least the wind was blowing against the door instead of inside it. It was a small comfort, but she was thankful for it.

She slid down the wall, stretching her tired and sore feet out. Her stomach rumbled, and she pulled open the bag. Anna just stared. The package had been heavy, but she hadn't dared look inside when she left the woman's home. Anna knew its weight was worth more than gold and had gladly taken the goods.

Now opening the bag, she saw that inside sat two apples, two sandwiches, biscuits, a tiny jar of jam, a small bottle of milk with a stopper in it, carrots, and cookies. There was even a small spoon for the jelly. Tears pooled in Anna's eyes. Did this woman even know how she had saved and was still saving, her life?

Anna unwrapped one of the sandwiches, eating slowly, savoring each bite. She wouldn't hurry through it. It was to be savored and appreciated. The bread was fresh, just like the bread the Reinholds made in their bakery.

Her mind wandered to Peter. Was Peter now a soldier? Did he still care about her and her family? She would probably never know. Her last memory of Peter was his father holding him back when all the Jews in the neighborhood were loaded on the trucks destined for the ghetto.

Next, she pulled the stopper from the milk bottle and took a few gulps. It was cold and creamy. Last, Anna ate one of the cookies. She wouldn't waste a thing. The rest was for tomorrow, and for however long she could make it last. For now, her stomach was content, and she drifted off to sleep.

Anna woke to snow piled around the door opening. She was cold, but not too wet. Daylight streamed through the crack in the doorway. She'd have to wait a couple hours before darkness would settle in and she could move on. Towns were getting closer, and she couldn't afford to be careless, especially since she had made it this far.

Trucks rumbled off in the distance and she could only imagine they were full of soldiers off to honor Hitler. Just thinking of what they were capable of made her want to vomit, but she didn't want to waste any food that had already fed her physically and mentally.

It seemed forever before daylight faded. The snow had stopped falling, which was both a blessing and a curse. She wanted her tracks to be covered, yet staying dry was appreciated. She packed up her bag of food, pulled her hat down and shoved open the door that was now half frozen in place.

The sky was scattered with clouds, a few stars trying to peek out, giving some light along the snow filled ground. The snow crunched under her boots and sounded loud in the night silence, and still she marched on. She decided not to take the road. It was too dangerous, too many people and trucks now. She had seen town signs and knew she was about twenty-five kilometers from home, or what used to be home. It was slow going. Anna had gone about five kilometers when she heard voices. She pulled up quick next to a huge oak tree and slid down the trunk. She quickly pulled dead leaves around and over her as best she could, pulling her cap down, and tucking into a small ball.

The voices became louder, closer, and she could hear what they were saying. Kids, they were just kids, but even they were dangerous. They would run and tell their parents. She prayed they would leave. They were calling for what had to be the dog.

"Come on, boy," they called. "Come on."

Yeah, she thought. *Go on, you stupid dog!* She sat stiff against the trunk and waited. Pulling her hat up, she flinched when she saw a huge German shepherd staring inches from her face. "Go on! Get!" she whispered. The dog just stood there, tongue wagging, its rancid breath panting in her face. The boys' voices got closer, and if the dog didn't leave, she knew she was in trouble. They couldn't have been more than ten yards away when they called again, and the dog ran off in their direction.

"Good boy," she heard them praising the dog.

Finally, the voices faded. Anna got up, stretching her legs, stiff from sitting so long. She was a mess again, but at least she was clean underneath her clothes. She was still remembering sinking into the woman's warm bathtub. How she wished for it again.

The sun was starting to show, and Anna was seeing clusters of houses. She was on the outskirts of a farm community, which meant she was getting closer to town. Earlier, she had moved closer to the road, so she could find the road signs and confirm she was heading in the right direction. She had about fifteen kilometers until she reached home.

Anna's heart jumped at the thought of getting to her house, and yet, she knew it was no longer home. Still, she wanted to see it, at least one more time. Maybe the Reinholds would be baking, and she would get to smell the scent of homemade bread in the air. Just the thought made her mouth water.

Knowing she had to find a place to hide for the day, Anna moved farther into the woods and searched for shelter. There wasn't much, but she had become very resourceful. There was a small out cropping of rocks that would provide a shelter for her back and a slight overhang of about ten inches that could help keep the wind off.

Gathering ground brush, Anna laid it down to pad her from the cold ground. It would at least save some of her body heat. Next, she leaned branches against the top of the rocks, leaving the bottom further out, giving her room to lie down. She tried to make it blend in so it would look like the branches had fallen that way.

Before getting in, Anna took a fir branch and moved it over her tracks. She couldn't remove them all, but at least they wouldn't show right next to her shelter.

Slipping inside, she pulled the fir branch over her to camouflage her body and for warmth. It was tight, but it provided some relief from the cold, and her body started to warm up. Opening her sack of food, Anna pulled out the last half sandwich and bit into it. *Delicious,* she thought. The sandwich was cold, but she didn't care. She ate it slowly, wanting to enjoy every bite, picking the last of the crumbs from her dirty coat. Anna pulled the sack open again and removed the last of its contents. Pulling apart the last biscuit, she used the small spoon the woman had included and slathered the remains of the beautiful strawberry preserves over the top. She could smell the strawberries.

She sucked the smell into her nostrils, closing her eyes, taking her back to when she and her parents picked wild berries, and she and Mama would make homemade preserves. Slowly, she took a bite, but she didn't chew. She just let it sit in her mouth, allowing the smell and taste to take her back in time. Content, she laid her head down, pulled her hat down over her eyes, and went to sleep.

That evening, Anna woke to the moon high in the sky. It was cold but clear. Opening her lunch sack, Anna stared into it. She knew it was empty, but hunger made her open the bag, just to make sure she hadn't missed anything. At least she had water. She had kept the milk jar and refilled it with water every chance she got.

Anna poked her head outside, confirming the coast was clear. Crawling out, she stretched long and hard. Her body was getting used to being in a ball. *"What would a nice bed feel like?"* she pondered. She missed her family, her home, and her soft bed piled with her down comforter.

Well, I don't have time to reminisce, she thought. Home. Soon she'd be home, or at least she would get to look at it before she made her way to her hiding place. It was almost ten o'clock. She had slept too long. The sun would be coming up before she knew it. She didn't have much time.

She was getting near town. She could see the lights from the buildings. A few cars and trucks rumbled down the streets, unaware a young Jewish girl was sneaking her way back into town instead of out. Anna snuck up the back of her street along the wood line. Crouching low and careful not to make any noise, she moved along the edge of the woods until she had parked herself behind the brush. The leaves from all the trees except evergreens were long gone, leaving her exposed. The bushes would have to suffice for cover.

There it was, her home. The bathroom light flicked on, and a few minutes later, it went off.

"How dare someone else live there!" she fumed, wanting to run into the house and tell them to get out! It was her home, hers, Mama's and Papa's. They lived there! But she sat still. Her mind raced with anger, but she knew she had to stay silent, unable to do anything about it.

She looked over to the Reinholds' bakery. She could almost smell the bread and her mouth watered. Her mind wandered to Peter. Was Peter there? Did the Reinhold's sell bread to the family who lived in her house? Probably, how could they say no?

Anna just stared at her home and the Reinholds'. It seemed like hours, but it had been only minutes. Anna knew she had to leave so she could get to her hiding place before daylight. Slowly moving back from the bushes, she made her way to the edge of the tree line. One last look back; that's all, just one. Anna turned and soaked in one last look. A light flicked on and Peter's silhouette framed his bedroom window. Peter was standing, peering into the darkness, while Anna stood in the dark, staring into his bedroom. Tears tracked down Anna's face.

"Oh, Peter, Peter," she whispered. "I miss you."

Peter looked out his window, searching for something he wasn't even sure was there. Thoughts of Anna pierced through him. He knew she didn't think of him the same way, but his heart loved who it loved, and he had never been attracted to anyone else. Peter rubbed his eyes and ran his hands through his hair.

He was so tired, physically tired from baking fourteen hours a day for the repulsive Nazi army, and mentally tired of pretending to love helping the Fatherland. Most of all, he was so tired from worrying about Anna and her family.

He was awake, so he might as well get the ovens going and start the day. Pulling on his clothes, he shuffled off to the bathroom and then downstairs to start another monotonous day. He'd surprise his father by getting an early start. As he descended the stairs, yesterday's garbage greeted his nose. Trying to hold his breath, Peter grabbed the garbage tin and headed out the back door. Just as Anna was going to leave, the Reinholds' back door opened. Peter came out carrying a bag of garbage. Anna sucked in her breath. Pulling the metal lid off the trash can, Peter slipped the garbage in, turned, and stared off into the woods. Anna froze. She could swear he was staring straight at her. Could he see her? Did he know she was still alive? Did he even care? Peter stood there for a couple of minutes staring into the woods. The moon lit up the trees, and he could have sworn there was someone there.

I must be even more tired than I realized, he thought. All the extra baking for the German army was wearing him out. He hated baking for them. The only good thing that came from it was he didn't have to worry about joining Hitler's army. He was exempt, but the bakery was commanded to help keep the armed forces fed. He was thankful for that, but Hitler repulsed him. Look what he had done to Anna and her family.

Peter slipped back inside, the thought that someone might be there haunting him. His mind went to Anna and her parents. He was so angry that his father had held him back the day they were loaded on the trucks. They were treated like dirty cattle, and the neighbors were scum that took them away. What was wrong with people today?

Anna slipped into the woods. Instinct took over and her feet automatically led the way to her hiding place. Her mind was unattached to her body, her mind racing with thoughts of Peter, her home, and her parents.

It was hard going in the woods at night, but a little over three hours later, the farmer's field and her new home appeared in the distance. The sun was just starting to come up as she reached the berm, her hide out. A light spiral of smoke swirled from the chimney telling Anna, the farmer was home. She crept up to her hiding place, squatting at the forest's edge, not sure what she'd find.

She waited, looking, listening, feeling her surroundings. Everything was silent except for the light wind weaving through the trees. All that time in the ghetto had made her senses sharp. Slowly, she crept to the mound in the middle, using a swag of brush to remove her footprints as best she could.

Pulling the fake branch door open, Anna crawled inside. It had been over two years since she had been there. She didn't know what to expect. It was dark, and she didn't have a flashlight, but she knew Papa had left the candles and matches just inside the doorway on the left. Anna's hand searched for the box and found it. She grabbed a candle, and then let her fingers search for the metal tin containing matches. *"Got it!"* She sighed with relief.

Anna tried opening the tin, but the lid was stuck. She pulled hard, and the tin burst open, the matches flying into the air. Anna sank down on her knees and cursed. She had to find at least one match. She ran her hands over the cold dirt floor until she felt a small stick, a match.

"Please God," she prayed, "help me." Anna struck the match, and a small sizzle broke the silence, emitting a small orange flame. The sulfur swirled up her nostrils but to Anna, it smelled good.

Lighting the candle, she moved it around the room to see what her new home looked like. To her relief, everything looked the same as she and Papa had last left it. She quickly searched for the spilled matches. It wouldn't do to let them soak up moisture from the ground. She needed them. After picking up all she could find, she pulled a candle holder from the box, placed the candle in it and set it near the bed.

The cot was set up on the south side, the sleeping bag on top, still rolled from the last time they had been there. Anna unrolled the bag. She was exhausted. Crawling inside with her clothes still on, she let the warmth hug her. This was the best bed she'd had since they'd had to leave their home. She blew out the candle, pulled the bag over her head and slipped into a deep sleep.

****

CHAPTER SEVEN

"**M**ove, move it!" yelled the soldier. Joseph Feiner shuffled along with the others, moving as fast as his emaciated body could go. The ghettos were being cleaned out. Everyone was being transferred to the concentration camps, or as some knew, "the death camps," the last place to die. Joseph's coat now hung on his frame; two sizes too big. His once fine hands and polished nails he'd kept in excellent shape for working with small tools and fine gems were now filled with dirt, broken and cracked.

The soldiers pushed everyone with the butts of their guns toward the rows of trucks. If you stayed in the middle of the crowd, you could avoid the brunt of a soldiers' anger. Reaching a truck, Joseph hoisted himself with all the strength he had left, throwing his valise up first. He rushed to the back of the truck to get away from the open end where the rain and snow could get you. Everyone was pushing him forward, and he landed on the bench at the very end. *Lucky*, thought Joseph. He could lean against the truck cab and sleep. The truck was overloaded, packed like sardines, but at least it saved body heat.

The truck growled, roared to life and then lurched forward. Everyone jolted, grabbing each other for balance, trying not to fall on those sitting on the truck floor. The trucks picked up speed. Joseph missed the fifty pounds he had lost the last couple of years. Every rut they hit went through him like a knife. Leaving the ghetto, he had made sure to grab Miriam's last handkerchief, his most precious possession and tuck it into his shirt sleeve. He had dabbed her perfume on it just like she had done for Anna. He pulled it out and drew in her smell.

When they had left the ghetto, it had started to snow, but now, hours later, it was a blizzard. Joseph felt lucky he was crammed back in the farthest corner. Those at the other end were getting soaked. He tried to sleep as the truck rolled on and on. It had been hours since they had started on this journey.

The soldiers didn't stop for anyone to relieve themselves unless it was for them. Prisoners couldn't leave the trucks, which left the truck reeking of urine, making Joseph pull his scarf up around his face, Miriam's perfumed hanky tucked under his nose.

He kept his eyes closed. The scent of her perfume took him back in time, to when his family was all together. His thoughts went to his wedding, and he remembered how beautiful Miriam was. It had been a simple wedding but perfect. Almost ten years later; Anna had been born. He had marveled at how he thought his life had been perfect before, yet Anna had brought so much more. He kept his mind from thinking of what might be happening to Anna now. He couldn't think of it.

The truck's wheels hit every pothole on the roads and jarred everyone from their seats. It was all he could do not to fall off the bench, sprawling on the poor people sitting on the truck floor. Finally, the wheels screeched to a halt, the high pitch of the brakes making his ears ring, and the truck's gates were yanked down.

"Get out! Out!" the soldiers yelled. Joseph again stayed in the middle of everyone to avoid the butt of a gun. Everyone unloaded, standing in the blowing snow. They were ordered from the trucks and pushed into railcars.

The cars were made of wooden slats, where you could peek out and watch what was going on, but they gave little protection from the wind and snow. Anyone who moved too slow was automatically shot. Joseph quickly jumped in and slunk down the slat wall.

An hour later, the cars were overflowing with men, women, and children heading to their final destination. The wheels rolled along the tracks, winding and turning, making some people sick. There was nowhere to throw up except where you were standing or sitting. If you had to use the bathroom, you tried to make it to the corner bucket, but multiple times, the contents were sloshed and spilled over the car floor. Men attempted to pee through the slats, but most of it ended up spraying the walls.

It had been two days when the wheels screeched to a stop. The doors rolled open, and the soldiers started pulling people out of the doors. Many were dead from exposure and malnourishment. The stench was so bad, guards covered their noses with one of their hands and with the other, pushed everyone toward a huge compound, screaming at them to hurry up. A huge sign above the gates read, *Auschwitz*.

The outside of the compound was lined with barbed wire fencing. Twenty feet in, another row of barbed fencing ran parallel to the first one. Beyond the fencing was an open area that led to rows and rows of buildings. Towers stood at each corner, soldiers watching, waiting for someone to run.

"Line up!" yelled one of the German officers. As they all started to form a line, a young man about twenty years old, turned and bolted for the opening hoping to make it to the woods. His run was short lived, as shots rang out and he slumped to the ground. He brought his head up slightly, his hands digging into the snow and then he went slack. Scarlet-red blood soaked into the snow, like a strawberry snow cone. No one followed his attempt. They all silently honored his courage, but no one had the desire to follow in the few footsteps he'd taken.

They all lined up, and an SS officer questioned each person. After being questioned, some went to the left and some to the right. It wasn't hard to figure out which line you wanted to be in.

"Occupation?" yelled the officer.

"Jeweler," replied Joseph.

"To the right," he barked, and pointed. It was the line you didn't want. It was mostly old men, women and children.

Joseph hesitated, and then, with as much confidence as he could muster, he said, "My hands are strong. I can work long and hard. They're used to working long days. I can also make beautiful pieces of jewelry for the officers, for their wives and loved ones."

The officer glared at him, his eyes piercing into Joseph. Joseph prayed God would intercede. He'd heard rumors and knew the line on the right was certain death. The officer motioned to the left, and Joseph hurried past him before he could change his mind.

****

CHAPTER EIGHT

Anna woke with a start. It took a moment to get her bearings and realize she was safe now and no longer had to run. She lay back down, sinking into the warmth of her sleeping bag. It had been so long since she'd had the luxury to relax and not have to try to be invisible. Finally, she propped herself up on one elbow, and did a visual of her new home. Left of her cot were the three boxes full of food, and underneath her cot were additional boxes with clothes, a small allotment of tools, and the flashlight. Just inside the doorway was the box of candles, matches, and odds and ends. Anna's stomach growled, reminding her she hadn't eaten in almost two days. Unzipping her sleeping bag, she threw her legs over the side. It was cold, her breath puffing white against the air. A fire would be ideal, but she didn't want to take the chance on someone being out and seeing smoke. She opted to wait until dusk, when everyone would be inside. Still, she needed to eat.

Going through the boxes of food, Anna chose a jar of home-canned peaches. Finding the can opener in the box, she popped the lid. Pulling a fork from the box, she speared a slice of peach and popped it into her mouth. She didn't chew, she just let it sit there, the juice pooling in her mouth, enjoying its flavor. The sweet juice dripped down her chin. Slowly, she chewed, wanting to enjoy every moment. Mama had canned these peaches. She closed her eyes and ran a picture show of Mama putting the fruit in scalding hot water to peel the skins off, cutting them into slices, and then stuffing them into jars for canning. Tears streaked down Anna's cheeks as she took in the memory and ate the peaches her mother's hands had touched. She ate half the jar, and then drank half the juice before putting the lid back on, placing it safely back in the box.

Next, she took the small shovel and started to dig for the box with the money and jewels they had hidden the night they thought the Nazis were coming for them. Anna remembered where to dig, and she dug until she hit what she was looking for. There it was; her future. She knew there was more out in the woods by the river, buried under the crooked tree but she'd leave that until later or when she was desperate.

Next Anna went through the box of clothes. The clothes she had on were worn and dirty. They had been through two years of ghetto life and living on the run; it was time for fresh clothes.

Anna pulled a pair of pants out that she and Mama had bought at the market. They had paid a pretty penny, but Papa had insisted she have pants if she had to live in the woods and move around. She didn't look forward to stripping down to nothing with no fire and in the dead of winter. Goosebumps pricked her skin as she peeled off her ragged clothes. Anna pulled on clean underwear, which felt wonderful. She'd only had three pair for the last couple of years, and they were tattered to shreds and dirty. Changing your underclothes, any clothes, was at the bottom of the survival list in the ghetto. Just having warm clothes, filthy or not, made you rich.

Quickly, Anna pulled on wool stockings, her khaki pants and then a brown plaid flannel shirt and a dark brown sweater vest. She started to laugh. Here she was in boys' clothing, and all she could think of was how color coordinated she was. Mama had always indulged her ever consuming fashion needs. The pants were huge, but she had a piece of rope and she looped it through the belt loops, making a belt.

After she finished dressing, she dumped the tattered rags near the door, deciding to bury them later when it was safe. Burning them would produce too much smoke but it was important, as Papa would tell her, not to leave any evidence she was there.

She had a long day ahead of her. She couldn't leave her new place during the day, since it was too risky. Night would still have to be her daytime.

Peter was up early. His day always started at five-thirty in the morning but today he was wide awake and up at four o'clock. He couldn't get over last night. Maybe he was just tired, but he could have sworn he saw someone out in the dark by the bushes, and then at the edge of the woods.

Well, he was up so he might as well start work early. He and his father had orders from the Third Reich to make bread for the army. It wasn't a request, it was demanded. Not complying meant death or the front lines. They did it, but not because they wanted to help Hitler's cause. Peter had wanted to refuse, but his father had convinced him it was what was best.

"Bread is a staple for the army and our country," said his father, "so it's a gift that we have a bakery. You can't help Anna and her family if you're at the front or dead. You need to harness your anger and focus on survival, just like Anna's doing."

His father flushed with frustration over his son. He knew Peter was very protective of Anna and her family. Peter wasn't the only one who loved her. His father never said much but when Anna was around, his heart was lighter, he smiled more, and he was always making lemon cookies, Anna's favorite. How many times had Peter's father said to him, "You know, Peter, when you're older and are looking for a wife, don't go far from home. I know there's a girl here for you." Peter would just chuckle. His father knew he never looked beyond the neighbors' door.

Peter had loved Anna since he was fourteen years old. Somewhere in between being young kids riding bikes and turning into teenagers, his heart had turned. He knew Anna didn't feel the same way, but it didn't matter to him.

Pulling on his work clothes, Peter headed down the stairs. He needed to make over a hundred loaves, and it was demanding work. He was tired every day; it never stopped. It was rare to have a day off. Peter was almost glad he worked all the time; it meant he had less time to think about the Feiners.

****

CHAPTER NINE

Anna opened the tin and put some of the money in her pocket. She didn't know what each day would bring, so having money made her feel safer. She reburied the rest, knowing she still had the money the officer's wife had slipped in her coat. At some point, her food would run out and her money would be gone. She needed to think about how she was going to survive. There was nothing else for Anna to do but lie down and think until nighttime, letting her mind wander over how she could stay safe and fed.

Papa had tucked a few books into the boxes to surprise Anna. She would save them for another day. For now, she tucked herself into her sleeping bag and dozed off and on, dreaming of her family and Peter. She was accustomed to her night being day from being on the run. She could only travel at night, so her chances of being caught were less, and this would continue to be her normal routine.

Anna roused from sleep, rubbing her palms over her eyes. Dusk was setting, and she could finally get outside and move around. First, she was going to eat, so she'd have some energy. She lit a candle and pulled out the open jar of peaches. Finishing off every slice, she drank down the sweet, sticky juice, tapping the bottom of the jar, determined to get every last drop.

Finally, taking her tongue, she licked the inside neck of the jar and set it down. Later tonight she'd open some meat for protein but right now, she was going to head down to the creek and get water. After that, even though she knew she shouldn't, she was going to go back and see her old home and the Reinholds' bakery. Maybe she'd see Peter.

It was late, and Peter needed to head to bed, but he couldn't. He wanted to wait and watch the tree line. Would someone be there tonight? He pulled up a chair near the window, flicked off the light, sat down, and watched.

Anna had walked in the dark for at least three hours. Not bad timing considering she constantly had to be on her guard and work her way through the woods without light. She snuck up to the edge of the wood line and crouched her way over to the two bushes she'd sat between last night. She snuggled between them, trying not to move the branches too much. She sat still, trying to take small breaths, but it was cold out, and her freezing breath puffed white into the frigid air. She tried to hide her breathing, pulling her coat collar up, wrapping her scarf around her mouth.

The lights in her old house were on. She could see the silhouettes of people moving about her bedroom. It looked like two young kids. She wondered if they had thrown all her things away, or if they'd kept them as their own. Anna wasn't sure how she felt about that. Part of her didn't want them to have her stuff, but the other part of her had memories in her belongings and didn't want them thrown out. It wasn't the kids' fault their parents were Nazi sympathizers. They had learned hatred from their parents; it wasn't something they were born with.

She looked over at Peter's bedroom window. It was dark. He was probably sleeping. Her thoughts went to him, picturing his face, always smiling at her, his dimples deep in his cheeks. His eyes were such a beautiful blue. She used to tease him about how unfair it was that a boy had eyes that a girl would die for. Peter always chuckled and would tell her his eyes were only for her. Even now, Anna could feel herself blush just thinking of how Peter would look at her when he said it, warmth moving up her neck. She knew her cheeks were now pink, but it wasn't from the cold. She had never thought of Peter as a boyfriend, but she had to admit, he was a good catch. The other girls in the neighborhood had always been jealous of all the attention he had given her.

Peter sat at the window staring into the dark. There was a hint of the moon, casting a sliver of light over the night. He studied the bushes and tree line, looking for something out of the ordinary. His eyes were so tired, but he wasn't going to give up. His lids drooped, but he forced them open. Then he saw it! A motion in the bushes. Something was out there!

Peter yanked his binoculars off his nightstand. Even in the dark, he focused in on the area and could tell it was a person. He couldn't tell if it was a man or a woman because they were tucked so far back into the bushes. Even though the figure was crouched down, he knew the person was not tall. Now what? he thought. At least he knew he wasn't crazy, but his mind raced to decide what to do next. He was staring out the window, never suspecting Anna was staring up at him.

Anna was freezing and needed to get up and move around. It was time to head back to hiding. She scooted back on her bottom, slowly, trying not to give herself away. Just as she started to slide into the forest, a door slammed. Anna bolted around, hiding behind a tree. A man was standing outside her house, taking out garbage. A woman followed with a small bag of stuff, handing it to what must be her husband. Their voices carried, and Anna listened intently.

"Don't forget to take the garbage out in the morning after breakfast," said the woman. She was a little taller than Anna, but much heavier. Her stomach protruded out rather far, making Anna wonder if she was pregnant or just fat. Anna's anger surfaced, hoping the woman was just fat and not having another Hitler baby. She hated her. She was living in her family's house.

"I don't want the house to stink up while we're gone for the weekend, so make sure you do," she half-scolded.

"Yes, I will," said the man, sounding disgusted. He was very tall, but he wasn't missing any meals. It sounded like his wife ran the show. Anna hated him too. The man stepped back into the house, the back door slamming again.

Anna's heart was beating wildly. They were leaving for the weekend, tomorrow. She dared to think of sneaking in for a look at her home. She knew it wasn't smart, but she didn't know if she could resist. She turned around and scurried deep into the forest, heading back to camp.

Peter had seen a figure at the tree edge. He had stood there for a few minutes. The family who had taken over Anna's house was outside. Once they went in, the figure left. Peter needed to know who it was, and why they would stalk the neighborhood, especially his back yard.

****

CHAPTER TEN

Anna was getting proficient at trudging through the dark forest. She was careful to wipe away traces of footsteps when she got to an area that her boots weren't walking on brush. She didn't need to leave bootprints. Anna drank from her canteen and noted she needed to replenish. Working her way to the creek, she dipped the canteen below the water and filled it back up, her hand frozen for her effort. She decided she would come back with a bucket and get some water to wash herself down. Her last bath had been when the nice woman at the farmhouse had invited her into her home. Every time Anna thought of her, she said a prayer of thanks. God had surely put that woman in her path.

Making it back to camp, she dug a small hole about ten inches in diameter and six inches deep, like Papa had shown her. The ground was hard, slightly frozen, but she worked at it until she'd reached her goal. She prepared to make a small fire. She needed the warmth and she'd heat some water to clean herself and have a warm supper tonight.

Papa had set aside dried moss and branches just for building a fire but had given advice not to rely on always having it. She had picked some wood up on the way home that wasn't too wet and would dry inside for use later. For now, she'd use what Papa had stored. She didn't want it too big, she just needed to make some hot coals. She didn't expect anyone to come out this far at night or even during the day. She could gamble on a fire at night better than the daytime, though.

She crisscrossed small dry sticks into the hole, added some dry moss, and then added larger sticks, crisscrossing them again. She lit the match, holding it to the moss. The flame started small and then grew, catching the moss and sticks on fire. One by one, larger branches were added. Yellow and orange flames licked the branches, warming the place up quickly. Anna crawled outside and checked how much smoke was coming out. The last thing she needed was for a smoke alert to the enemy, which was everybody at this point. Her fire was so small that Anna could barely detect any smoke, even though she was specifically looking for it. She breathed a sigh of relief, feeling safer.

Crawling back inside, she grabbed a large metal bucket and emptied its contents. Grabbing the empty peach jar too, she headed out to the river. It was about a quarter mile away. She had her flashlight but would only use it when she was so deep into the trees she could barely see. She'd chance using some light over breaking a leg in the dark forest.

Once at the river, she hurried and filled the bucket three-quarters of the way full, then cleaned and filled the mason jar all the way up. Hauling it back to camp was hard. The water was heavy, and Anna was in poor shape. She had little muscle left from the meager food and horrible living conditions in the ghetto, but she struggled back, continuing out of sheer willpower. She was determined not to splash it all out before she got back to camp.

It had taken her about an hour to haul water. Nearing her hideout, she realized she could see her small fire from outside. She hadn't bothered to set the door back in place. How stupid! She was furious with herself. She hadn't left a trace of smoke, but she had left full view of the whole inside of her camp, lit up like the screen at a picture show. She needed to be more careful!

Crawling back inside, she set the bucket and jar of water down and then crawled out and covered her tracks. Back inside, she set the door back in place, fitting it snugly, tying it on both sides to hold it closed. Finally, Anna relaxed.

She stoked the fire to get more coals and then let them burn down before she set the bucket on top of them. Alongside the bucket, she added some sticks letting the flames lick the sides. She didn't need the water boiling, just warm would be nice. Her camp was warm enough that she could no longer see her breath in the air, so she shed her outer coat. Rummaging through her food supply, she pulled out a can of meat and a jar of pickles. Anna would heat the meat, but the pickles were for now! She popped the lid and pulled out a homemade pickle.

"Mmmm," she moaned as she bit into it. They were cold and crunchy, just the way she liked them. She pulled out another and another, savoring each crispy bite. Anna had to stop herself from eating the whole jar and making herself sick. She put the lid on and set the jar back in the box.

Testing the water, she dipped her index finger into the bucket. A few more minutes and it would be warm enough. She scrounged through the wood box for a washcloth and towel she knew her mother had packed. Anna smiled. What didn't Mama think of? Anna let the water continue to heat while she stripped naked. Her clothes discarded she wrapped the washcloth around her hand and pulled the bucket of water off the fire. Pulling the coals farther apart, Anna set the opened can of meat on the outer coals. She'd let it get hot while she washed. Kneeling on the ground, she sank her hair into the bucket, and then pulled it out, letting the excess water drip over it. She lathered her hair with lavender soap and scrubbed until she thought her hair would fall out. She lowered her head back into the bucket and rinsed the soap, working her fingers into her hair.

The Mason jar had been sitting by the fire, warming, but it was still cool. Anna picked it up and poured it over her hair. The cold hit her like ice after the warm water. Her breath caught in her throat, and she had to force herself to breathe. Quickly, she squeezed her hair over the bucket, wrapped the towel around her head and flung her head back. She shivered.

The bucket of water was now barely warm. She put it back on the coals to heat, but dipped her washcloth in and soaped it up. She scrubbed her face, neck and arms, rinsing the cloth into the water every once in a while, to rinse off. She quickly finished, wrapping a blanket around her back, leaving the front open to the fire. She put her clothes back on and pulled the bucket to the door. By now the meat was sizzling. Anna pulled out a fork and slowly ate the whole can of meat. Her thoughts were only to eat half, but she was too hungry to stop. She would pace herself after this, but not today.

Mama and Papa had thought of everything. She had a set of silverware, real silver. Mama said that she might as well eat in style. It was better than leaving it to the Nazis. There was a comb, brush, lotion, toothbrush, and handkerchiefs. Mama's touch was all over this box of goods, and today, it came to good use.

Anna brushed her hair out by her fire. There were hours before daylight when her sleep would finally come. What to do until then? Unlatching the door, Anna hauled the now cooled bucket of bath water outside and carried it some ways into the woods. She poured it into some brush, under the trees. She had to be careful of everything she did, especially near her campsite.

"No trace, invisible," she could hear Papa say.

Slipping back into her hut, she pulled the door shut and stoked the fire. Tomorrow she'd have to gather some wood and kindling, but for now, she was just going to relax. Winter was here, and the harsh weather was only a sampling of what was to come.

****

CHAPTER ELEVEN

Joseph and hundreds of other Jews who were saved from the extermination showers were herded into a building and instructed to strip off their clothes. Next, they were sent to the showers, had their heads shaved bald, and were given a set of blue and cream striped clothes that everyone called "striped pajamas." Everyone looked the same, young, old, rich and poor. It was hard to distinguish one person from another. Everyone got a number tattooed on their left forearm. You were no longer a name; you were just a number.

Dressed in thin, shabby pajamas, they were led to a long drab wood building. Exhausted, Joseph thought at last he could lie down. Once you stepped inside, what you thought was as bad as it could get, got worse. Hundreds were already inside, lying on wood bunks, multiples to each. There were no mattresses, just hard wood. Even underneath the bunks, men lay on the cold floor. Men sat up against the walls, anywhere there was space. The building was overflowing with bald headed, striped skeletons. Joseph found a tiny place and quickly sat down next to a bunk, squeezing next to another man. Exhaustion took over, and he fell asleep.

Morning came early. Today was the start of learning the harsh rules and reality of living in a concentration camp.

Standing out in the cold, they waited for roll call. They stood there for hours. Men who dropped were hauled off to their graves, whether they were breathing or not. The cold bit into Joseph. He no longer had his wool coat, just the thin, threadbare pajamas. He missed his coat but most of all, Miriam's handkerchief that had been tucked in the pocket. There was no getting it back.

Finally dismissed, they were given breakfast. All Joseph could do was stare at it. It was a gray watery soup, mainly water. Joseph watched the others and did as they did. He didn't need any unwanted attention. Drinking down the liquid, he did as the others did and lined up for a work assignment.

A German guard barked out the assignments. You didn't question it. Joseph recognized a man a few ahead of him. He asked for a different assignment. The guard looked at him, slipped his gun from its holster, and shot him in the head. The shot echoed throughout the camp as his body dropped with a thud to the dirt, blood pooling around his head. Pointing to the next two in line which included Joseph, the guard yelled at them to take him to the ditches. So now he had his assignment and it would last all day, and days beyond.

Keeping his head down and mouth closed, Joseph grabbed the dead man under the shoulders, and the other man grabbed his feet. The other man never said a word; he just moved his head in the direction they needed to go. Joseph knew he would make this man his mentor. He needed to learn the ropes so he could get out and find Anna.

****

CHAPTER TWELVE

Peter was up again at dawn. He was still tired from last night. He had sat by his window watching the shadow of someone sneaking around behind his and the Feiners' house. Why would they sit there in the dark, in the cold? His heart twisted. He wanted to it to be Anna, but that would be impossible. You just don't walk out of the ghetto. Besides that, he had heard from soldiers coming into the bakery that they were now cleansing the ghettos, and those still alive were being taken to concentration camps.

Peter pulled on his work clothes and climbed down the stairs. The bakery was warm, and Peter was thankful for that. If he wasn't working feeding soldiers, he'd be up on the cold front trying to kill someone or being killed. His father was right, at least now he could concentrate on finding Anna. He had done some digging every time soldiers came into the bakery for rolls and pastries. He pretended to hate the Jews, but he was trying to find out where they had taken Anna and her parents. The only information he had gotten was the name of three ghettos that they may be in.

He had gone to the ghettos and searched. He couldn't let the soldiers know he was looking for a Jew, that he was a Jew lover. He went to the ghettos on the pretense of bringing goodies to thank the soldiers for cleaning up their neighborhood. He'd take a box full of pastries and cookies as offerings to the soldiers he hated. While they ate all the treats, Peter would dig for information that could lead him to the Feiners'. Each time, he left disappointed.

The disappointment always hung heavy on Peter but knowing he had left each soldier with a belly ache from extra ingredients he had put in the dough, lifted his spirits a little. He could visualize them doubled over in pain or running for a place to yank their pants down before they messed them. It took a good half day for them to start having stomach pains so there was no way they could associate Peter with their problems.

Despite all of his searching, he hadn't gotten anywhere. He still had no idea where the Feiners had ended up.

Peter's mind couldn't stop going to last night. Who was it? He was determined to find out. He was going to solve the mystery. The day seemed to never end. He had tons of bread to bake, and then there was the normal neighborhood customers and stationed soldiers that would come in for a snack or dessert for later. Finally, his father locked the front door and they cleaned up the bakery, ready for the next day. Peter and his father headed up the stairs, exhausted.

His father pulled out a loaf of bread from earlier in the day and sliced four pieces. It was common for them to just eat a sandwich and coleslaw for dinner before retiring to bed. There was never enough time to do anything but eat, bathe, and head to bed. Peter took the sandwich from his father and sat down at the table. His father looked over at Peter.

"You worry me. You don't seem yourself these last few days. What's the matter?"

Peter didn't want to worry him, and he didn't need anyone nosing behind the bakery, until he figured out who was stalking the premises.

"Nothing, Father," he lied. "I'm just tired from all the work, and I haven't slept well lately". At least part of it was true.

His father nodded in understanding. He was always exhausted too. He would look at his son and think that this was a terrible way for Peter to spend his youth. In the end, he was satisfied knowing that Peter was safe here and not at the front with the army. It was a huge blessing. His father put his hand on Peter's shoulder.

"Try and get some sleep, son," he said, and padded off to his room.

Peter knew he wouldn't get any sleep tonight either. He was planning on watching the back for his unknown visitor. He planned on leaving some cookies and a note out in the bushes. He wanted whoever it was to know he was not an enemy.

Hours passed. Finally, Peter slipped down to the bakery.

Grabbing a few almond and hazelnut cookies, he wrapped them in waxed paper and set them in a tin with a message.

"I watch you at night and I mean no harm. Please consider this a gift. Can you tell me who you are and why you are here?" He closed the box and headed to the back of the building. It was dark, and the new neighbors were gone for the weekend, so he didn't need to worry about anyone watching. He got to the bushes where the person had hidden and slipped the box between the two trunks. If it was still there in the morning, he'd bring it back in and try again the next night. He would not give up.

****

CHAPTER THIRTEEN

Joseph was rail thin and he had a cough that never subsided. They called this a death camp for a reason. The only positive thing that came from being in the camp so long was he had gotten a coat and a cramped bunk to share with two other men. You were lucky if you had a bunk instead of a small spot on the cold floor. Joseph always chose the middle. You could draw off what little body heat two skeletons could give you. It was better than nothing.

His friend Jacob had gotten some medicine from the infirmary where his cousin worked but so far it hadn't done much. He could only get minute amounts without the soldiers finding out. His cousin was putting his life on the line sneaking cough syrup out. If they caught him, there would be no chance to defend himself, it was a quick and precise death. Joseph was barely holding on. He kept going for Anna, and because he had promised Miriam, he would use his last breath to find her. He prayed for Anna every day.

Working the graves brought some satisfaction to him. Each time he laid a body on the pile, he had to smile inside. There was one Jew they didn't get; his Anna.

Even though he had managed to get a coat, it didn't offer a lot of warmth over the thread-bare pajamas. His clothes hung huge on his skeletal frame. He had no gloves and the worn-out shoes gave little to no protection or warmth. You were considered a rich man if you had a pair of socks, holes or not. Joseph still considered himself lucky. These few precious belongings kept him closer to living and finding his daughter.

He had been on the work detail carrying the dead to the incinerator ovens for months now. If it weren't for Anna, he wouldn't even try to survive, he would will himself to die without much effort, but he had made a promise to his wife.

The wood cart was loaded high, three to four bodies piled on top of each other, their hands and feet hanging over the cart edges. They all looked the same, even their faces. It was a pile of naked skeletons with hollow, sunken cheeks, and eyes that didn't even look human anymore.

When he had first been assigned to the detail, Joseph had vomited for the first week. He couldn't afford to lose any precious nourishment, so he had forced himself to come to terms with his situation, choosing not to see the bodies anymore. The one time he had, trying to be respectful, he recognized someone from the old neighborhood. Her nakedness was sunken over her bones, making Joseph feel sick. The Nazis didn't even have the decency to let the dead keep the pajamas. They were taken off and reused. He couldn't help but think, *"This could be me one day."*

Joseph and Jacob pushed hard, trying to get the cart to start rolling. The ground was full of potholes and it was hard to avoid all of them. Once you hit a deep one, you were back to starting over, hoping you didn't lose any bodies from the cart. One final shove and the carts wheels finally moved. They pushed on. Getting to the ovens where they burned the bodies gave you physical relief, but the anguish of what they were doing to them made you mentally ill.

Joseph was glad he didn't have to unload the dead. He was only responsible for loading and getting them to the ovens. He always kept his hands on the cart, even when it wasn't rolling.

You never knew when the guards would think you weren't working and whip or shoot you on the spot. They would shoot you just for looking at them. He had learned long ago to keep his head down and never look the guards, especially officers, in the eyes. He waited for the cart to be emptied. *How many bodies have lain on here?* he wondered. *Too many, for sure.* The cart was empty too fast, but he gripped the handles and pulled backwards. Losing his footing, Joseph slipped and spilled onto the ground, his hand landing on an officer's boot. The officer kicked him hard and shoved him off, swearing at him.

"I'm sorry, I'm sorry. "Joseph spoke with his head down, waiting for him to pull his pistol.

"You!" barked the officer. "Are you Feiner?"
****

151

CHAPTER FOURTEEN

Anna had fallen asleep for a long time. Waking, she knew she had been dreaming. She had dreamed it was a beautiful sunny summer day, and she and Peter had gone down to the riverbank on their bikes and ridden all day. Peter had brought lemon cookies, Anna's favorite, and two bottles of soda. The day ended with dinner at her house, with Mama making her and Peter's favorite, fried chicken, steamed dumplings, and green beans. Mama topped it off with moist chocolate cake. Just as Anna was about to take a bite, she woke up.

Not fair, she thought. *I should have at least gotten to eat the cake!*

Her fire had pretty much gone out except for some warm coals. She stretched, pulled herself out of her sleeping bag, and added a few sticks of wood, fanning it to get the flames going. The sun was setting, which meant she could get out into the woods. Anna felt refreshed. Having bathed made her feel like a new person. Her head no longer itched from her dirty hair. It felt silky and smooth again. She had brushed it dry over the fire last night.

First things first, Anna knew she had to eat. Not knowing what her future food situation was, she would eat light. Opting for a couple of pickles and some deer jerky, she sat on the edge of her cot and ate slowly. Food was a precious commodity. She slipped a piece of jerky in her pocket for later and then set the bag back into the box.

The fire had died to low embers, and rather than put it out, she decided to just let it be. She would go for a warmer living space and hope nothing would catch on fire while she was gone. It wasn't something Papa would have done but, she was alone now and making her own decisions.

Anna pulled her coat and hat on, then grabbed her scarf and flashlight and headed out the door.

Having overheard the couple who now occupied her old home say they were going out of town for the weekend, Anna headed to the old neighborhood. She knew what she was going to do was risky, but she didn't care.

She was getting good at navigating through the woods in the dark with no light as she headed to her old house. Occasionally, she switched the flashlight on, but she didn't want anyone to see it, and she didn't want to wear the battery down. It was about eleven at night when she finally arrived. Instead of heading to the bushes, she crouched at the tree line and watched. All the lights were off in her old house and Peter's. She stayed there for about an hour, watching and waiting. Finally, she moved, running to the shed behind the house. It was freezing outside but she was sweating. Her arms and legs felt like rubber as she made her way to the back door. Again, she stood perfectly still except for her heart, which beat like a loud drum. She swore it was going to wake the Reinholds. Anna tried the door, but it was locked. She reached above the door jamb, and sure enough, the key was still there.

She slid the key in and slowly turned the knob, opening the door a couple inches, and then pushed the door open farther. It creaked just like it used to. She slipped inside and closed the door, turning the knob so the lock wouldn't click. She waited and waited, realizing she had been holding her breathe the whole time. She forced herself to breath, letting the air in and out. Memories flooded in as she moved into the house. The shop where Papa had worked and sold jewelry was filled with boxes and furniture. Some of it belonged to her family, and some must belong to the current occupants.

Anna's ears were still attentive to any noise she didn't recognize. Carefully, she made her way up the stairs to the living area. The stairs squeaked in a familiar way, but other than that, the house was silent. Anna stepped into the kitchen.

The house still had familiar smells and she soaked them in, breathing deep. Anna wanted to cry, but was determined not to let her emotions take hold while she was still in the house. They had kept the table and chairs. A coffee cake was in the middle of the table, wrapped like it was ready to go somewhere but had been forgotten. Anna recognized Mama's dish towels lying on the counter. She fumed, wanting to take them all back to her camp. Her anger choked at her, her nails digging into her palms.

Stop, she thought. *I have to stay focused.*

Slowly, she moved down the hall and stopped at her old room. The same tiny yellow flowered wallpaper adorned the walls. The room didn't look the same other than that, and Anna was thankful. Moving over to the dresser, she noticed two small wood jewelry boxes, and then, her eye caught it.

Her small silver box that used to hold a couple of her necklaces sat in between the two boxes in the middle of the dresser. The new occupants' children must have wanted to keep it. Anna picked it up and moved her fingers over the box. It had been given to her by her grandmother. She started to put it in her pocket but decided against it. She didn't need for anyone to notice she had been here. She wanted to be able to come back. Anna knew that thought was absurd, but she couldn't help it. She set the box back on the dresser, then turned and headed to her parents' room.

The room still smelled the same to her. She looked around the room, looking for anything that belonged to her parents. Resting on the dressing table was Mama's hair comb. Anna knew it belonged to her because Papa had set three large rubies in it. Papa had taken her everyday favorite comb she held her hair up with and set rubies in it.

The comb was old, and Papa used to tell her to buy a new one, but Mama wouldn't.

"This was my mother's comb, and I love it, "she would say. "I get to have a piece of my mother with me every day." Papa understood. The comb was old and worn, but irreplaceable.

The day before Mama's birthday, he had taken her hair comb late at night when she was sleeping and set the rubies in it, along with two small diamonds on each side.

The next day, on her birthday, Mama found the comb on her dresser. She went between crying and humming all day. She pulled her hair up, twisted it in a bun, and set the comb so all the gems could be seen. Anna could still remember the looks her parents had exchanged all day and thinking she hoped her married life would be just like theirs.

Anna slipped the comb in her pocket. She didn't care if she noticed it was missing. The fat Nazi slob was *not* going to wear it! Anna justified taking it by thinking the woman would probably think she had lost it herself.

She knew she had been in the house too long. She had a long walk back and certainly didn't need to be caught. Making her way to the back door, Anna slipped outside, silently closing and locking the door. She slipped the key back to its hiding place. She dashed behind the shed and then made a run for the trees. Little did she know, Peter was at his bedroom window.

Peter had been seated by his window for hours, waiting. He was hoping the stranger would come tonight. He had tried to keep his eyes open, but he kept drifting off. He needed to go to bed. Getting up, he stretched and took one last look out the window. His eye caught some movement.

Grabbing his binoculars, he zoomed in. It was so dark but there it was, not in the bushes, but heading into the woods. It was a man, wearing pants, a heavy coat, a scarf, and knit cap. The man was short, almost too short for a man, so he thought he must be a teenager. Somewhere in Peter's heart, he had wanted it to be Anna, but he knew it was ridiculous he had even thought that. He would not give up trying to find her. He wanted the war to be over and Anna and her family to be okay.

Well, obviously this teen is hiding for a reason, he thought, and he was going to help him. He was probably homeless and hiding from the Nazis. Maybe he was Jewish like Anna. He wouldn't find out tonight, but he wasn't going to give up. Exhausted, Peter fell into bed and drifted off to sleep.

The day started with a blizzard. Peter's heart sank. In this weather, his night visitor more than likely wouldn't come out. Still, he was going to stay on track with his plan. Reaching for his coat, he slipped out the back door and headed to the bushes to see if his package of cookies was still there. His heart sank when his hand landed on the tin.

Snow was really starting to come down by the time Anna made it halfway back to her camp. Would she ever call it home? She doubted it. There was nothing homey about it. As she neared camp, a blizzard was in full force. Even inside the woods, snow was covering the ground. Anytime she saw a piece of wood that looked dry, Anna picked it up. There would be no way she'd be able to go out in this weather once she got back to camp. With all the snow, Anna didn't worry about covering her footprints. Finally, she was back. She pulled the door covering open and crawled inside. Dropping the wood in the back, she shook her cold and cramped arms, getting back the circulation.

Getting wood was going to be a daily chore from now on. She couldn't afford to be caught in this kind of weather without wood. She was getting lax in preparing for winter, too focused on seeing her old house. She didn't have room inside, but she'd have to set up someplace close that she could put wood and keep it drying. Anna inspected her small fire pit. The fire was out but the coals were still slightly warm. *Good*, she thought. *It won't take a lot to get it going.* With the temperature plunging into the low teens, she needed to keep warm.

****

CHAPTER FIFTEEN

F einer? Are you Feiner?" the officer yelled at him again.

"Yes, yes." Joseph nodded, still waiting for a bullet to pierce through him. His eyes remained down, waiting.

"Are you the jeweler?" The officer rested his right hand on his holstered gun.

"Yes," said Joseph again, his voice more confident than he felt. Maybe this wasn't his day to die.

"Come with me! Schnell! You," he pointed at Jacob, "get someone else to take his place. Tell them Major Heinz said you need a replacement."

Jacob nodded, grabbed the cart, pushed it hard to get the wheels going and disappeared quickly, not wanting the wrath of the major.

Joseph stood there by himself, sweating out of fear, despite the cool temperature.

"Come with me!" barked the major as he strode off toward some of the nicer buildings. They got to a small plain wood building, and the major walked inside, commanding Joseph to follow. Joseph kept his eyes down.

The major turned and looked at Joseph, eyeing him up and down.

"You said you were a jeweler. Some of the officers want jewelry for their wives and girlfriends." He let out a little laugh, knowing some were just flings they kept secret from their wives.

"The major pointed to four boxes sitting on a wood slat table. "You'll find some of what you'll use in there."

Joseph slowly moved to the boxes and peered inside. His stomach churned. Piled high in one of the boxes were teeth, nothing but teeth with gold laid in them. They hadn't even washed them off; dried, caked-on blood covered the roots. Bile rose up his throat, threatening to spew all over. He gulped, swallowing the sour taste back down.

Joseph looked in the other boxes sitting on the table, and a wave of relief came over him. There were no teeth. They were piled high with jewelry the Nazis had confiscated from all the belongings that had been brought in suitcases or hidden in clothing when they first got to Auschwitz. It was obvious the Nazis didn't want or like it and were willing to have it remade.

"What else will you need?" asked the major.

"I'll need a torch, gloves, small jeweler tools."

"Go to the storage facility and get what you need," the officer said, cutting him off. "I'll check back in a couple hours, and I expect to see you set up!"

"Yes, sir." Joseph nodded. "Excuse me, sir. It'll take a lot of time to get the gold off, and if I had an assistant, then I would be able to concentrate on doing

160

the delicate and precise work faster. I'm sure you're all anxious to have your pieces made. The man I was with has worked with metal before."

The major stopped, angry that Joseph had the audacity to speak to him.

"Get him, but you better show results!" He turned, yanked the door open, and stepped into the cold.

Joseph waited a minute and then rushed out the door, looking for his friend Jacob. He found him at the ovens. Rushing up to his friend, Joseph tried to catch his breath. He grabbed Jacob's arm and tried to explain he was going to be his helper making jewelry for the Nazis.

"They collect the gold teeth and hidden jewelry and want me to make new pieces for them! It's in a building that has heat! I told them it would take too long on my own, so they agreed you could help," explained Joseph. "Hurry. We need to hurry back."

Just then, a soldier came, swinging his whip up, ready to strike.

"Get to work!" he screamed.

Jacob picked up the carts handles but Joseph hurriedly told the soldier that Major Heinz had put them on a new assignment and wanted them to report at once.

Joseph waited for the soldier to strike, his hand starting to bring the whip high in the air, but instead he lowered it.

"Well then, what are you waiting for? Go!"
****

CHAPTER SIXTEEN

T he blizzard was still going strong, and Anna knew she shouldn't go out in it, not even to see her home or Peter's. She wanted to, but her father's voice kept nagging at her to stay put.

"Most of all, be safe," he would say.

Anna's fear of being on her own was subsiding, and her confidence was growing stronger, but she wasn't going to be stupid. For now, she'd stay put.

Sitting in a small, cramped place by herself, made Anna miss everyone even more. She was starting to feel sorry for herself, but down deep, she knew she was lucky and would just have to be strong. Still, she wanted someone to share her loneliness with. Seeing Peter hadn't helped, it had made her miss everyone more. Besides, it wasn't like Peter knew she was watching him.

The snow blew hard, whipping around camp constantly pulling at the door. Anna had ripped off two strips from a blanket and tied them to each side of the door. The thirty plus mile an hour winds were trying their best to win.

Everything was frozen, including herself. Again, she could hear Papa tell her to be resourceful. Anna was quickly finding out what that meant but it wasn't easy.

Anna had no idea whether it was night or day unless she poked her head out occasionally. She scratched the days off in the dirt to track how long she had been at camp. Seven scratches stared back at her. She had been here for three days before the storm and was into her fourth during. She had to get out of here or she'd go insane. Besides, she was going to need wood, bad! She'd freeze to death if this storm didn't stop.

Peter was frantic. He knew it was no good to watch from his window every night, especially on such a snowy night. But he wanted to. After a long day of baking, he tried to watch but his eyelids constantly slipped closed and he would nod off only to suddenly jerk awake from falling off his chair. It was futile to watch during a storm. Snow swirled so fast you could hardly see out the windows. White, that's all you could see, day after day.

Peter had finally given up taking his tin box of goodies out to the bushes. He'd have to start back up when the weather eased up. He couldn't help but wonder if Anna was alive and weathering this storm.

Anna lay in her cot, bundled up in all her clothes, snuggling deep into her sleeping bag so all you could see were her eyes. She had so many clothes on it was hard to zip the bag. She had tried to pull the two brown wool blankets on top too, but it was hard when you had so many clothes on you could barely move.

It reminded her of when the Nazis broke into their home and she and her parents had pulled on layers of clothes before they were loaded into the trucks heading to the ghettos. The thought made her shiver even more.

She kept her fire stoked but minimal, so she could conserve wood. She didn't know if she could find her way back in this storm, or even find wood in these conditions. Eating consisted of dried deer jerky and a few sips of water she kept in the Mason jar near the hot coals to keep it from freezing. Still, her lips would meet huge chunks of ice each time she took a sip.

Anna had to laugh at herself. She thought back to the coffee can she first had to pee in when they arrived at the ghetto. Now she was using an old pan, so she didn't have to go outside. She wasn't sure if she had moved up in the world or down. Either way, she had no desire to brave the cold just to drop her pants. *Men had it easy*, she thought. She hadn't minded not eating or drinking much just so she didn't have to bother getting in and out of her clothes, but the stench was starting to get to her.

Scratch number eight was marked in the dirt, but Anna could no longer hear the wind howling outside. Forcing herself to get off the cot, she crept to the door and poked her head out.

It had finally quit snowing, and the wind was now only a slight breeze. *Thank God*, she thought. She built the fire up with the pretense of getting out now and getting more wood. She could afford to use more and to eat something solid and warm. She swore her insides were frozen solid.

Her canned goods were still well stocked, but she knew they wouldn't last forever, and then she'd have to figure out what to do. Hunting squirrels in the winter was not ideal.

The fire sizzled, the flames licking the now frozen can of meat she'd opened and set on the coals. Her stomach growled long and loud as if anticipating it was now going to get fed. Today she was going to have a full course meal. She welcomed the smell of cooking meat, closing her eyes and pretending Mama was making a roast with potatoes, carrots, onions, and hot bread fresh from the oven. Grandmother's beautiful china, goblets, and real silver utensils adorned the dining room table.

The fire snapped, bringing Anna back to reality. Still, if just for a few minutes, she had been transformed back in time to when life had been good. She ate slowly, savoring the taste and warmth of her meal. Even if it was canned, it was delicious, and she wasn't going to waste any of it, not even the juice. She let her taste buds soak in the flavor, closing her eyes and letting her imagination run. Finishing it all off was a cracker heaped with berry preserves and her favorite, one of Mama's half-frozen dill pickles.

Satisfied, Anna wiped off her knife and fork, setting them back in the wooden box. She needed to get rid of her garbage and collect some wood. Pulling her knapsack out, she put her trash in, pulled the cord tight, then headed out the door.

There wasn't any snow to blow over her tracks, so she made sure to use some brush to pull snow over her footprints. Anna snuck off into the woods.

****

CHAPTER SEVENTEEN

P eter," called his father. "We have an extra-large order today. It's going to be a long day so let's get started early."

Peter was deep in sleep for once and had to force himself to open his eyes. He had given up watching for the late-night visitor and wasting good sleep time. He hadn't given up on finding out who was out there, but it was impossible during blizzard conditions. Besides, he had been slacking lately, and it was unfair to his father. Peter felt bad, but he would make up for it.

"Ya, Father," he called back from his bedroom. "I'm getting up. I'll be down in a few minutes." Peter pulled himself up, stretched long and hard, arching his back as far as it would go. Pulling his clothes on, he padded off to the bathroom. He looked in the mirror. Staring back at him was a young man with broad shoulders, an unshaven face and dark purple circles under his eyes.

"I'm so tired of all this. How long will this last?" he asked the person in the mirror. If it had been just him, Peter would have left when the Nazis had taken the Feiners' off to the ghetto. Hitler disgusted him.

Peter brushed his teeth, shaved, ran a comb through his unruly blond hair and stared into the mirror again. *Better,* he thought. His ocean blue eyes stared back, and he thought of Anna teasing him about how unfair it was for a boy to have beautiful eyes like his. Peter's heart ached.

Peter and his father had been baking all day long with handling the army's orders along with daily customers who came into the shop. The chime over the door dinged again, and Peter looked up to help a customer. A German SS officer stood there, staring at Peter. The officer looked Peter up and down, his eyes piercing through him.

"Good afternoon," Peter said. He felt like his voice didn't sound like himself. He was forcing himself to talk. "What can I get for you, sir?"

"You can get me some hazelnut cookies," he said abruptly, "and you can tell me why a strapping young man like you is here, and not at the front with all the brave men serving the Fatherland. We need strong men at the front." Anger edged his voice, and his stare was accusatory.

Peter stood frozen in place, scared to say anything. After all, this man wasn't just an officer, he was an SS officer. He could shoot Peter right now, for no reason, and nothing could be done. Peter sucked in his breath and blew it out slowly.

"Yes sir," Peter sighed, pretending to agree with him. "I've argued this point until I'm blue in the face."

He began shaking his head back and forth. "I say the same thing, yet I'm stuck here baking bread for the army instead. It bothers me that I can't join the front, but I have to stay here and bake useless bread."

The officer mulled over Peter's comment. "Ah, I see. You want to join," the officer said, more as a comment than a question. He didn't expect an answer from Peter and Peter didn't offer one. The officer bobbed his head up and down repeatedly, understanding Peter's predicament, yet his gray cap with the huge skull ornament adorning the front never wavered.

"Yes, it must be hard to be left behind, but bread is essential for our troops. It may seem worthless to you, young man, but we must all help the Reich as best we can."

"Yes, sir." Peter nodded. "I feel I could do more. I want to do something that is more useful to my country." Peter almost choked on the lie. All he could think of was how he hated this man, and that he had no desire to help extinguish the Jews. He loved one of them!

Peter handed the officer a box of cookies as he pulled money from his perfectly pressed pants.

"Oh no!" exclaimed Peter. "I couldn't take your money after all you're doing. Please, it's my gift today."

The officer smiled, slipping his money back into his pocket.

"You should be proud, young man. We each help the Fatherland in our own way."

Again, Peter nodded. "I'll remember that." The officer finally left, the door chiming behind him.

Peter's father stepped up behind him. "You handled that well, son." Peter could see his father was shaking, but so was he.

"Danke," said Peter, touching his father on the arm. "I hate them, and I spit on his cookies," he said calmly. Peter looked up at his father, and they both burst into laughter.

"Son, sometimes it's the little things that bring huge satisfaction." They both burst into laughter again.

****

CHAPTER EIGHTEEN

Anna made it to the river, only to find it frozen over. *Great*, she thought, *now what?* She was afraid to walk out onto it, in case the ice gave way. There would be no one to hear her yell for help, in fact, no one who would care, even if they did hear her. They'd just as soon let her drown.

Grabbing a large thick stick, she walked about a foot onto the ice, staying close enough to the river's edge in case she had to jump to safety. She stabbed hard onto the ice, putting her full force into it. She kept stabbing the ice, slowly chunking tiny pieces, making a small hole. Water spread onto the surface, and she gave a final whack. Water gurgled up, and Anna grabbed her mason jar, quickly filling her bucket halfway. She didn't need to splash water on her boots during the walk back, and she didn't need water for a bath in this weather! She hurried and stepped off the ice just as she heard it crack.

Struggling with the bucket, Anna worked her way back to camp. She set it in the bushes near camp and headed off to find some wood. It was going to be hard considering the amount of snow that had fallen over the past few days, but she needed wood to keep from freezing. She moved farther in, hoping there would be less snow to contend with. Scouring near the tree stumps, she found branches hidden under some fallen trees and tapped the snow off. She'd have to set them near the fire to dry out some. She couldn't afford to have a wet, smoky fire alert the farmer.

Heading back to her camp, Anna looked up, and realized she hadn't even thought to pick wood from the other berm piles. Then it struck her, she had been so focused on survival that she had forgotten to look in the wood berm that Papa had used for storage. Anna dropped the pile of branches from her arms and snuck up to the storage area he had used for extra supplies. Excitement surged through her. It was like celebrating her birthday! You didn't know what you were going to find, but you knew it was going to be good!

The opening was tiny, but Anna pulled herself in. She had no idea how Papa had gotten in considering how small the space was. It was dark and Anna pulled her flashlight from her coat pocket. She always took it with her, but rarely used it, to conserve the battery. Papa had taught her to let her eyes adjust to the dark. It would keep her safe and give her an advantage from those who may be tracking her.

Anna's mouth dropped open. Inside were two wooden slat boxes containing jars of canned food, a wool blanket, an extra pair of hiking boots larger than her current ones, candles, matches, extra batteries, and lastly, wood stacked in every space and crevice available.

Anna plopped down in the middle of everything and burst into tears. Papa had thought of everything, not once, but multiple times and it had cost him a fortune to get all of this. Everything cost Jews ten times what it cost everyone else. There was no way that Anna could disappoint her parents. She was not only going to live but she was determined to thrive!

Anna's hands caressed each item, knowing what went into getting it and putting it there for her. She came to what looked like an empty mason jar, but she could see paper was curled up inside it. She unscrewed the metal ring and popped the lid off. Unrolling the paper, she could see that Papa's handwriting graced the first page, and Mama's was on the second. She uncurled the letter to lay it flat, pulling her flashlight up to the page.

My Dear Anna,

If you are reading this letter, then things have turned the way I thought they would. I wish this weren't the case, but I rejoice that you've found your way to camp and found our letters. We thought our life was complete until you were born, only to realize it was never near that point without you. You're a wonderful, smart, loving daughter who always brought joy to us. You're strong and I know you'll succeed in our plan for you to live beyond what your mama and I may get to. Please don't be sad. We lived a happy life and are satisfied knowing we've taught you what love is when you marry and have children of your own.

Anna was crying so hard she could no longer read. She pulled her coat sleeve up, wiping her eyes and runny nose. Pulling the letter back under the light, she kept reading.

I've tried to think of everything that will help you begin a life in secret, but I know that I can't predict everything you'll encounter. Trust your instinct; it will serve you well, Anna. You've always been independent enough that you can learn to use the resources around you and you're smart enough to stay safe. I'm very proud of you.

It's okay to be afraid. Fear can be a good thing; it can keep you safe. Know that each day will bring something different. Some you'll be prepared for and some you can't. In time, try to make your way to Switzerland, Israel or America and start a new life. I hope we've left you with enough money and supplies to help you live, but most of all, we leave you our love. No matter what happens, you'll always have it, and no one can take it away from you.

Love, Papa

Anna wept uncontrollably now. Her eyes were just about swollen shut and snot dripped from her nose. Tears splashed onto the letter, and Anna tried to wipe it dry with her sleeve. She flipped to the second page, where Mama's beautiful cursive handwriting caressed the paper.

A soft waft of rosewater rose off the page, making Anna smile. Mama had always dropped rosewater on her letters. She said it added a sense of yourself to the person you were writing to. It was like the person could feel you there with them. Anna could now appreciate what she meant. Setting the flashlight over the page, Anna read.

My Dear, Dear, Anna,

One day there were two people and then three, and life was complete. You were such a tiny baby, yet you brought such huge love and joy into the world. What you brought to my and papa's life was so immense, we could never measure or imagine it. I watched you grow from that tiny baby into the lovely, beautiful, young woman you have become. You've grown in spirit, independence and strength that every mother wishes for her daughter.

I pray that you will not only survive but find the love and joy that your father and I have had. Marriage is work, compromise, respect and most of all love. Find that Anna, give that, and enjoy your life.

Don't get stuck on the trivial things that in the long run, don't matter. Have children and relish in the joy they bring.

Be strong yet don't let these times in your life define what your life will be. It won't matter if you live through this ugliness if you can't find the beauty in moving forward.

Most of all my lovely daughter, I love you. I hope that we'll see each other again in this life, but if not, I'll be waiting for you after. I will be waiting for you either way. I love you Anna.

Mama

Anna felt the letter slip from her fingers to the dirt floor. Two photographs fell alongside it. She picked them up and ran her finger over them, as if she could feel her parents through her skin.

The first one was of her parents holding her as a baby. On the back, Mama had written she was about nine months old. They were sitting on the park bench in the park where her and Peter would ride their bikes. The second one was of her and her parents at the ocean. Papa had closed the store for the whole weekend, so they could spend family time together. It was rare that he could take a whole weekend off.

She had been about twelve. She remembered that day as if it were yesterday. The sun had been out, and they had pulled off their shoes to run through the surf. She had built a huge sandcastle with a moat, and Papa had filled it with ocean water. Eventually, the waves had won over the castle, and it had slowly disappeared into the water.

They had laughed all day, had ice cream, supper on the boulevard, and to end the day, they had watched the sun set into an orange ball that gradually disappeared. Papa had called it a "glorious day." It had been.

Anna rolled the letters up, took one last scent of her mother and put the paper back in the jar. Running her fingers one last time over the pictures, she dropped them in too. They were the only pictures she had left now. Someday, she would pull out those pictures and show her children their grandparents and tell them all about the wonderful parents she had been blessed with.

Anna put the jar back in the wood box and turned the flashlight off, putting it back in her pocket. She gathered up some dry wood in her arms and scooted back out the door. She tossed the wood into her camp and went back for what she had gathered in the woods. She'd store it in the storage area Papa had made her, so it could dry. She'd make sure she put new wood back when she took the dry out. She'd make Papa proud. Anna pulled the bucket of water from the bushes and set it inside her door and pulled pine branches over all her footprints, leaving no trace.

What a blessing, she thought. She hadn't even thought to look in the small berm. She had forgotten all about it, maybe because of exhaustion, being overwhelmed, or both. Pulling her heavy coat off, Anna snuggled into her sleeping bag, smiling. *Today,* thought Anna, *I'm just going to do whatever I want.*

I'm going to celebrate! Reaching from her bag, she pulled out the food she liked best and ate to her hearts content.

Before she knew it, she had fallen asleep. Hours later, a huge snore woke her from her slumber. She had slept so deep that drool had left a huge wet spot on her sleeping bag.

Peeking out the door, she saw that dusk had settled into darkness. It was still safe for her to leave camp and get back before the sun rose. Anna knew where she was going to go. She had gotten remarkably familiar with the woods and how to get to her old house. Sometimes, she took a different route, so she didn't wear a path down in one place. She didn't want anyone wondering where the path led.

****

CHAPTER NINETEEN

Peter looked out the front store window, wishing it was five o'clock. He wanted to lock the door. The last fifteen minutes of the day seemed to drag. He was sure it was because he watched the clock and prayed no one would come in. Town was now swarming with soldiers, and he was sick of having to wait on them.

The ticking on the large cream clock continued. *Tick, tick, tick.* It seemed that it was ticking at him just to annoy him. Someday he was going to yank that clock off the wall and smash it! *Tick, tick, tick,* Peter watched, waiting for the big hand to strike five. Just as it was about to tick for the last time, marking five o'clock, the door chimed, and in walked the SS officer who had been in before.

"Heil Hitler!" The officer swung his right arm high into the air in the familiar Nazi salute.

Peter had no choice but to do the same, but it was done with as little enthusiasm as he could get away with. The officer smiled at Peter.

"I got here just in time! I had to do a little sprinting to make it," he exclaimed, huffing from his run.

Peter was not happy to see him, nor that he had come in just when he was ready to turn the lock on the door, pull the shades and call it a day.

"I have to say," the officer said with a chuckle, "those cookies last week made a hit with my wife and her ladies club. I thought I'd surprise her with something new for tomorrow's club day. Do you have any suggestions?"

I sure do, thought Peter silently, smiling through his gritted teeth. He had some good suggestions, but he was sure the officer wouldn't like any of them. Peter was extremely agitated and hoped he could keep his anger in check. Right then, his father came around the corner.

"Oh," exclaimed Mr. Reinhold, "Peter, we have a last-minute guest, and I see a valued repeat customer." His father sounded cheery, almost to the extreme, which was his father's way of telling Peter to watch his words.

"Major Holtz," the officer said, extending his hand to Mr. Reinhold. "You must be this wonderful young man's father."

"Yes." Mr. Reinhold nodded. "I am. I'm an extremely lucky man. He works hard to make sure our troops have bread even though his heart's desire is somewhere else." *If the officer only knew that Peter's heart's desire was a Jewish girl,* he thought.

"Yes, I understand," said Officer Holtz. "I could put a good word in for you, Peter, but unfortunately, we need you here. I would love to have you in service with me, young man, but I think our Führer would give me a demotion for taking such a valuable asset away from the mouths of our troops."

"Your words are very appreciated," Peter lied, struggling to keep the disdain he felt for the vile man out of his voice. "I've taken on a new appreciation from our conversation last time. You've let me know that my job here is important and, of course, I want to do what the Führer needs."

"Oh good." Holtz smiled.

Peter wanted to vomit the words he had just spoken. Before the officer could start talking again, Peter asked what he could get him, so he could get rid of the creep. The man repulsed him.

"Perhaps that wonderful coffee cake." The officer pointed toward the cookies. "And some butter cookies. Yes, I think that would be perfect. Of course, those cookies won't make it home, though." The officer laughed and winked at Peter.

Peter laughed a fake laugh, wrapped the items up, and this time, took his money.

"Thank you," said Peter. "We appreciate your business, and you enjoy these goodies."

"I will, I will," the officer said with a toothy smile.

"Here, let me get the door for you," Peter said, as he rushed to pull the door open, so he could get rid of him.

"Well, thank you." He smiled again. "Hard working *and* polite," the officer praised. "Your father raised you well."

"Oh yes, he certainly did," Peter agreed, nodding his head, his blond hair falling over his eyes. As soon as the officer stepped outside, Peter closed the door, locked it and pulled the shades.

"I have a feeling we've become his new favorite pastry shop." His father snorted.

"Yes, I think you're right," growled Peter, flicking his hair back into place.

"Well, did you spit on his cake and cookies?" His father snickered.

Peter smiled up at his father, a grin so big there was no denying what Peter had done when the officer wasn't looking.

"Well what do you think, Father?" They both laughed so hard they were soon both crying. Oh, how good it felt to laugh, just like he and Anna used to.

Peter was relieved he had finally gotten rid of the SS officer. He was so tired of keeping up the farce of being a loyal German. He just wanted to find Anna and her parents and escape from a country he had grown to hate. Yes, he hated Germany for what its citizens had turned into, for the things they thought and believed. How could they follow an insane man? Peter had grown up loving his country. Germany had always been beautiful, full of generous and caring people. One man and the stupidity of its citizens had turned his country ugly.

As he finished cleaning up the bakery, Peter turned off the lights and followed his father up the stairs to the kitchen. Even though he wasn't hungry, he took the sandwich his father offered and sat down at the table across from him. Neither he nor his father spoke. They were both too tired for small talk. They ate their dinner in silence, cleaned up the dishes and headed to bed to wake up to another day, just like every other day.

"Good night, Father," Peter called as he headed to his room.

"Good night, Son," his father called back. "I love you. Get some sleep tonight."

"I will." Peter didn't know if he would or not, but he'd let his father think he would. The snow had quit falling last night, and he had meant to leave his tin of goodies in the bushes tonight, but he was too exhausted to go back downstairs and into the chilly night air. He didn't have high hopes the visitor would come anyway.

Pulling his pajamas on, he crawled into bed and pulled his down comforter up around his neck. Minutes later, light snoring rose from the covers.

****

CHAPTER TWENTY

J oseph and Jacob made their way to the storage building and stepped inside. The room was cold. The Germans didn't feel the need to waste heat on prisoners. A guard was stationed in the corner, watching everyone who came in and out, making sure no one could steal something.

Pushing his list across the counter, Joseph said, "I have a list of items I need in order to make jewelry. Officer Heinz sent me." He kept his head down, and his voice was so low that the attendant could barely hear him. All prisoners knew to be as inconspicuous as possible.

The attendant just nodded and scurried off, leaving Joseph and his friend alone with the guard. Both kept their hands on the counter and their eyes down. Boxes of tools were dropped onto the counter, and Joseph and Jacob quickly picked them up, making a hasty quick exit. Stepping into the crisp air, they felt relieved they were out of the guards' view. With arms loaded, weighing heavy with tools and machinery, they made their way back to their building.

****

CHAPTER TWENTY ONE

The night was cold, but at least the snow had subsided. Anna wished for a light snow to cover her tracks, but she wasn't in charge of the weather. At least she felt like God was looking after her. That thought made her feel bolder.

The snow crunched under her boots, loud in the silence of the woods. Anna's ears were tuned into any unfamiliar sounds and she was careful to duck into the brush occasionally to wait and watch for anything or anyone who shouldn't be there.

Tonight, she was going to go see her home and Peter's. Having found her parents' letters, she felt empowered to go home. She moved swiftly through the woods, taking a slightly longer route in order to avoid beating down a regular path. It would take her a good forty minutes longer, but it was necessary. Papa had told her not to get comfortable.

"Getting comfortable can lead to mistakes," he had said.

The last twenty minutes Anna had to push through a lot more brush, but she finally made it. There in front of her was home. Seeing the lights were off, she peered over at the Reinholds'. All the lights were off there, too. Anna didn't care; she just wanted to see her home. She nestled herself in between the two bushes, pulled her scarf up around her mouth and nose, and just stared at the windows.

Anna woke with a start. Dawn was just beginning to peek on the horizon. *Oh my gosh,* Anna panicked, her heart was pumping wildly in her chest as she realized she must have fallen asleep. She needed to leave immediately, but her hands and feet were frozen. Anna tried to pull herself out of the bushes, but her extremities refused to work. Slowly, she crawled from the bushes and up behind a tree. She rubbed her hands together and blew warm breaths into her gloves. She could feel the warmth against her palms work down to her fingers. She did this about ten times, until she could finally move her fingers with some ease.

Her feet were so cold. She stood up, trying to stomp her feet up and down to get the circulation flowing. Standing up exposed her, and she prayed no one was up yet. She still had to get into the woods and back to camp. Her feet started to tingle, which was enough for her to start moving.

Anna clumsily moved into the tree line and made her way to camp. Little did she know that a familiar face had opened the back door and was staring right at her.

Peter rushed back into the bakery, grabbed his jacket, and pulled the back door closed. As the door closed, he reached for the screen door, but it slipped from his grasp and slammed against the doorjamb with a loud bang. He hadn't bothered to pull on his snow boots, he couldn't take the time or chance of losing his secret visitor.

Anna's head jolted around, hearing the door bang. She realized someone had come outside. She needed to hurry, and she needed to head someplace dense, so they couldn't follow her tracks. Today was not going to be an easy day, she thought. She could kick herself for being so lax and stupid. She wasn't feeling so bold anymore. Placing one frozen foot in front of the other, she made her way north, toward camp. She had been trekking through the woods for about five minutes when she heard a voice not too far off.

"Wait, please wait! Please, stop. I want to talk to you. I can help you if you need it. Please!"

Anna stopped short, sucking in her breath. It was Peter! She recognized his voice. Her heart beat faster, and a warm feeling spread through her. She wanted to stop. She wanted Peter to catch her, but she knew she couldn't let him. Papa had told her not to trust anyone.

"Even the Reinholds?" she had asked.

"No, not even the Reinholds," Papa had replied, shaking his head back and forth, his eyes sad. "We can't trust anyone. Not even our friends. Only trust God."

Anna started to move quicker into the bushes, sweeping a fir branch over her footsteps as best she could.

Peter was running through the brush, calling out for her to stop. His feet were soaked, his canvas shoes frozen now. He'd have to slow down soon.

Peter called out again, his voice closer. Anna started to panic. He was heading in her direction, and soon he'd be able to see her.

Scanning the area, she found a clump of green bushes around the trunk of a huge fir tree. Anna crawled into the middle of them, careful to cover her tracks. She scrunched down deep, pulling the brush up around her, setting the fir branch she had used to cover her tracks, on top of her head. She then scrunched down even farther. Her jacket was a deep brown, and her knit hat was black, helping to camouflage her into the scenery. She could see her breath and quickly pulled her scarf over her mouth.

"Hello?" called Peter. "I'm a friend, you can trust me. I want to help you, please! I leave you a tin of pastries in the bushes where you hide. I don't care if you're Jewish or not. I just want to help."

He had stopped right in front of Anna. She could see him through a small spot in the bushes. He was turning around in circles, looking in every direction. He looked so good to her, even handsome. She wanted to jump out of the bushes like a Jack-in-the-Box, throw her arms around him, but she stayed put. It seemed like hours that Peter stood there, looking, but she knew it was only minutes. Poor Peter looked miserable. His face was beet red from the cold, his pants were soaked up to his knees, and his shoes were covered in snow and ice. He had to be freezing.

He sighed deeply, tucked his cold hands into his coat pockets, and turned toward home. The last thing Anna heard was him mumbling that he wanted to help, and they could trust him. She felt sorry for him. He looked so sad, but she was to trust no one.

She waited about ten minutes, to make sure Peter wasn't waiting in the distance, watching. She knew from the look of his shoes and clothes he couldn't stay out in the cold long. Finally, she got up, stretched her legs, and pushed herself out of the brush. Her feet felt like they were still half frozen, but she needed to get back to camp and away from Peter.

As she hurried to camp, Anna's thoughts went to Peter's words. Did he really mean no harm? She believed him, but she still wasn't ready to throw her fears out the window. She needed to heed Papa's words for now. She wanted to run up and grab Peter and just hug him until she was too weak to hold him any longer, but for now, she would have to just watch him from a distance.

Hours later, camp came into view. She had never approached or left during daylight. She was shaking, but it wasn't just from the cold. She was afraid she would get caught. She had been careless, and she hoped it would not cost her more than she could afford. Slowly, Anna crept to the edge of the field, peering from behind a tree. She waited and watched for any signs of life. The farmer's chimney spiraled smoke, letting her know there was probably someone in the house. So far, she'd been lucky. Since she had been living in camp, she had only seen someone a couple of times, from a distance. Still, she waited. She didn't need to be impatient and give herself away.

Far off in the distance, Anna saw movement. Someone was out by the barn, but Anna was so far away she couldn't tell if it was a man or a woman. She waited until they went back inside the house.

"Thank goodness." She sighed. Slowly, she worked her way up to her hut, brushing her footsteps away as she went. Crawling inside, she collapsed onto her cot, spent. Her arms ached from brushing her footsteps away and she swore her feet were blocks of ice.

The fire still had some coals in it, so Anna put a couple of branches on it. The wood sparked the fire to life and slowly produced warm, orange flames. Even though Anna could see her breath, it was much warmer in her camp than it was outside.

Pulling off her boots, she gently massaged her feet and set them near her tiny fire. Before she had left last night, she had set a pile of rocks on the edge of the fire pit. Papa had shown her this when they had gone camping years ago. The first time she had seen him do it she had laughed so hard, but now she had a new appreciation for his ingenuity. With a smile on her face and memories of her and Papa, she pulled an extra pair of socks from her box and threw some of the warmed stones into the bottom of them. Slowly, she pulled each sock over the socks she was wearing, adjusting the stones onto the bottom of her feet and a couple on top.

"Oh," she groaned in pleasure. She could feel the warmth spread through her feet, tingling them back to life.

****

CHAPTER TWENTY TWO

Peter trudged back to the bakery, his feet now ice cubes. He opened the back door and slipped inside. His father was there in the bakery working dough into loaves of bread. He looked up at Peter in surprise, staring at the frozen young man in front of him.

"Peter! Where were you!" he exclaimed. "You're a block of ice! I thought you were upstairs! What in the world were you doing?" His father stood there, his hands on his hips, flour covering his arms and apron, staring at him.

Peter knew he had to fess up to what he had been doing but he really didn't want to. He knew he'd have to listen to his father lecture him that he wasn't being careful, that he needed to toe the line and not bring any more attention to them. Still, he couldn't just let someone sit out there, spying on them, not knowing who they were.

Peter looked his father in the eyes as he spoke, gauging his reaction.

"Someone is spying on us," said Peter. "They sit in the bushes late at night and early morning and watch our place. I saw him this morning as he was leaving. I wanted to find out who it was, so I tried to follow him. Maybe he needs help."

He was right, his father wasn't happy. His father never yelled. He always spoke softly when he was upset or disappointed. Sometimes Peter wished he would just yell at him. His father was such a patient man, and it reminded him, that in regard to that, Peter didn't take after him. Now with the soldiers crawling all over the city and in everyone's business, he knew he needed to be careful, but it was hard.

His father shook his head back and forth, whispering.

"Peter, Peter, Peter. You work so hard, and you worry so much about Anna and her parents. Maybe you just thought you saw someone? You can't be running off into the woods chasing people, imaginary or real. If there is someone out there, you can't have the neighbors thinking you're trying to help someone that may be against the Fatherland. We've talked about this, Peter. Spitting on the officers' pastries is one thing, but helping someone that may be considered a traitor will get us both killed."

Peter hung his head, his wet hair dripping onto his face. The ice on his shoes was now melting, forming puddles around his feet. Pulling his coat off, he hung it on the wall and looked into his father's eyes.

"Father, I just have this feeling this person needs help. I've watched him for weeks from my bedroom window with my binoculars. This morning, when I came out with the garbage, he was standing behind a tree along the wood line. He started to run when I saw him. What if it's Mr. Feiner? We have to help!"

Peter's arms were now swinging in the air, his emotions needing more than a verbal outlet. Peter's voice rose as he tried to convince his father he was doing the right thing. His father let out a deep sigh.

"Son, you have a kind heart, and that's one of the things I love about you, but it's also something that will get us in trouble. I know you well enough that I am sure you won't stop looking or wanting to help, but you need to be extra careful. You can't go off into the woods calling out and alerting the neighbors, especially those that now live in the Feiners' house."

Just the mention of the new neighbors in Anna's house made Peter's face turn red with anger and his hands curl into fists. He hated them for taking the Feiners' home and would never forgive them. Peter hardly acknowledged them. They acted like they deserved the house and that the Feiners were garbage.

"They are the trash," thought Peter.

"You must use discretion," his father admonished. Putting his hands on his son's shoulders, he looked him squarely in the eyes, letting him know he was serious. "You must be extremely careful. Promise me."

Peter nodded his head. He didn't say anything else. Pulling his shoes off and setting them by the ovens to dry out, he headed upstairs for dry clothes. He pulled his hand through his wet hair. "It's going to be a long day," he mumbled.

****

CHAPTER TWENTY THREE

It had been a long trip back to camp and Anna was exhausted. Her feet had finally gotten their feeling back, and she took the extra socks off, setting the rocks back on the fire's edge. A jar of half frozen peaches had sufficed for breakfast and lunch today.

What she wouldn't have done for a Reinhold pastry! Anna thought about what Peter had said about leaving a tin with pastries for her every night. She pictured the tin, bright silver, but what did he put inside? That was the mystery. Was it something she liked? He didn't know it was her. In fact, he thought she was a man.

Anna knew Peter well enough to know he would be relentless in trying to find out who was hiding by his house. She would have to lie low for a while. She was getting a little too bold. She could see her father shaking his head in disapproval. Yes, she would lie low, but only for a while.

It had been more than a week since she had been to the house. She was still afraid Peter would be diligent in watching for her, and as much as she wanted to see her home and watch for Peter, she'd stay put. Making good use of her time, she decided to do an inventory of her food supplies. She wasn't afraid of clothes issues but once you ate your food, it was gone!

She needed to find out what she had left and calculate how long it would last. Besides, she didn't want to wait until she was completely out and starving to death. Those conditions would make you take risks you normally wouldn't.

The weather had warmed a little bit. Spring was finally arriving, and soon she wouldn't have to worry about freezing. On the other hand, she'd have to worry about the farmer and where he'd be plowing and planting crops.

Anna tucked into the storage berm and started going through the boxes of food. Papa and Mama had really stocked her with loads of food and essentials, but she had been hiding now for over two months. She desperately needed to know what she did and didn't have, and how long it would last.

Pulling the first crate off the top of another, she started to pull all the items out, mark the contents on her notepad, then carefully tuck it all back into the crates. There was one crate completely empty now. She'd use the wood as kindling, since it was nice and dry. Nothing was wasted.

Pulling the second crate out, she repeated the process, picking each item out, counting it, and then placing it back in the crate. This crate was only a quarter filled, if that. Anna frowned, knowing she didn't have much left, but she had lasted a long time on what she had been blessed with. She set the one empty crate over with the others that had been emptied over the months. She reviewed her notes, mentally acknowledging she was going to need more.

A half of a pound of flour, one can of meat, two jars of pickles, one jar of peaches, a can of beans, less than a quarter pound of dried deer jerky that Papa had shot and smoked, and some carrots that had grown so much fur on it she knew she couldn't eat it, remained. Included was a small tin half full of hard candies.

Anna opened the candy tin, popping a lemon one in her mouth. She loved candy. It was a special treat that her parents had surprised her with. Sucking on the sweet, hard candy, it almost felt like her parents were with her. Anna smiled to herself, mentally picturing them.

Making sure everything was stacked and covered, Anna crawled back out, covered her footsteps and snuck over to her hut. She had one old fruit box left in her living quarters that had barely anything left in it. Sadly, her list had quickly diminished and only included a half-eaten jar of peaches and one can of beans, enough for three meals if she ate sparingly.

I need to make smaller meals, she thought. She was heavier than when she had been in the ghetto, but much slimmer than before the war. She and her parents had anticipated she'd grow when they'd purchased clothes to hide. She had grown taller, but her weight had gone the opposite way. The boy's pants they had bought were still being held up by a rope. The waist rippled with extra fabric, but at least her pants stayed up.

By Anna's calculations, she would have about two weeks she could stretch her food out if she was lucky. She had to figure out how to replenish, and catching squirrels was not going to do it. She knew what she had to do, but the thought scared her, making her shiver. Trying to live could still be the death of her.

She had no choice. She would have to go out into the open and try to purchase food. She didn't think she'd be any good at stealing, and it also went against what she believed. No, she would go to a town that wouldn't recognize her and try to buy food. Maybe this was where the blessing Papa talked about would really help her; she didn't look Jewish. Tomorrow might be her last day of freedom, so tonight would be her last chance to see home again. If she was lucky, maybe she'd see Peter, and maybe he had left her a surprise in the bushes. She'd have to be quick tonight and not linger.

Even though Anna knew it was a bad idea, it had been over a week since she had been home, and she could no longer resist. "Just a quick look," she mumbled to herself. "Just a quick look, check the bushes, and leave." She only hoped she wouldn't get emotional and screw everything up.

It was dark out already, but Anna wanted to give herself another hour before she left. She preferred to wait until almost eight o'clock, so she'd get there close to eleven. She needed to try to outsmart Peter. When he had seen and followed her weeks ago, he had seen her after midnight.

She'd go the short route tonight. She'd still have time for a nap and to clean up before she would go to town. Anna checked her watch, which was worth its weight in gold. Papa had slipped his watch into her pocket before she had gone to the dead pile. It was the only personal possession he'd had, and he had given it to her.

Anna had protested, but he wouldn't hear anything about it. He had wanted her to always know what time it was.

"It will keep you safer," he'd said.

Even though Anna's body clock was good at calculating time, having a watch allowed her the luxury of being exact.

Anna passed on eating before she left. After doing inventory of her food situation, she decided to see if Peter left anything first. She lay down on her cot and let her mind go back to good times. She pulled Mama's hanky up to her nose and sucked in the smell. The scent of her perfume had faded a bit, but there was still a hint of Mama.

Tears trickled down Anna's face. She wasn't sure if living in these conditions was even worth the hiding, but she had promised her parents she'd live, and she was going to do her best to uphold her promise.

Besides, how long could this war and hatred for the Jews last?

The hour had ticked away, and Anna pulled herself off her cot. Using her boot, she kicked the coals away from each other so they'd cool down. Pulling on her coat, she squeezed out the door and snuck off into the woods, making sure not to leave any footprints.

The night air was cold, and you could see your breath, but the snow had finally subsided and hadn't dropped a flake for days. It had warmed up to about thirty degrees and she was thankful. Ten degrees versus thirty was an enormous difference. The sky was filled with clouds but at least they weren't snow clouds and it kept the air warmer. A clear sky always made it cold.

Traipsing through the woods, Anna still had some icy snow to contend with from previous days, but she was grateful it wasn't deep, and it wasn't everywhere. She kept to her determined route, stopping frequently, ducking into some bushes, watching for movement, making sure she wasn't being followed.

Seeing movement, Anna froze when a white rabbit darted through the trees, taking cover. Anna smiled, imagining a nice fat rabbit being roasted on a stick over her campfire.

"If you only knew how lucky you are tonight little guy," she whispered. Getting up, Anna got back on course. Approaching the edge of the wood line, she crouched low, sitting on the haunches of her legs, and watched. Her breath cold against the air, she wrapped her scarf around her mouth and up over her nose. Finally, she laid down on her stomach and slowly, inch by inch, crawled up to the bushes. The snow was packed into the ground and helped her slide along.

It was close to eleven o'clock when Anna had gotten there, and the only lights on were the back-porch light from Peter's and lights from the oven area in the bakery shop. That meant Peter or Mr. Reinhold was up, or perhaps both. Someone was working late, probably cleaning up.

Sitting between the bushes, Anna moved her hand around until it settled on a hard box. There it was, the silver tin tucked deep into the brush. Her heart skipped a beat, and her mouth watered. She was dying to open it. Peter was still putting food out.

I was right, she thought, *he'll never give up.*

Pulling off her gloves, Anna popped the lid off. Inside was a holiday! There were two brotchen rolls, Anna's favorites. It was a soft white bread with a light crispy crust. She loved to eat them at breakfast with her Mama's homemade jam. Her mouth watered just thinking about it. Next, she pulled out an apple danish, setting it gently on the tin's lid so it didn't get dirty. Last were two linzer tart cookies.

Outside of the Reinholds' lemon cookies, these were some of her favorites. They were double layered cookies brimming with raspberry filling and topped with powdered sugar. Anna's stomach growled, reminding her she hadn't eaten anything all day. Anna willed her stomach quiet, promising she'd feed it when she returned to camp.

Putting all but the danish in her jacket pocket, she pushed the lid back on the tin, setting it quietly back into the bushes. Anna stared off to Peter's and smiled. Tonight, she was going to have a little piece of home, thanks to him.

"Thank you," she silently mouthed in his direction. She had always loved Peter, not ever the way other girls did, but lately, her heart had changed some. She had a new appreciation for him and couldn't help but feel something for him, something she had never felt before. If only a war hadn't started, but then again, would her feelings for him have grown under different circumstances? She wasn't sure, but what she did know was that she really missed him.

Anna wasn't sure where to put the pastry without squishing it and getting it all over her clothes.

"That'll be a mess," she thought. She'd use the tin but wanted to leave it, so he could fill it again, at least she hoped he would. She held up the golden-brown danish with the white vanilla icing drizzled over the top, inviting her to take a bite. She slowly and gently sunk her teeth into it, her tastebuds coming alive.

"Yum." She sighed, savoring the treat as the flavors exploded in her mouth. It was apple, and the pieces still held a slight crispness to them. The Reinholds' never over baked their danish. She took another bite of the fluffy pastry letting it sit in her mouth, enjoying it longer, before she started to chew. She took another huge bite and then slowly, popped the last of it into her mouth, wiping her hands over her lips to get the final bit, licking her fingers clean.

The rest of Peter's goodies tucked securely in her pocket and a letter she couldn't read until she got back to camp, she scooted out of the bushes and headed back. She couldn't afford to linger. Tomorrow would bring what it would bring. She had no control, but tonight was her night and she was going to revel in her happiness. Anna's heart sang with joy, her scarf covering the huge smile on her face.

****

CHAPTER TWENTY FOUR

Peter pulled off his apron, hung it on the hook, locked the doors and shut off the light. Father had not been feeling well and had headed upstairs hours ago. He had kept trying to work, but Peter could see he wasn't well at all. He kept insisting his father go to bed, that he'd be fine handling things on his own.

"Father, I've been working in the bakery since I was five years old. I'll be fine. You need to go upstairs before you make me sick too." His father had finally agreed.

Peter worked hard to get everything cleaned up and ready for the morning. He wanted to be able to watch his window for a while. The last week had proved fruitless in seeing the visitor but he continued his vigil of tin goodies in the bushes. He set them out when he knew the neighbors would be in bed, asleep. Tomorrow, before the sun came up and he started work, he'd check the box. He prayed he wouldn't be disappointed again.

Peter's father had gone to bed as soon as he'd gone upstairs. He could hear a light snoring coming from his father's room.

Good, thought Peter, *he's getting some rest.* Today had been especially hard. Not only had his father been ill but they had been extremely busy. The army had added more bread to their orders, to handle the extra soldiers stationed in town and up at the front. He wondered how many other bakeries had turned into Hitler's suppliers.

It was common for soldiers to come into the store to buy cookies or something sweet. Peter was getting good at hiding his hatred. Some of them he felt sorry for. From listening to their conversations, you could tell they didn't like being in the army, and they were not serving of their own free will. The only difference between them and himself was, he was a Jew lover, literally.

Peter had not seen Officer Holtz for the last few days, and he was thankful. It was common for him to come in a couple times a week now to pick up goodies for his wife's gatherings. Peter absolutely hated the man, yet the officer thought Peter was a wonderful, loyal Nazi. The man's tongue never stopped wagging, thinking Peter was his friend. Sometimes he would come into the bakery and linger, just chatting away. Little did Officer Holtz know that Peter was getting as much information as he could about what was happening to the Jews, and not for the reason the officer would have supposed. As far as Holtz knew, he thought Peter hated them as much as he did. Peter smiled to himself. If he only knew.

The next morning, Peter rose while it was still dark outside. The moon was still out, hiding behind cloud cover, fighting to be seen. Peter dressed quickly, brushed his teeth, shaved and pulled a warm cloth over his face. Tucking his head inside his father's door, he saw he was still fast asleep, his chest rising and falling with each breath, a slight snore escaping from time to time. He tiptoed down the hall and made his way downstairs, trying to avoid the steps with loud creaks in them. *Father must really be sick,* he thought. He was hoping he'd take the entire day off, but he had doubts that he would.

He turned the ovens on to heat them for the day's work, and then yanked his coat off the peg, slipping it on before he silently snuck out the back door. He made sure not to slam the screen. It was four thirty in the morning, so there was zero chance of anyone being up. Peter snuck over to the bushes, watching for anyone's lights to come on. He'd promised his father he'd be careful. Moving his hands around the base of the bushes, he pulled out the tin, disappointed it was still there. He headed back to the house, knowing he'd be working out his frustration on bread dough.

Back in the bakery, he angrily pulled his coat off, throwing it on the peg. Yanking his white baking apron from its hook, he pulled it over his head, messing up his hair in the process.

He opened the box to throw out last night's contents, and stood staring into the tin.

"I must be dreaming," he thought. He pushed the lid back on and stared at the box again. A minute passed.

Peter wanted to yank the lid back off, but he was scared it wouldn't be empty after all. Perhaps he had only seen what he wanted to see. Slowly, he pried it off again and looked inside. Nothing! Peter ran his hand through his unruly hair and danced around the room. He wanted to scream in delight, but he kept silent, so he didn't wake his father. Peter's smile showed all his straight white teeth and his deep dimples. His face hurt from smiling so much.

"Thank you, God!" he whispered. He held the box up to his chest and thought about what to do next. He had a confirmation someone was out there, but he still didn't know who. Would they read his letter and believe him? Would they let him be their friend and help them? Peter set the box under the counter and started the day's bread and pastry preparations. All day his smile told his customers he was a happy man.

****

CHAPTER TWENTY FIVE

Anna had gotten back to camp about one-thirty in the morning. She had only stayed at her house for less than fifteen minutes. She had a lot to do to get ready for today. She needed to mentally and physically prepare to go out in public.

She made mental notes of what she had to do. First on the list was to get water and heat it for a much-needed bath and hair washing. It had been a few weeks since her last one. She stoked her fire a bit, so she'd have coals to warm up the river water. The river still had some ice on it, and heating it took time and firewood. Taking a bath was her least favorite thing about living in camp. It took a lot of work and it was cold being stripped naked in this weather. She would have to make sure her hair was completely dry before she left camp. She couldn't afford to get sick. If she got pneumonia, there was no one to take care of her and nowhere to go.

Anna dug up the tin Papa had hidden in the dirt near her cot. She opened the tin and pulled out some more money to add to what she had already taken. Remembering things cost more since the war, she pulled the tin open again and took another small wad of bills from the box. She set the money on her cot and reburied the tin.

Grabbing her bucket, Anna made her way to the river, dunking the bucket in until it was three-quarters full. As usual, she filled the glass jar full too and headed to camp. Pulling her camouflaged door open, she crawled inside and set the pail on the fire, adding pieces of the empty crate to get the fire burning faster. She slipped outside to make sure she wasn't sending up smoke signals to unwanted visitors.

Setting her towel and clean clothes on her cot, she dunked the tip of her finger in the bucket to see if it was hot yet. Still cool, she waited another half hour and rechecked it. Anna smiled, feeling the water was now toasty warm. She pulled the bucket off the fire and stripped naked.

Holding her breath, she dunked her head up to her neck into the bucket and pulled it back out, letting the water drip back into the bucket. She didn't want to make a big mud puddle inside her living quarters, and she would need all the water she could save. Lathering up her hair, she scrubbed it well and then rinsed if off, dunking her head all the way as she worked the suds out of her hair. Anna pulled her hair out, twisted the water out, then pulled it up, rolling it up into a bun, using Mama's favorite comb to hold it in place. Despite having a wool blanket around her while she washed her hair, once her head left the warm water, it felt like it was freezing. Anna shivered in her nakedness.

Pulling the blanket off, she hurried and scrubbed herself, hard, getting the weeks' worth of dirt off her face and body. She had to admit, she smelled much better. She dried herself off, quickly wrapped the blanket around herself again, undid her hair and used the damp towel to squeeze as much water as she could out of it. Anna pulled her underclothes on, buttoned her blue blouse, and pulled a navy wool jumper over her head. Last, she pulled on her blue wool stockings and then her hiking boots. She'd take her good shoes with her and change them before she left the woods. Her clothes hung too large on her slender frame but there was nothing she could do about it.

Deciding to leave the pail of water inside, she set it to the side to wash clothes in later. It was a little dirty, but she used water until it turned brown. She took her time drying her hair, constantly brushing it to keep it straightened.

It would be a good four hours before the sun would be up, but she couldn't afford to fall asleep and miss leaving early in the morning. Picking up one of the books that her parents had surprised her with, she started reading.

The sun had finally made an appearance. Anna worked the coals apart so the fire would die down before she left. Today, she would cover her fire with a metal garbage lid she'd found in the woods near her old house. She hadn't known what she'd use it for at the time, but it had turned into a good find. Sometimes, when the coals had worked themselves to small embers, she would lay the lid over the coals and put her stocking feet on top, letting the warmth seep through. She couldn't always have a fire, but keeping her feet warm helped wrestle the cold. She hoped that the lid would keep the coals warm until she returned, so she could easily restart her fire. Remembering Peter's note, she pulled it from her jacket pocket.

Dear Visitor,

I've watched you from my window and would like to know who you are. I wish you no harm. I only wish to help you. It doesn't matter if you're Jewish or not.

Your friend

She knew he hadn't put his name on it in case it was intercepted by someone. It would mean death. She crumpled up the note and threw it under the garbage lid to burn. She thought about Peter's words. She knew he was probably telling the truth. He was a kind soul who was always for the underdog, the person who needed help, needed defending. She smiled, imagining Peter's face smiling, his huge dimples deep on both sides of his cheeks. A warmth rose through her and she wished it would stay with her forever.

Anna shook herself. "Get a hold of yourself," she mumbled to herself. "You have to stay focused." She had to stop thinking of Peter, or she'd end up doing something stupid. Anna shook off her thoughts and focused on her dangerous journey ahead.

Today, she'd be heading in the opposite direction of home. She couldn't go to Dusseldorf, where she grew up, as too many people knew her. No, instead, she'd head north to Solingen. She had been there before, prior to being shipped to the ghetto. Papa had insisted she know the layout of the town, just in case. She now thought how lucky she was that he had thought of just about everything. The only thing she wasn't prepared for was the demand for papers if she got stopped by the Gestapo.

Anna went over the list of what she wanted to achieve in town, knowing she needed to get in and out as quickly as possible. Towns were swarming with soldiers now who could randomly ask to see your papers. The thought of getting stopped made her shiver.

She was scared and practiced pretending she ran into a soldier, trying to figure out how to act and sound. If she sounded nervous, they were bound to be suspicious and ask to see her papers.

It was time. Anna pulled on her brown wool coat Mama had made Papa put in the clothes box. "She can't wear a boy's jacket if she has to go out in public," Mama had admonished him. "She needs to look normal." Papa had mulled the information over and agreed. There was no star on this coat, or the jacket she wore when she was out in the woods. Any trace of the Jewish star was a dead giveaway.

Anna had brushed her hair out straight while it was drying, finishing by pulling one side up behind her ear with a hair pin.

The money lay on the cot, and Anna picked it up, putting half into a small purse and the other half into her coat pocket. "Always keep your money in multiple places," she could hear Papa say. Last, she tied the laces of her oxford shoes together and slung them around her purse strap.

Taking a deep sigh, Anna crawled out the doorway, careful to get as little dirt as possible on her. Taking the little husk broom, she brushed over her tracks and tucked the broom under some branches by a tree at the forest's edge. Anna silently disappeared into the woods.

****

CHAPTER TWENTY SIX

Peter had been excited all day long, thinking hard on what he would put in the box for tonight. He was so anxious he could barely think straight. His plan was to stay up tonight and watch from his bedroom window for sure.

He had a lot to do and got to work with extra speed this morning. He didn't want his father to feel he had to help today, and he wanted to be done in time to take a nap before he watched for his late visitor. It was going to be a long day, but worth it. Peter hummed to himself all day long. Nothing was going to destroy the way he felt after opening the tin box. If he couldn't help Anna, then the least he could do was help someone else. He was so disgusted with his neighbors and the soldiers stationed in Dusseldorf. How could they think they were any better than someone who was Jewish?

Anna's walk in the woods was hard. It wasn't a path she was used to taking. A few times she had pulled the compass out to make sure she was still bearing north. Snow spattered the forest floor along with pinecones, slick leaves, and moss.

Anna had about a half mile left to town when she put her foot down and it jetted out from underneath her. Flipping up into the air, she landed on her back and head with a thud, whacking her head on the hard-packed ground. She lay there for minutes, stunned, her head throbbing. Slowly, she sat up and propped herself against a log. Her head pulsed with pain and a wave of nausea hit her. Anna laid her head in the palms of her hands and just sat there. A half hour had passed when she finally lifted her head and slowly stood up. Again, the nausea hit, and Anna sat back down. This wasn't good.

"I probably have a concussion," she whispered to herself. She knew she needed to head back to camp, but she was so close to her destination, she didn't want to give up. The last thing you should do with a concussion was sleep, so she stayed with her plan.

She sat there for another fifteen minutes and finally pulled her coat off and brushed the dirt from it. By the time it had been brushed multiple times, the coat looked good. Her shoes were covered in dirt, and Anna pulled out a hanky and rubbed them clean.

Anna was determined to keep going. She was so close now that giving up didn't seem like an option. She didn't know if she'd have the guts to try again after today. Anna pulled on her coat and started to walk. It was a slow walk, but her feet were moving one in front of the other. Every fifty steps, she would lean on a tree for a few seconds convincing herself to keep going. Her head throbbed with every movement, but she was now only half a mile from town.

Anna mentally tried to put the pain out of her mind and focus on walking. Sitting down on a log, she untied her boots, slipping them off, and then tucked each foot into the oxford saddle shoes. She took out a handkerchief and wiped the toes of her shoes off again. Her hiking boots were pushed into the brush, then she moved leaves over the top of them. The oxford saddle shoes were a little small confirming Anna's feet had grown. Her toes pushed into the fronts of the shoes, making Anna want to curl her toes down to avoid squashing them. There was nothing she could do about it but suffer through it. Her head still throbbed so maybe she wouldn't think of her poor feet.

Anna lowered her head, closed her eyes, and prayed. Letting out a long sigh, she stepped out of the woods and made her way down the hill toward town. Town was busy, and Anna wasn't sure if that was good luck or bad. So many people being around made it easier for her to blend in, but it also meant more people who might recognize she was Jewish.

Making her way down the main street, head throbbing, Anna looked for the shops she and Papa had checked out on their visit together. She pulled her list out, checking it. Candles, matches, food, and if she could afford it, she'd try to find a second-hand store for some larger shoes. Anna passed a few soldiers standing in a group, laughing, and she quickly passed by, making sure her face was turned away. A few feet later, an older gentleman tipped his hat and smiled at her. "Good morning," he said. Anna didn't trust her voice yet, so she just nodded and smiled.

The street bustled with people, young and old, and soldiers. Mothers pulling their kids places they didn't want to go, men with briefcases in hand, heading to work and most noticeable were the soldiers at every corner and in the shops. Her stomach was in knots and despite the cold, her hands felt clammy. She continued to make her way down the sidewalk, trying to be inconspicuous. *Keep walking, keep your head up high, be proud,* said Anna, over and over in her mind. *Don't give yourself away.*

Reaching the dry goods store, Anna pushed the door open, a little bell ringing, announcing her entrance. Anna was now sweating, and her head throbbed.

Two or three people were already in the store, waiting for their purchases to be rung up.

"Hello," called the clerk. "Can I help you find anything?" Anna looked the woman in the eyes and smiled.

"Yes, candles, please."

The woman pointed to them, and Anna scurried over to get them, so she could pay and get back outside. She also picked up two big boxes of matches. As she set it all on the counter, the salesclerk smiled again and rang up the purchase. "My, you're buying a lot of candles," she remarked.

Anna didn't know what to say. Was she being obvious by buying so many? Were ten candles too many? Anna looked at the woman and smiled.

"Yes, my mother loves to light candles at dinner. I guess she's just a romantic," Anna said, sighing deep and winking at the woman.

"Well, your father is a lucky man, then," the woman said, smiling back at Anna. "With that beautiful long hair and pretty smile, you'll be having a handsome husband one day," she said. "You better look out for these young soldiers. They love to keep their eyes on our young girls."

"Thank you." Anna nodded. "I'll watch out for those soldiers." Anna smiled, paid the woman and quickly grabbed her package off the counter, hurrying out the door. She had done it, she thought. She had fooled them, and even made conversation, leaving them none the wiser she was Jewish. Anna laughed inside. This was too easy.

Crossing the street, Anna stepped into the grocer's and stood in line. So far, so good. No one pointed to her, making her feel like she stood out. Papa was right, so far; her non-Jewish appearance was a blessing.

"What do you want?" bellowed the heavyset man behind the counter. "Speak up, girl, I don't have all day!"

"Oh, yes, yes," spoke up Anna. *Be brave, be brave,* she said to herself again. Anna was now the only one in the store and she was glad. "How much for the canned meat?"

"It's two blue rations a can," he barked.

"Oh," said Anna hesitantly. Ration cards…she had forgotten you had to have ration cards for some things. Something like candles, you could buy with money, but food was another story. "I'm afraid my parents are out of ration cards, but I have money." She smiled big as she said it.

"Are you trying to get me arrested? No ration cards, no goods," he yelled at her. The man's face was beet red, like he was ready to explode. She didn't need the Gestapo coming in to see what was wrong.

"I'm sorry. I'm really sorry," she mumbled. "I'll let my parents know." That was the last thing she said as she rushed out the door.

"You do that!" he screamed after her.

Anna's head was racing a mile a minute, and her hands and legs were shaking. She managed to walk down the block and get away from the grocer's, so she could get a hold of herself. She was visibly shaken and needed to calm down. She still felt nauseated and her head was pounding. Just as she thought she was getting calmed down, an older woman approached her. Her gray coat was a little raggedy, and her shoes had no color left on the toes, but she had a beautiful light blue cashmere shawl wrapped around her neck and an ornate pin set with what looked like real diamonds and blue sapphires adorning her coat.

"Are you all right, miss?" She was a few inches taller than Anna. She was bent over, looking into Anna's eyes. Anna couldn't speak. She was frozen with fear. "I say, miss, are you all right? Can I get you some help, a soldier perhaps?"

Anna bolted upright and stared at the woman. Her face held wrinkles around her eyes and mouth, and her hair was a soft silver.

"No, thank you," whispered Anna. The woman had kind eyes, but she didn't need anyone drawing attention to her.

"Oh, you look a little frazzled, dear. I thought you might need some help. This war makes life so hard."

"No, thank you," she said again.

"Where were you heading?" the woman asked. "Can I give you some directions?"

"I was just looking for the bakery," Anna lied. She didn't want the woman to know she had already pissed off the grocer.

"It's just down the street and around the next corner," the woman explained, pointing down the street. "I wish I had rations for bread," mumbled the woman, more to herself than Anna. "If I had money, I'd buy on the black market." The woman's eyes opened wide, shocked at her own comment. Fear covered her face. "I shouldn't have said that!"

Anna could tell the woman was now the one flustered. Anna put her hand on the woman's arm.

"I understand," said Anna. "The war is hard. I'm in need, the same as you."

The woman relaxed, studying Anna. Anna smiled back at her, letting her know her secret was safe with her.

"I don't have ration cards for some things, and I don't know what I'm going to do," Anna volunteered.

The woman didn't say anything for about thirty seconds, and then moved closer to her.

"There is a market here you can buy from, but you have to know someone, and it isn't cheap." The woman looked around to see if anyone was watching them.

"Please," Anna pushed. "Can you tell me where I can buy? I'm getting desperate." How desperate, the woman didn't need to know. It wasn't just that she had run out of items, Anna couldn't even get ration cards in the first place.

The woman sized her up again and leaned in even closer.

"Go down the block, turn left, go another three blocks and then to the blue house on the end. Tell them Greta sent you. It'll be trouble if you get caught, for you and for them. Be careful."

Anna nodded her head up and down, assuring the woman she would be.

"Good luck to you, dear," said the woman. She took Anna's hand, gripping it between her own, giving it a warm squeeze, then turned and walked off in the opposite direction.

Anna hurried along, making sure to avoid the soldiers. If they were on her side of the street, she quickly crossed over to the other side. When they showed up on that side, she switched back again. If she couldn't avoid them, she pretended to be window shopping until they were busy with someone else, and then she quickly walked past them. They would randomly ask for papers, and she had none.

Finally, Anna found the building. Trying to be nonchalant, she looked up and down the street to make sure it was clear and then climbed the steps and softly knocked on the door. The door opened a couple of inches, and two eyes peered out at her.

"Yes?" said a voice from behind the door. "What do you want?" Anna hesitated a bit, but she was here, and she needed a way to replenish her goods.

"I need some items," she said. She was still scared someone would know what she was up to. "Greta sent me."

The woman pulled the door open, poked her head out, looked Anna up and down, decided she wasn't a threat, and pulled her inside the house.

"Do you have money?" asked the woman, her hands resting on her rather large hips.

This woman isn't missing any meals, thought Anna. "Some," she said.

"You look awful young to be buying here," said the woman, looking Anna over. "You sure you have money?"

"Yes," said Anna, trying to control the anger that was starting to well up inside her. She just wanted to get what she could and get out.

"What are you looking for?" she asked. Anna noted the woman was all business. There was no warmth to her demeanor. *Just as well,* she thought. *I don't need any friends.*

"Canned meat, potatoes, flour, and baking powder."

"Hmmm," mulled the woman. "I'll be right back. Stay here, and don't answer the door." Anna just nodded. It was about ten minutes later when the woman came back with a sack filled with stuff. One by one, she pulled the items from the bag for Anna to look at.

"I can give you four cans of meat, six potatoes, a pound of flour and a small tin of baking powder. Do you see anything else you want?" the woman asked, standing guard over the stack of food, eyeing Anna closely.

"Cheese, sugar, and tea," said Anna. She knew she was going to pay a high price for all of it, but the more she bought now, the less she'd have to come back. Besides, she figured, why not go for the moon?

"There's a half pound of sugar and tea and a pound of cheese." The woman quickly added everything up. "With the pound of flour and other items, I can let you have it for forty Marks," she said, eyeing Anna on whether she was an easy sell or not.

"Hmmm," Anna sighed slowly. "I wish I could afford it, but I have other things I need too. What can you really do?" she asked, eyeing the woman back, seeing if she would budge. She needed to establish a rapport with the woman for the future, but she didn't want to be an easy target, either. Her money needed to stretch as far as she could make it last.

The woman huffed, acting disgusted, and told Anna none to nicely that she had to make a living too, and that Anna was lucky she was willing to sell to her.

"If you don't like it, go somewhere else!"

Anna stayed silent for a minute. Finally, Anna looked at the woman and spoke. "Thank you, but I guess I can't afford any of it." Anna tucked her hands into her pockets and turned to go. Just as she was reaching the door, the woman called out.

"Well, I need to make some money, but I can give you a little better deal. I can't go any lower than thirty-five, and that's my final offer. Take it or leave it. If you don't want it, someone else will. Those dirty Jews have made our lives miserable. They've brought nothing but disease and hardship on us."

Anna's back stiffened and she wanted to slap the woman for her hatred and ignorance, but instead, she held her head high, pulled the money from her pocket, and handed it to the woman.

"I need the bag, too," said Anna curtly. She had forgotten to bring a bag and the person who sold her the candles had just wrapped them in paper. The woman acted disgusted that she had to give her the bag too, but she put everything inside and handed it to Anna, complaining that next time she needed to bring her own bag.

Anna didn't want to think about next time. She hated the woman, but she knew she wouldn't let her hatred stop her from getting what she needed. No, she'd probably be back.

Once again out on the streets, Anna was careful to blend in. She had decided to forget about the shoes. She'd had enough for one day! Anna quickly moved down the street, heading back to where she had hidden her boots. Just as she rounded her last corner, *smack!* She slammed right into a soldier! Anna tumbled onto the sidewalk, holding her aching head from this morning.

"Oh my gosh!" exclaimed the soldier, as he tripped and fell, trying to grab Anna and keep her from falling.

"Oh my!" he exclaimed again, looking straight at her. They were both spilled all over the sidewalk, looking ridiculous.

The soldier burst into laughter, and then looked at Anna and blushed.

"I'm so sorry," he said. "I had no idea you were coming around the corner. Are you all right?"

Anna pulled herself upright and quickly grabbed her bag, thankful nothing had spilled out, giving her away that she'd been at the black market. Anna was holding her head with the other hand, moaning.

The soldier was now leaning over her. "Here, let me help you. You may need to see a doctor." Anna yanked her arm off her head and quickly got up.

"No, no, I'm, I'm all right," she lied. She felt nauseated and a little dizzy, but she was more scared he would ask for her papers. She had gotten this far, and now she had literally landed in the arms of a soldier.

"Are you sure?" He put his hand on Anna's arm. "You look rather mangled," he said. He was trying not to laugh.

Anna yanked her arm away, and he laughed even harder.

"I'm sorry, Miss…?"

"Oh, dear," thought Anna, *"we're going to get into names and papers."* She didn't want to give her real name. *A name, a name,* she thought quickly. "Margaret," she blurted out. The name was that of her best friend back in the old neighborhood, although they were sworn enemies now.

"Please forgive me," said the soldier, now smiling at her. "I am sorry, really! I tend to laugh in odd situations when I don't know what to do or say," he said, still smiling. "I'm Franz." He held out his hand.

Anna took his hand, revolted that she had to touch the Nazi filth. Here he was being nice, but she knew if he wanted to, he could be ugly, and she would be at his mercy and probably dead. She quickly released his hand.

"It's quite all right; my fault as much as yours," she replied. Anna pulled her bag to her side and started to step around him.

"Good day," she said and started down the street.

"Wait, wait," called the soldier.

Anna froze. *This is where he'll ask for papers*, she thought. She was as good as dead!

"Please, can I make it up to you with lunch?" He smiled a huge smile, one front tooth slightly crooked but showing a nice row of white teeth, his chestnut hair falling over one eye. He wasn't very tall, a bit under six feet, with a straight narrow nose and nice green eyes. His green uniform made his eyes stand out. Anna noticed he was a rather nice-looking man, but he was still a Nazi.

"Thank you, no," said Anna, now shaking with fear.

"I've definitely harmed you, Miss Margaret," calling her by her fake name. "Look at you, you're shaking."

"I'm fine, really," lied Anna. "I'm just a little shaken. I have to go, but thank you for your generosity." Anna turned to leave.

"At least let me walk you home. I can't leave you in this state. Besides, maybe I can talk you into having lunch with me in the future," he said, his confidence surging.

Oh my gosh, thought Anna. She had to think quick.

"I really appreciate your offer, but my boyfriend wouldn't like me showing favor to a young man other than him." Anna smiled.

"Oh!" he said, his smile disappearing. "Well, I'm sorry for me, but he must be a happy man."

Not wanting to make him angry, and still afraid he would ask for her papers, his attitude changing, she led him on a bit. "Perhaps we'll run into each other again," she said smiling at him, "and if I'm not with anyone, I'll definitely have lunch with you. Fair enough?"

He was smiling again, eagerly nodding his head. "Yes, please," he said. "Maybe it's still been my good fortune to have run into you." He chuckled. "I'm stationed in town at the Justice building, just ask for Corporal Franz Schmidt."

Smiling at him, Anna waved goodbye, trying not to look like she was rushing to get away from him. He waved back, a huge smile on his face.

If it weren't for Hitler, Anna thought, *we'd probably be friends.* Her heart was still beating wildly, plus her head was aching from her fall in the woods this morning. Running into Franz had made her question if she should ever come back. She had a long way to go. She waited a good fifteen minutes to make sure Franz had left and wasn't following her, and then she slipped up the hill and back into the forest. Finding her boots, she put them on, thankful to get out of her shoes that were at least one size too small, cramping her toes. Her head was throbbing now, the grocery bag pulling on her shoulder. Anna headed south, toward camp.

She couldn't compare Peter to Franz, she thought. Peter had way more going for him. He was better looking, he wasn't a Jew hater, and he was kind-hearted, not that Franz couldn't be kind. He had shown concern and kindness to Anna, but only because he didn't know she was Jewish. Franz was nice looking, but his Hitler loyalty detracted from his looks. Still, Anna wondered if he was a Nazi because he wanted to be, or because he had to be?

She was exhausted, and it was hard going back to camp. The sun was quickly sinking beyond the horizon, which would leave the woods extremely dark. Her headache hadn't gotten better. If anything, it was worse. She was barely putting one foot in front of the other. She had about another half hour to go and could hardly wait to lie down in her cot and succumb to sleep.

****

CHAPTER TWENTY SEVEN

P eter was busy setting loaves of bread in the oven. He would normally make bread, a couple pastries, and two types of cookies today, but with his father sick, it would be only bread and rolls. They made bread every day, but only made sweets every Monday and Thursday. Today was the exception. Lately, there were less and less people buying sweets with the ration situation, so they'd probably go down to only one day a week soon anyway.

Flour and sugar were becoming harder and harder to get, but since they were commissioned by the army, they got as much as they needed. Little did the army know that the Reinholds said they used more than they did and sold the rest for other ration coupons.

People could barely afford bread, let alone goodies. Peter had noticed the decline in business, so as much as he hated the army, he was thankful they were buying bread from them. He didn't mind taking their money or selling on the black market, because, after all, Hitler had started this ugly war. Business would be normal, and he'd still be living next to the Feiners if it weren't for that horrible man. He couldn't help but wonder where Anna was.

Anna stumbled back to camp and laid on her cot for a good hour before she could muster the energy and strength to raise her head and get up to make a fire. Her camp was cold, and she needed to get warm. She was positive she had a concussion, but at this point, she didn't care. She wanted warmth and sleep.

She pulled the metal cover off the fire pit and was lucky enough to find a couple warm coals, making it easier to start a fire. Grabbing some dry kindling and ripping a few pieces of precious paper from her notepad, she crumpled it up and laid it on top of the warm coals. Crisscrossing the kindling on top of the paper, Anna blew slowly onto the coals until the paper ignited, and red and orange flames licked around and through the kindling. Satisfied, she added a few small sticks and sat back on her cot.

Anna sat there, mulling the day over in her head. She had passed the test of blending in. No one had suspected that she was Jewish. She had even passed the test with a soldier, face-to-face. Still, she wasn't sure she wanted to go back to the black market unless she was extremely desperate. She had no intentions of running into Franz again.

It had been a long day, but it was finally over. Peter had made the army's quota and finished with a few types of rolls. He cleaned up his work area, hung his flour caked apron on the hook, and sat down on a stool. He was exhausted. Sweat dripped off him as he sat there, processing the day. How had life gotten so complicated and ugly? All he wanted was to go back in time to when no one hated each other, and neighbors didn't suspect each other of being traitors. If it wasn't for his father, he'd take off, make it across the border, except he knew he couldn't really do it without knowing what had happened to Anna.

Peter got up and grabbed his tin from under the counter and opened it. *What to put in the box tonight?* he wondered. He was hoping his visitor would come back. One of these times, he was going to find out who it was.

Setting the lid on the counter, Peter laid waxed paper in it and put two fresh sourdough rolls in and then a couple cookies in the tin, folding the wax paper over the contents. Slipping a note on top of the wax paper, he set the lid securely back on, so it couldn't pop off.

It was dark out, but the neighbors would still be about, so Peter needed to wait until their lights were off. While he waited, he might as well make good use of his time. His stomach was growling, so he scarfed down a sourdough roll and then started preparing for the next day. He set out all the contents they'd need and made the dough for the cookies, setting it in the refrigerator. It didn't take long to make the cookie dough. They only made a quarter of what they had before the war. The preparation would mean tomorrow would be a much easier day for him, especially if his father was still sick.

Father always seemed to be out of breath lately. *I need to pick up more of the work and make it easier for him.* Peter loved his father, and his heart sank thinking that the man he loved was having a tough time lately. This war was wearing on him.

The clock hit ten-thirty, and Peter knew his neighbors would be in bed. He grabbed his coat off the back-door peg, grabbed the tin, and slipped quietly out the backdoor. He was careful to keep an eye out for the nosy neighbors watching from windows. He shoved the tin between the bushes, making sure no one could see it, and snuck back into the bakery. Peter was tired. It was time for bed, but little did he know, Anna was just waking up.

Anna's body clock told her it was time to be up and about. It was one in the morning but after being out all day, when she would normally be sleeping, she was still exhausted, and her head still ached. The throbbing had stopped, but she still had a headache. She flipped open her sleeping bag and slowly sat up. The fire had died out, and it was cold, so she threw on a couple of small branches. That done, she shined the flashlight over the wood slat box that held medicine her parents had stocked. Pulling out a bottle of aspirin, she unscrewed the top and shook two out of the bottle, washing them down with a gulp of water. She hoped her headache would subside.

She wanted to go see if Peter had put out another box, but her body wasn't going to let her. She opened the pickle jar and pulled out a crispy dill pickle, crunching down with a large snap. It wouldn't be long before she wouldn't have Mama's pickles to enjoy.

She'd miss them, but most of all, she'd miss knowing that her mother had lovingly made them for her, and she'd never have them again.

Anna was so burned out, she didn't have it in her to hike out to her home. Her heart was in it, but her body said no. For once, her body won over and she tucked back into her sleeping bag, pulling the covers high over her chin. She quickly dozed off, thinking of Peter.

Peter sat by his bedroom window ready with his binoculars. It was past one in the morning, and he knew he had to go to bed. He was disappointed, but he'd check the bushes in the morning. He might miss the visitor, but he hoped they had found the tin again and that it had been helpful. Miles away, Anna was now awake and hard pressed to keep anything down.

Anna's stomach ached, spasms doubling her over in pain. She felt sweaty all over, yet chills shook her body. All she could think of was, she had the flu. In between the shaking and stomach pains, nausea would hit her, and she'd reach for the tin pail. She no longer had anything in her stomach, but she continued to dry heave, trying to coax something up.

All she could do was lie on her cot, try her best to stay warm, and keep her pail nearby. Every so often she managed a sip of water and a few bites of peaches. By the third day, she had managed to finally keep something in her stomach, but she was so weak, she barely made it off her cot. Little by little, bite by bite,

Anna's strength slowly showed improvement, but she wouldn't be going anywhere anytime soon.

The stench in her camp made her want to throw up all over again, and she knew she had to air it out and get rid of the pail's contents. She was at least thankful she hadn't had to do more than vomit and pee in her pail, the benefits of not eating.

Shaking terribly, Anna buttoned her coat tight, wrapped her scarf snugly around her neck, and pulled her hat down over her ears. Pushing the door of her hut open, she struggled out the opening, carefully pulling her pail behind her. It was quite full, and she didn't want to accidentally spill any of its contents inside. The thought made her stomach heave, and she yanked her scarf off her face to suck in fresh air.

Anna's legs felt like rubber after having little to eat and lying in bed for days. She made her way into the woods, not bothering to cover her tracks. It was all she could do just to walk.

Finally, she neared the river where she discarded her pails contents under some brush, and then rinsed the pail in the river multiple times, using a fir branch to scrub the inside and outside of it, then rinsing it one last time. What she wouldn't do for a good scrub herself, but she was too weak, and it was too cold. She picked up her pail and made her way back to camp.

****

CHAPTER TWENTY EIGHT

Almost two weeks had gone by while Anna tried to recover her strength. She really wanted to see Peter now that she was feeling better, but it wasn't as safe as it used to be. Nazis were swarming everywhere, and they were the one thing she needed to avoid.

The Russians were trying to take over northern Poland and the United States and their allies were marching to Germany. Either way, if any of them succeeded in defeating Hitler, it was said you wanted to be captured by the Americans. Anna knew she'd have to move on soon. Germany was being bombed, and she needed to figure out where to go next. If she was lucky, she'd run into the Americans.

Before she left, she had to go see Peter one more time, though. She wished she could see him in person, touch him, let him know she was okay, but she knew she shouldn't. She should let the view in his window suffice.

It was still light out when Anna slipped out of camp, but she wanted to get a head start and be able to stay longer, in the hopes that she'd have a better chance to see him. Her plan to move on meant this was going to be her last chance.

Anticipation of seeing Peter had made Anna get to her home sooner than she should have. Dusk was just starting to set; the night sky was not there to protect her. Sneaking up to the bushes, she moved in closer to town. She could see soldiers strolling the streets, hands on their guns, asking residents for their papers. Anna shivered but it wasn't from the cold. She squatted, tucking herself as small as she could.

Twenty minutes had passed, and the sun was finally disappearing when a dog started barking, straining on its leash that the soldier was holding. Anna stayed still but knew she may have to make a run for it. The dog kept barking, pulling hard on his lease.

"What's up boy?" the soldier asked, exciting the dog even more. The barking was relentless, and it was trying to drag the soldier toward her. The soldier looked up toward Anna, giving the dog a slight release on the lease. "Come on, boy, what did you find?" The soldier was giving the dog lead right toward her! Several other soldiers followed him, egging the dog on. Down deep, Anna knew she had sealed her fate. She had stayed one day too long.

The soldier released his hold and the dog darted toward her, its lips pulled up in a huge growl, its yellowed fangs ready to tear into its prey. Anna rolled herself toward the woods trying not to be noticed, then bolted up and started to run. Behind her, she could feel the dog's breath on her, snarling, and then its teeth buried themselves deep into her coat, pulling her skin away from the bone. The dog was almost as big and as heavy as she was. She tried to get up, but the dog was biting her everywhere. The most she could do was cover herself, waiting for the soldiers to pull him off.

"Major, down!" yelled the soldier. The dog immediately stopped and sat on command, but stayed ready to lunge at her the first chance it had.

The soldier yanked Anna off the ground, his gun drawn, and the barrel end snug against her temple.

"Well, what have we here?" sneered the soldier. "Look at this, boys, we have ourselves a little Jew boy hiding from the Führer."

The only thing Anna was thankful for was, they thought she was a boy, or they'd all take their turns with her. The soldiers didn't want to live with the Jews, but they didn't mind raping them.

The young soldier holstered his gun and grabbed her arm. Pain surged through Anna from the torn flesh the dog had ripped through, but she stayed silent. Pushing her forward, the group of soldiers formed a semi-circle around her, giving her no chance to run. It wouldn't have mattered anyway; the dog was their insurance she was not going anywhere.

Peter heard the commotion and stepped outside the bakery. A young boy was being held by a soldier, who was yelling he was a Jew and needed to be shot. Officer Holtz had been heading to the Reinhold's bakery and came over after hearing the commotion.

"I caught him spying from the trees!" yelled the soldier. "He's a Jew! My dog found him and took him down, sir. Good boy, Major."

The crowd was growing, taunting the soldiers to shoot him. Officer Holtz calmed the crowd, telling them to go about their business and not the Führer's. The crowd dissipated, leaving only the soldiers and Peter.

"Your papers!" he barked at Anna, throwing his arm out to take her papers from her. Anna hesitated, knowing she was caught, and death was knocking at her door.

"Your papers, boy, now!" yelled Holtz. Anna stayed silent.

Holtz slapped her across the face, his fingers leaving huge welts across her cheek, her face turning bright red.

"Who is your family? What is your name?" barked Holtz again, starting to pull his Luger from its holster.

Peter waited, wanting to learn the boy's fate. He was angry. If he was Jewish, he was doomed.

Anna moved from one foot to another, rubbing her gloved hands together. She looked up, her eyes meeting Peter's. Tears streamed down her face, her voice quivering.

"My name is Anna Feiner."

Peter's mouth dropped open. He stared at Anna, not believing what she'd said. He couldn't have heard her correctly. The boy didn't even look like her. She was dressed in boys' brown wool pants and a brown plaid flannel shirt, two sizes too big, and a brown jacket that hung huge on her shoulders and past her knees. Her dirty hiking boots finished the look. He looked deep into Anna's eyes when recognition hit him full force.

Holtz moved forward, grabbing her cap off her head, and Anna's beautiful chestnut hair tumbled down over her shoulders. Peter watched as if in slow motion, Holtz slipping his Luger from his hip, aiming it at Anna's head.

"No!" exclaimed Peter.

Holtz stopped short, released the trigger and stared at Peter. Anger spewed from Holtz's eyes. How dare he talk to an officer of the Reich that way.

"No!" exclaimed Peter again. "I want to do it!" Peter's face twisted in anger. "Please, let me have the pleasure. I can't ask my comrades at the front to do everything when this is in my own neighborhood."

"Have you ever killed anyone?" questioned Holtz, frowning at Peter.

"No," said Peter, trying to stay calm and keep his voice even. "I've handled a gun a lot and killed plenty of animals. I want to do this," he pleaded. Peter looked Holtz straight in the eyes, begging him. "Let me do this and show you I can do more than bake bread for the Führer."

Mr. Reinhold looked on, stoic, his face blank of emotion. He didn't dare step in, or his son would be dead too. His heart sank, hearing Peter would be happy to kill Anna. He wasn't the Peter he knew.

Anna couldn't believe what was spewing from Peter's mouth. She had believed his note that he meant no harm was for real, not a ploy to kill Jews! Now she knew he felt the same as every other Nazi. She lowered her head, so she didn't have to look at him, tears spilling, uncontrolled, down her cheeks. Soon it would be blood spilling over her.

Holtz smiled at Peter. Slapping him on the back, Holtz handed him his gun.

"You make me proud, Peter. Yes, you said you wanted to join your friends at the front. We can't afford to lose a good baker that feeds our troops, but I can let you have your moment."

Anna was spinning, bile rising in her throat. All this time she thought Peter had hated the Nazis, but now he was confessing his loyalty to Hitler! Anna almost *wanted* to die. The one person she thought she could trust besides her parents was Peter. He had never really meant what he said in his notes, she realized now. He just wanted to catch a Jew.

"Well, Peter, you have my blessing." Holtz smiled his approval.

"I'll have no Jewish blood in front of my bakery where I bake for our troops. I won't dirty our beautiful city with her filthy blood!" Peter grabbed Anna's mangled arm, holding her tightly as he pulled her toward the woods. "She can be left in the woods for the coyotes to finish where I leave her bloody corpse," he proclaimed savagely.

The corporal who had caught Anna started to go off with Peter, but Holtz called him back. "No, let the young man have his pleasure with her too. This is something he can do alone," he said, grabbing the soldier's arm.

"Have at her, Peter!" he yelled after him, laughing.

Anna's mind whirled. *He's going to rape me too,* her mind screamed. She had so misjudged him. She felt like vomiting, but she wouldn't give him the pleasure of letting him see her fear.

Peter pushed her into the tree line until he was sure they were far enough for no one to see. Anna looked back once. She wanted the last thing she would see and think about to be home. Memories flooded her brain, making Anna's stomach and her head ache.

A hundred feet into the forest, Peter picked a spot that was surrounded by thick brush. He wanted privacy for what he was going to do. He turned Anna toward him, pulling her chin up so he could look into her eyes. Anna stood stiff and silent.

"Oh, Anna," he whispered. "I'm so sorry." He leaned over and kissed her on the forehead, and then on the cheek. Slowly, he brought her toward him, wrapping his strong arms around her, feeling her body against his. How he wanted to be with her.

Peter's strength was apparent. All those days hefting flour and sugar and rolling dough had made him strong. He was taller now too, by at least three inches. Here she had been having feelings for him and now he was not only going to kill her, but rape her first. She looked at him, saying nothing. His dimples were deep as ever, and his beautiful blue eyes watered with tears.

"Lay on your stomach, Anna," he choked. "I'm going to fire two shots into the ground. You need to wait a good half hour before you leave. If they come back here, you play dead." Anna yanked her head up, staring at him in shock.

"What? You're not going to kill me? I thought you wanted me dead?"

"No!" exclaimed Peter. "No! I can't let those Nazi filth kill you and I certainly can't do it myself. I love you, Anna, I always have! From the time I was fourteen years old, you've been the only one for me. I'd rather them kill me for trying to save you than give that filth what they want!"

"So, you meant what you said in your notes?"

"It was you?" Peter's mouth dropped open. "You were the one in the woods?" Now it hit him, she was coming back to see her house.

"It was me," she said, cocking her head to one side, staring at him. "I wanted to see home and to see you. I have no one left. I know Mama is gone, and Papa, well, God only knows, he could be dead too."

"But where have you been? They took you to the ghetto. I've looked for you everywhere. I took pastries to the soldiers, so I had a reason to go in and look for you, but I never found you or your parents."

"I escaped, and I've hidden in the woods. Papa and Mama left me some food and living essentials and money. We hid them a long time ago. We found a place to hide and filled it with things I'd need to survive." Anna shrugged.

"I'm so sorry," he whispered, pulling her close to him. This time she responded, hugging Peter tight. "I've tried so hard to find you. I even had to befriend Officer Holtz, so I could get information on what was happening to the Jews. It never helped, and then he thought we were best friends and never stopped coming into the shop. I despise the man, but God turned it into a blessing. You can't come back here again, it's too dangerous. I'll leave you food every few days where we camped when we were kids. It's some distance from here, but you can't come home anymore. I'll be there this Wednesday afternoon."

Anna just nodded her head, acknowledging what Peter had said. She was wrong about him, he was a good man, one she cared about.

"We need to finish this, Anna. I need to go back and tell them I finished you off." Anna lay on the cold ground, waiting for the shots to ring out. Peter pulled the gun up and fired! Two shots sped their way into the dirt near her, leaving both their ears ringing. Anna lay still.

Pulling his pocketknife from his jacket, Peter rolled up his sleeve and made minor cuts on his arm, letting blood spill around Anna and over her clothes. If anyone came to inspect the dead, they'd think the blood was hers. The gun hung loose in his hand. "I love you, Anna," he whispered, then he turned and headed back to the street. Walking with purpose, Peter swung around the corner, meeting Holtz and the other soldiers. Peter smiled big, making his dimples dig deep into his cheeks, and pretended to zip his pants for show.

Holtz was all smiles as he slapped Peter on the back. Peter smiled back, handing him his Luger.

"How was she, Peter?" He laughed, throwing his head back. The soldiers all laughed along.

"Best feeling I've ever had, in more ways than one." He laughed suggestively.

"Good job, Peter. I guess if I ever get short a man and we can get you away from the bakery, I'll get you assigned to my unit." He slapped Peter on the back again and then brought his arm up, "Heil Hitler!"

Peter snapped to attention, bringing his arm high into the air, saluting him back. "Heil Hitler!"

Holtz dismissed the soldiers and turned to leave.

"Thanks for the favor," Peter called after him.

Holtz turned, waved, shaking his head and laughing again.

Letting out a huge sigh, Peter slipped into the bakery and went looking for his father. He felt so joyful he couldn't stop grinning. His father sat on a stool by the ovens, his head in his hands, weeping.

"Father, what's wrong? Today is a good day! The best day ever!"

His father pulled his head up, staring at Peter with his blood-shot eyes.

"You, you killed her! You killed Anna!"

"No, no!" Peter pulled his father up and hugged him tight. "Today, I saved her! I couldn't shoot her; I love that girl! I pretended to kill her, so she could sneak out of here. I never thought Holtz would be of any value to me, but today, he was my best friend." Peter hugged his father again, a large grin wide across his face.

"So, she's alive?"

"Yes!" exclaimed Peter, his excitement hard to contain. "I knew she wasn't killed in the ghetto or camps. I would have felt it. I found her against all odds, and I'm going to help her stay alive."

Peter's father hung his head and started crying again.

"I'm sorry I doubted you, Son. You sounded so convincing that you wanted to kill her."

"I had to, or they wouldn't have believed me. It's okay. Anna is safe, and that's all that matters."

"You're bleeding, Peter!" exclaimed his father. "You're bleeding badly!"

Peter had forgotten about his arm. His adrenaline had been pumping so fast, he didn't feel any pain.

"I needed to leave blood in case they came back to check. Blood would ensure they thought she was dead and that I'd shot her." Peter grinned.

His father hugged him tight, careful of his arm.

"Today you've made me the proudest I've ever been of you. I've always been proud, but today, you were a man. I can go to my grave knowing you're all your mother and I could have hoped for."

"Thank you. I'd like to think I'm a lot like you." He grinned, hugging his father again.

"Come, let's get you cleaned up and bandaged."

"Sounds good." Peter was exhausted, and what he'd done finally hit him. He couldn't believe he had confronted Officer Holtz and convinced him to let him kill Anna. He had pulled it off. For once, he appreciated Holtz thinking they were friends. Holtz could just have easily shot him for being insubordinate and interfering with the SS. It was a onetime deal.

Anna lay on the snow packed ground, Peter's blood oozing onto the snow, scarlet red against the stark white. She carefully started counting, one minute, two minutes, three minutes…ten, fifteen, until she reached a full thirty minutes.

Slowly she moved an arm and waited. Nothing happened, telling her it was probably safe to sneak away. Ever so slowly, she moved the hair away from her eyes, so she could see. Her body felt frozen from lying in the icy snow, but she didn't let it stop her from crawling farther into the forest. Finally, she stood up, ducked behind a tree, and searched the area. She listened for movement and voices, but heard nothing but the slight wind rustling the trees. Still stiff from the cold, Anna slowly started back toward camp, breaking into a full run as her numb limbs awakened.

Snow had started to fall, another God-given gift. Her footsteps would be invisible soon, the feathery snow filling her tracks.

She couldn't even think right now; her brain was fuzzy trying to take everything in. Once again, she had escaped the Nazis. Anna knew she had more than just Peter and luck on her side. God was part of this plan.

The sun had set, and Anna was glad. She was better off in the dark. She knew her way around the woods and instead of taking the fast way back to camp, she took the most difficult. If anyone was going to be looking for her, they'd think she took the easier path. Papa had always told her to do what was least expected. Besides, if they were going to find her again, they were going to work for it.

Working her way back, her mind went to Peter. She didn't even know what to think. She had really thought he was going to kill her. The viciousness in his voice had been more than convincing. *He's a pretty good actor,* she mused, rethinking everything that had happened, and then him telling her he had loved her since he was fourteen. Anna's face was red from the cold, but she felt her cheeks flush thinking of what Peter had said.

She had felt rescued by Peter when she discovered the tin box in the bushes, betrayed when he said he wanted to kill her, but now, she knew exactly how he felt about her. Her mind reeled. He loved her but how did she feel about him? She had always loved Peter as her friend, but now she felt something different and it wasn't just because he had saved her. A spark had been ignited.

A couple of long hours passed before Anna finally saw the farmer's house and barn. Even though the snow was now thick in the air, the chimney smoke told her she was back at camp. Knowing she was so close, spurred Anna's feet on faster than she had ever moved.

Reaching the edge of the woods, Anna hid behind the tall evergreens, making sure the coast was clear. Quickly, she pulled her camp door open, crawled inside, and burst into tears. There was no warmth in her camp, the coals had long turned from fiery red to cold black. She knew she needed to thaw her arms and legs out to avoid frostbite. Her arms worked clumsily, her arm torn from the dog was throbbing and bleeding, but she tried to pull kindling from her box and the matches from the silver tin.

Lighting a candle, she searched for her wool blanket and pulled out her pocketknife. A good pile of lint would start the fire more quickly. Learning this trick had been Papa's godsend to her.

Opening the knife, Anna stroked the knife against the wool blanket over and over, stroking hard enough to create a small pile of lint. Placing the lint in the middle of the cold coals, she made wood shavings, setting them on the lint, and then crisscrossing kindling on top. Striking the match, its sulfur smell filled her camp. Holding the match to the lint, a small flame erupted and grew, filling the room with much needed light and warmth.

Anna smiled. *I've gotten pretty good at starting a fire,* she thought. *Papa would be proud.* Thinking of her parents, about what had happened today, she broke down and let the tears spill like rain again. *I deserve a good cry,* she thought. She was mentally and physically exhausted. Finally, she pulled her coat off and grabbed her first aid kit.

Opening the box, she pulled out the salve and bandages, hoping she wouldn't have to use the needle and thread to stitch up her arm. Her arm throbbed but she knew a torn arm was better than a bullet in her head. Her coat had thankfully gotten most of the dog's aggression, leaving only a two-inch gash in her flesh. It was still bleeding, but she didn't think stitches were necessary. She washed it out, applied some salve and wrapped a thick layer of gauze around it. Finally, she lay back on her cot sinking into exhaustion.

****

CHAPTER TWENTY NINE

Joseph and Jacob set up shop, settling into their new jobs.

Let's get started before they change their minds about wanting jewelry," said Joseph. Jacob took one tooth at a time, prying the gold off the way Joseph had shown him. The gold dropped into the jar, piece by piece, clink, clink, clink. The teeth were discarded into the wooden box on the floor.

When he first glanced into the box of teeth, he had felt the nausea rise, just like it had for Joseph. He hadn't been sure he could do the job, but Joseph had calmed his mind, telling him that as horrible as it was, those who had unwillingly given up their teeth would be happy that someone's life was being saved. Jacob had reconciled himself with it, but it still repulsed him.

Pulling the wax from the boxes and all the other items he needed, Joseph got busy designing wax molds to pour rings and stone settings. He scanned his brain for some of the elaborate but easier jewelry he had made in the past. He wanted to get something going quickly to keep the Germans on his side.

The door blew open, and a corporal stomped in, slamming the door behind him.

"Here!" He shoved a large, cumbersome box at Joseph. Joseph gazed into the box, and what stared back at him, turned his stomach.

"Danke," was all Joseph could say. The corporal grunted, yanked the door back open and left, slamming the door behind him.

"What is it?" asked Jacob.

"More teeth," said Joseph. "I have a terrible feeling we'll have an unending supply." They both shook their heads and went back to work.

A jar with a pile of gold sat at the back of the table and the white and yellowish teeth lay piled in a box on the floor. At least they knew the teeth were from adults. The young didn't have teeth bad enough to warrant gold fillings. Three wax molds lined Joseph's table, waiting for him to melt the gold and fill their cavities.

Joseph's cough continued to linger, making his breathing labored. Even though Jacob had gotten him a small amount of penicillin, he still struggled to get well. His cough racked his body, making his lungs burn, but still, he concentrated on his work.

The afternoon sun was setting low when the major walked in.

"You can go back to your bunks and return tomorrow after roll call," he said with cool authority.

"Yes, sir," Joseph nodded. Jacob stood stiff, his hands at his sides, head down.

"Sir, we could work longer and get more done if we just slept in here. I'm sure you're anxious for your wife's gift, and so are the other officers, of course. It takes warm hands to do this kind of work and this way we won't have to waste time getting our fingers warm in the morning."

The major cocked his head at Joseph, mulling it over. He knew he was being played but he could also see the value in it.

"Get some wood and make your cots. You still need to check in with Sargent Heimer before you start work in the mornings."

"Yes, sir. Where would you like us to have meals sir? I can stop in the middle of a piece, but it tends to take more time and creates more errors."

Joseph knew he was probably pushing it, but he had gone this far, so why not a little farther? He knew men enjoyed giving their loved ones' jewelry, he had counted on making a living on it. Beads of sweat lined Joseph's forehead as he waited for the major to respond.

"You," he barked at Jacob. "You'll go to the kitchen and bring your meals back here. I better see results." His gaze penetrated through them.

They both nodded with a straight face, but underneath they were smiling. Getting food from the kitchen was a thousand times better than standing in the soup line.

It had been three days living in their own building and both Joseph and Jacob could tell the positive changes it was making in their lives. Joseph's cough still racked his body, but he wasn't going to ruin his new position. The building had a wood stove that kept them warm throughout the day and night and the building didn't have cracks in it where the heat could escape. They didn't have to fight for a place to sleep, or worry about catching lice, and the food was far better. Even though Joseph's cough was the same, he could see the difference in his weight already.

He vowed to himself he would make gorgeous jewelry, so the Germans would keep wanting it. As much as he hated the Nazis, he had a goal and that was to find his daughter.

Holding up a gold ring in an Art Deco design with facets to hold a large stone and two smaller on each side, Joseph was pleased with his work. He didn't have his jewelry tools from home, but he'd make the ones he had work. The gold shone. Now he just had to decide what stones to put in it.

At that moment, the major walked through the door. Jacob jumped. He was always nervous anytime a soldier was nearby. They were always mean and unpredictable.

Joseph kept his head down. "Sir, I've just finished the first setting and need to decide which stones to use. Perhaps you'd like to pick them out and I'll finish this for your wife."

The major strode over to Joseph's table and inspected the setting that held no stones. It shone brightly, and the work was impeccable. Smiling, the major tilted his head, putting his hand up to his chin, stroking it in thought, deciding what he wanted.

"Emeralds, "he finally said. "Yes, emeralds, my wife's birthstone. Her birthday is next week, and this will be the perfect gift."

Joseph set the ring in a holder and pulled a small box toward him. In the box were precious and semi-precious stones that had been pulled from jewelry taken off the dead and those who tried to hide them in their clothing or suitcases. It was common for the guards to find family jewels and heirlooms sewn into the hems of dresses and hidden compartments. What no one counted on was, as soon as you arrived, you were quickly stripped not only of your clothes, but your dignity and life as well.

Joseph looked through the pile pulling out six emeralds, the largest almost two carats. With tweezers, he picked up the large emerald and explained to the major he was checking for size and clarity. Not all stones were worthy of making it into his wife's ring.

"If you look through this eyeglass you can see if there are minute scratches, or if the stone has large imperfections." The major moved over to Joseph and took the eyeglass and looked at the stone, and then the others. He was impressed to see real differences in each stone he looked at.

"It's amazing, you can't tell by just looking at them." His voice was almost friendly before he realized who he was talking to. Returning to his gruff self, the major clicked his heels, admonishing he better find the best in his wife's ring, and left.

Joseph turned back to the ring and began setting the stones. He was going to make it beautiful, so he would have a chance to stay alive and find his daughter.

Hours later, the ring was finally complete. It sparkled just like the beautiful pieces he had created when he worked in his shop at home. The emeralds were a deep green, one and a half carats in the middle, one carat each next to the middle one, then three tiny diamonds flowing down each side. It was beautiful. He hoped the major would like it, he prayed he loved it.

Setting the ring in a small velvet box, Joseph went back to working on the next order. A pair of earrings for another officer. He had asked for blue sapphires. Joseph started by sketching a few ideas on paper before deciding and then he pulled the wax out to make the molds.

Jacob sat silent the whole time, picking and prying gold from the teeth. He was always afraid he'd be caught saying the wrong thing when the Nazis walked in. Better to be silent and alive was his motto. Clink, clink, more gold in the jar. It bothered him to be doing this, but Joseph was right, at least in their deaths, these people were saving someone from the gas chamber.

Joseph's back ached from sitting on a stool, hunched over all day. He needed to get up more, but there was such a huge list from the officers that he dared not waste a minute. He'd rather have a sore back than be dead. Besides, the major would be strolling in at any moment. There was no reason to get sent back to his old job.

Jacob was headed out to get something to eat when the major pushed the door open. Jacob immediately stepped aside, allowing the major plenty of room. Keeping his head down, he waited until the door was clear, then hurried out. He preferred to not be present.

Slapping his black leather gloves against his palm, the major moved to Joseph's side. "The ring!" He demanded.

"Yes." Joseph nodded, pulling the velvet box out. He popped the lid open, and the ring shone, the stones gleaming in the light. The major's smile told Joseph he was well pleased.

"I took the liberty of adding cascading diamonds down the sides, I hope you approve, sir," said Joseph in a low murmur.

"Yes, yes, it's beautiful! It's magnificent! My wife will be extremely pleased. She'll insist on earrings after she gets this. You can start working on them. Well done," said the major, smiling down at Joseph.

"Thank you, sir," said Joseph, keeping his head slightly down and his eyes on the floor. He was sure the major had no idea he was smiling.

The major closed the box, tucked it into his jacket pocket, and left.

Joseph realized he had been holding his breath, not knowing the reaction he would actually get. He knew it was a beautiful piece, but counting on how the officer would react was not a safe thing to do"

"One piece down, more to go," mulled Joseph. Pulling up his stool, he started on another piece. A bout of coughing began not long after, which made it hard to work with steady hands. It was becoming harder to set stones, and the pain in his lungs made it hard to breathe. The constant hacking made his eyes blurry with unshed tears, making it take too long to finish pieces.

Despite his worsening illness, in the days since he'd finished the major's ring for his wife, he had been barraged with orders from other officers.

One morning rose to a warm sunny day, a nice break from the bitter cold. Joseph opened the door and let the sun soak into his body. It felt like a spring thaw soaking through his skinny frame and the chill that had been shadowing him subsided slightly. He raised his face to the sun, feeling lucky he was still alive to enjoy it. He had been working so hard he rarely got outside anymore, which, considering what the other prisoners put up with, was fine with him.

Ah, stop daydreaming, he thought, and stepped back inside, pulling his stool up to the table.

Major Richter stepped in behind Joseph.

"Feiner," called the officer. Joseph spun around on his stool and immediately stood up, his stool crashing to the floor. He acknowledged the major, but kept his eyes down.

"Yes, sir. I, I'm working on your earrings," he stammered. His body shook, not knowing what to expect. He didn't dare pick anything up, his hands were shaking so bad.

"I'm impressed with your work. It's the first gift I've given my wife that I've seen her so excited about. Here's something for your hard work." The major held his hand out, offering a brown paper box tied with a blue string on it. Joseph hesitated.

"Thank you, but I was just doing my job."

The major continued to hold out the box, almost shoving it at him. Careful not to touch him, Joseph took the box, whispering thank you. The major turned and left. Joseph's mind was beyond understanding what had just happened. It was a miracle.

Jacob had been standing in the back, not wanting to interrupt or be noticed. His plan was to always blend into the background.

"What is it?"

"I don't know." Joseph gently pulled the string loose, opening the box. Inside were four linzer cookies. They both stared into the box in disbelief. Finally, pulling two out of the box, Joseph handed one to his friend. They each bit into a cookie, chewing slowly, wanting it to last forever. Neither could remember the last time they'd had a cookie or something sweet.

Finally finished, they licked their fingers not wanting to waste a thing. Joseph closed the lid, tucking the box out of view, hiding it from anyone else who may come in.

"There will be dessert tonight, my friend," he announced, the smile spreading across his face.

Jacob smiled back. "I can hardly wait." Word had gotten out about their work, and the list was now so long Joseph thought he was going to need another assistant. The power of happy wives and girlfriends was an amazing benefit.

Occasionally, a small treat would be delivered when a piece of jewelry was being picked up. They wanted to make sure their pieces were given the same care as the major's.

It was also common for a soldier to come in and suddenly turn the place over, including Joseph and Jacob's clothes, making sure they weren't stealing any of the gold or stones for themselves. Joseph was not about to tamper with being in the good graces of officers.

Late in the afternoon, Joseph noticed a shadow and turned to see the commandant standing in the door. Joseph jumped to his feet, his arm hitting the can of melted wax, spilling it.

"Sir!" Exclaimed Joseph.

"You the jeweler?" asked the commandant.

"Yes, sir." Joseph stood perfectly still, wringing his hands, staring at the floor. His heart sounded like a loud drum in his ears and was beating a mile a minute. He was sure the commandant could hear it.

"I need a special gift for my wife for our anniversary. What can you make?"

"What would you like, sir? I can draw out some designs but if you give me some ideas of what your wife likes and the type of stones she prefers, I can incorporate that into the piece." Joseph stood still, waiting for the commandant to speak. The spilled wax was now hardening but he left it alone, standing at attention.

The commandant stood thinking, his uniform immaculate, his gray jacket and pants fitting perfectly on his muscular frame. The most intimidating part was the large silver skull, on his perfectly set hat, staring at him. His boots were polished to perfection, and his whip held tightly in his right hand.

"I think a pendant would be nice, not too big but I'd like it to make a statement. She likes all types of stones, so you have some liberty on picking them. Coordinating earrings would be a nice touch. Have some sketches ready tomorrow morning, and I'll see what I think."

"Yes, sir." Joseph continued to stand still and remained quiet. The commandant turned to leave, his leather gloved hand turning the knob. He stopped, then turned and pierced Joseph with his steel-blue eyes.

"I have high expectations, so I suggest you don't disappoint!" Joseph didn't say a word, just nodded that he understood.

The door closed and both Jacob and Joseph took a deep breath. Setting the stool upright, he sat down and pulled out his sketchpad, his hands shaking. He'd have to calm down before he could sketch a thing. Jacob went about cleaning up the now hardened wax.

Joseph worked long into the night, making unique designs and setting various stones on top of the designs, so the commandant could get an idea of what the pendant and earrings would look like. Finally, his eyes drooping, unable to keep them open any longer, he stretched out onto his cot, pulling his thin blanket over him. They were lucky. Prisoners usually didn't get blankets, so as thin as it was, no one would catch him complaining.

Dawn came way too early, but he knew the commandant would be in soon. He was known for being an extremely early riser, but also for being surly in the mornings. Joseph did not look forward to today. It didn't take long before they heard the doorknob turn and the commandant strode in. Joseph and Jacob snapped to attention.

"Do you have something for me?" he asked. The commandant's six-foot-plus frame filled the doorway and his demanding voice sounded even louder in the small wooden building.

"Yes, sir," said Joseph, his eyes on the floor. "I have multiple drawings with various stones that offer you some options, sir." Stepping back, he pointed to his sketches. The commandant stepped forward and viewed the various drawings, the stones set in place on the drawings to show what the pendant would look like. Underneath the pendant drawings were samples of drawings for matching earrings. A smile spread across the commandant's lips.

Joseph stood silent, but noticed the look on his face. The commandant was a hard man and known for not being reasonable, caring or patient. Inside, Joseph's body shook, but he only hoped it didn't show on the outside.

"Good," commented the commandant. "Good. I like this one." He pointed to the last one. "I like the size and the design. The gems were nicely picked. I need it by Friday." He then turned and walked out the door, slamming it behind him.

Nausea overcame Joseph, and he ran to a bucket and heaved. His body shook uncontrollably. Jacob stood next to him, patting him on the back, trying to comfort him. He felt the same way, but it was time for him to be strong for his friend, who had saved him from certain death. He should be pushing dead bodies to the crematorium, but instead, he was in a heated building with better food. He owed Joseph his life.

It took a good thirty minutes for Joseph to get a hold of himself. Jacob had gone and gotten him some bread, hoping to settle his stomach. All the heaving had worsened his cough, but there was little that could be done for it.

Finally, Joseph sat at his stool and began working on the commandant's request. He only had two days to complete it, and it was going to be a tough deadline. Picking up his tools, he began designing the molds. It took all day to complete them. The sun had already set, and they were working by small lamps. The stones which had already been set aside, waited to be set. Joseph felt the pressure of making a piece that outdid all he had done before. If the commandant didn't like it, he was sure he'd be removed and taken to the gas chamber.

The next morning. Joseph rose before the sun came up. The day was cold, and he stoked the fire, setting his hands near the stove to warm the stiffness out. Working with gemstones required nimble fingers. One by one, the stones were set in place. It took half the day, yet he wasn't happy with it. He doubted anyone else would notice except a jeweler, but today, it needed to be perfect.

The pendant was molded of gold, in a teardrop design. A large two carat pink pear-shaped diamond set in the middle, with quarter carat white diamonds set around it. Then, toward the outer edges, shaped around the teardrop, small, deep pink tourmalines finished the pendant. The earrings were also teardrop. Each had a round one carat white pear diamond with small pink tourmalines set around it. The pieces sparkled under the light. A deep sigh escaped Joseph's lips as he held his palms on his back and stretched the stiffness out. He was done.

Hours later, the commandant strode in, ready for his wife's gift. His clothes, like usual, were impeccable, and his boots shone so much you could see yourself in them. His hat set securely and confidently on his head, the skull staring directly at Joseph.

Joseph rose, opening the mahogany brown velvet box he had made for it from a piece of clothing not fondly donated from the dead. The brown set off the gorgeous pink and white stones, sparkling from the box.

He could hear the commandant suck in his breath as he took the box from Joseph's hands.

"I hope you don't mind, sir, I took the liberty of slightly enlarging the stones and adding a little more brilliance."

"It's beautiful," the commandant acknowledged. "I like the tourmalines on the earrings."

"Thank you, sir," Joseph whispered.

The commandant snapped the box closed and left. The next day, two roasted chicken legs were sitting on Joseph's worktable. A smile spread over Joseph's face.

It had been three weeks since the commandant's wife's piece had been completed. The orders were non-stop now, so many that they had given Joseph another assistant. Joseph had been given permission to choose the person who would be given the job. He had to make sure they were capable of really helping and keeping up. The small building had little room, so having one more person in it meant they had to choose someone they could get along with.

Jacob's cousin, Simon, was the best choice. Jacob would show him the ropes on extracting the gold from teeth, and Joseph would teach Jacob how to pour the gold molds and clean the burrs off. Simon was shorter, so they made his cot smaller to slip under one of the others to save room. The duo was now a trio, and if the officers kept asking for more jewelry, they'd have to expand to a new room.

Simon had caught on quickly and just like Jacob, he had vomited for a couple of days until he had come to terms with his predicament. He knew, just like Joseph and Jacob, how lucky he was to be chosen for the job.

It was probably a good thing Joseph was teaching Jacob the ropes on pouring molds and some of the intricate work, because by now Joseph coughed almost non-stop, his hands clutching his chest, hoping it would hurt less if he put pressure on it. He tried to hide his pain, but both Simon and Jacob couldn't help but think Joseph may not make it. Jacob was determined to get some medicine, but the guards and officers were extremely cross these days, more than usual.

The enemy was encroaching. The distant hum of engines made everyone, guards and prisoners alike, look skyward. It was hard to tell if they were friend or foe, but something was happening. You could hear the ground pounding off in the distance, and the guards' reactions made it obvious something would happen soon. A hopeful thrill spread through the long rows of prisoner barracks.

No one dared to say anything, but you could feel the defiance mounting toward Germany. If only the troubled souls of the incinerated had been able to hold on longer, maybe there would have been hope for them too. Even though the jewelry shop was still working, no guards or officers had visited the past couple of days. They were all rushing around, and lots of trucks and cars were coming and going, but no one came in about jewelry.

****

CHAPTER THIRTY

It was Wednesday, the day Peter would meet Anna at their old campground. Her heartbeat wildly, anticipating seeing him again. She knew her heart had changed toward him. What used to be brotherly love had slowly been replaced with something deeper, a love that made her look at him and feel a desire unfamiliar to her.

Pulling her pack onto her cot, she put in the little bit of food she had left, an extra set of clothes, matches, her flashlight, money, and gems. She felt it was better to take her valuables with her whenever she left the camp from now on. She shoved it into the bottom of her pack and looked around to see if there was anything else she should take. Pulling on her jacket and wrapping her scarf around her neck, Anna slipped out the door.

The day was warm, noting spring was only days away. Anna was glad. She'd had enough of winter, and looked forward to not freezing half to death every day. She trudged through the woods, anxious to see Peter. It would take her a good couple of hours to get there, but she knew it was worth the effort. It had been years since she had been to her favorite camping spot. The memories flooded in as she made her way east. The evergreens gave cover, and the warm weather was starting to fill in the other trees nakedness. It was almost as if a war didn't exist.

"Father!" Peter yelled up the stairs. "I'm heading out. Will you be okay here while I'm gone?" Peter's father seemed to be tired all the time and out of breath more and more often. Thinking of his father made him mad. He was mad at the German army for being so demanding lately with the increased orders. It was getting hard to keep up. They were lucky to have the money and benefits from the work, but it wouldn't do them any good if it killed them doing it.

"I'll be fine," his father yelled back. "Be careful, Son."

Peter assured him he would, loaded his knapsack with sandwiches, cheese, extra rolls, and a canteen of water, then slung it onto his back and headed out the back door. Peter's excitement grew as he headed into the woods. It was going to take him a few hours to get to the old campsite, so he had left early, before the sun had started to rise. He wanted to make sure he didn't leave Anna waiting without protection. Peter had loaded his .22 pistol and slipped it into his jacket pocket. He made sure to take an extra box of ammunition in his pack as well. He didn't trust anyone.

The warmer weather made it much easier to move through the woods, and with no snow to tramp through, Peter broke into a sweat.

The war was homing in on Germany's large industrial cities. There had been bombings, and the

Russians, British, and Americans were closing in. He was glad. He just wanted the war to end, so he could be with Anna, and they could find her family. He had heard some of the neighbors talking, while in the bakery, praying things turned around, and hoping the Russians didn't take over. Peter hoped the Russians didn't invade as well, but if they did, it would serve everyone right for the atrocities they'd done to the Jews and unfortunate people who were part of Hitler's master plan.

Peter was accustomed to troops roaming throughout the city and the planes that constantly flew overhead, but of late, it hadn't always been the Luftwaffe that was doing the flying. Every time he saw a foreign insignia on the planes, he smiled inside.

Getting close to the campsite, his excitement soared. Soon he'd be with Anna. He still couldn't believe everything that had transpired, how he thought he had lost her, and then fate had brought her back. He needed to protect her, but he wasn't sure how. The cities were swarming with soldiers, and the government was so paranoid that if they thought you were even thinking against them, you'd disappear.

He needed to figure out what to do. It wasn't safe to bring her home. There were too many people who would recognize her and know that he hadn't really killed her. Even though she could hide in their upstairs, it only took one person to realize something was amiss and he, his father, and Anna would all be executed.

Finally, the campsite came into view. He waited, looking around, and then stepped out into the clearing. No one was there. He was scared she may have been captured trying to reach him. He worried not only about the Germans but also the British, the Americans, and the Russians. If he had to pick who to be captured by, he had heard that the Americans or British treated you the best. The Russians couldn't be trusted.

Suddenly, Anna stepped out into the opening, standing before him. Peter moved toward her slowly, not wanting to spook her. She was taking a big chance trusting him again and being out during the day. He took Anna's hands, looking into her eyes. Anna smiled up at him.

"Peter." The only thing she could trust herself to say was his name. Her mouth was dry, and she was shaking.

"Anna, oh, Anna," whispered Peter. "You came. I was afraid you might not come, that you might not trust me."

Anna was emotional, and she burst into tears. Peter wrapped his arms around her, holding her tight.

"It's okay now," he said softly into her ear. "Everything will be okay." He hugged her tight again, and gently pulled away from her, searching her face. "I looked for you and your parents, but I couldn't find you. I can't believe you're in front of me now, that I'm actually touching you."

Anna leaned into him, wrapping her arms around him. It had been forever since she had hugged or been hugged by anyone. Without hesitation, she gently kissed him. It was a simple, sweet kiss.

Peter relished the moment. He had thought about this moment since he was fourteen. "I love you, Anna. I'm so happy you're alive, that you're here." Gently, he pulled her against him and kissed her back, hoping he hadn't overstepped his bounds.

"I'm going to figure out how to get you out of Germany. The country's swarming with soldiers, and now that the war is at our front door, we have to find somewhere safe to go."

"I don't know if I can leave. I'm sure Mama is gone, but my father, I feel like he's still alive. I can't leave without him. He wouldn't know where to find me."

"You have to. This is what your parents would want. Everyday it's becoming more dangerous. Your father will find you and I'll never stop looking for him, I promise."

"She hesitated. "I just don't know anymore. I've been living in a wood berm not too far from here, and Papa knows how to find me there. Maybe I should stay there."

"Listen, we need to get you out of here. The Russians are marching toward us and I don't even want to think of what they'll do if they find you. We need to head towards the Americans; I've heard they're kinder. We don't need to decide today, but I'm going to find out what I can, so you can go someplace safe."

Anna didn't comment. She didn't want to think about leaving now that she had Peter here in front of her again.

Pulling open his knapsack, Peter reached for the sandwiches and extra food he had brought for her. They were both famished and ate with intensity. Anna was starving and practically gulped the food down. It tasted so good. Peter pulled the lemon cookies from his sack, smiling.

"And these are from my father. He said to remind you that he loves you."

She laughed something she thought she had forgotten how to do. She reached over and hugged Peter. "Give him this hug and tell him I love him too," she said as she smiled. Anna hung her head. Thinking of all the people she missed made her sad.

"I will," he said, pulling her into another hug. If he had his way, he'd never go home, but he knew he'd leave his father in danger if he didn't.

"Meet me here Saturday unless it's not safe. Here's extra food, and I'll bring more next time." Caressing her chin in his hands, he searched her eyes, and quickly but firmly pressed his lips to hers. "Be safe," he whispered, as he turned and headed toward home.

Anna snuck back into the woods, her pack a little heavier with the food Peter had brought, but her heart lighter than it had been in years. Her body tingled, remembering his kiss. She knew she loved him. It had taken a lot of years to see him that way, but she knew she'd love him forever. Her mind kept going to him even though she tried to concentrate on getting back to camp and not getting caught.

By the time Peter left Anna, it was early evening before Peter finally got home. He slipped in the back door, pulling his boots off, tossing them in the corner. He slipped out of his coat, threw his pack onto the counter, and yelled for his father.

"Father, I'm back!" He didn't hear or see his father, so he took the stairs two at a time, calling out to him.

"I'm in here," he finally called back. "I'm in the kitchen."

Peter stepped around the corner and saw his father sitting at the kitchen table, coffee steaming from his favorite mug.

"Did you see her?" he asked.

His grin revealed everything. "Yes, I did Father. She's good. I left her some food and told her I'd be back on Saturday." Peter's face flushed thinking of her. "I told her I love her. She said she loves me too." Peter smiled, his dimples deep from grinning so big.

His father smiled back at him. "I'm glad, son. You two are good for each other. Let's pray this war ends and Anna will be safe." His breath came out labored, his face paler than usual.

"Are you all right? You don't look well! Did you see the doctor?"

"So many questions." His father waved him off. "You know the doctor can't fix my problems."

"Father, you need to stop working. I'll take on the extra load. You need to take it easy and rest."

"No son, I don't! I started this bakery, and I have no intention of slowing down now. I see what a wonderful young man you've become, and I get to work with you. Let me enjoy these moments."

Peter shook his head knowing his father would do what he wanted. The last thing he needed was to have a disagreement with him. He looked at his father, realizing he had aged dramatically in the last couple of years. The stress of the war and the hours the bakery required had taken a toll on him. Peter was filled with sadness.

"Okay, Father. I just worry, and I love you. You always say I'm stubborn. Well, you know who I take after-*you*!" He chuckled.

His father laughed, rose from the table and gave Peter a big hug. Peter hugged him back, and then hugged him again.

"This last one's from Anna. She told me to give you a hug and tell you she loves you and thank you for her favorite cookies." His father smiled, his eyes lighting up when he spoke of Anna.

"God found a way to bring you together." He beamed. "Your mother would be pleased. She loved Anna, too. I'm going to bed, son, but I'll be up early to get started on the orders for tomorrow. I love you."

"Good night, Father. I'm so excited, I don't think I can sit still. I'll head down and get a start on tomorrow. Do you want me to wake you up for dinner?"

His father shook his head no, letting him know he'd had already eaten a bite. Shuffling off to his room, he waved a hand goodnight to Peter.

Peter went downstairs, pulled his white apron off the hook, and started on the next day's bread orders. He was worried about Anna and his father.

"When will life get easier?" he asked himself. He couldn't help but wonder how Anna was doing.

Anna was exhausted. She wasn't used to being up during the daytime. Coming back to camp took twice as long, trying to hide and ensure no one was following her. She was happy, though, tired but happy. She loved Peter, and finally had someone she could talk to and depend on.

Reaching camp, she checked the field and the farmer's house, to make sure no one was out. A roar came out of nowhere. Startled, she looked up into the sky and could see planes soaring over the treetops. There were at least fifty of them with a star blazed on their wings. She knew they weren't the Luftwaffe.

Inside she jumped for joy. *"Serves Germany right,"* she thought. *"Now they can all see what it's like for someone to hunt you down and kill you!"*

The roaring continued for a good fifteen minutes, and then she heard and felt the ground quiver. The blasts continued to shake the ground, and the trees swayed as the shock waves moved through the air. It was close, eminent danger was at her doorstep, but she didn't care. At least Germany was getting what they deserved. She thought of Peter and prayed he was okay. They were bombing in his direction. Had she found him just in time to lose him? No! She shook her head; she wouldn't let her mind go there.

The ground stopped quivering, and soon silence filled the air. It was so quiet that not a bird chirped, and the animals had long snuck off to find safety. Peeking around a tree, she could see a couple of people near the farmhouse, looking skyward. She couldn't see their faces, but their body language said panic was setting in. It was the first time the enemy had dared reach their front porch. Anna would have hoped they bombed the hell out of their house, if not for the fact it was too close for her own comfort.

Now that Germany had been infiltrated, Peter was right, it was time to move on. She looked forward to seeing him on Saturday. She prayed he was okay.

****

CHAPTER THIRTY ONE

The big clock on the wall struck ten o'clock. Peter yawned and knew he had to head to bed, or he'd be exhausted tomorrow. The good thing was, he got a huge start for tomorrow, so his father wouldn't have to work as long. Untying his apron, he laid it on the counter, too tired to hang it up, and dragged himself upstairs.

Looking in on his father, he saw his chest rise and fall, the blanket pulled high over his chest, and a gentle snore escaping. Peter went to the kitchen and made a quick sandwich before heading to bed. His head barely hit the pillow before he was fast asleep.

Five o'clock in the morning, the shrill of the alarm woke Peter. He had meant to set it for four, but it was too late now. He pulled himself from his deep sleep, running his hands through his rumpled hair. Throwing his legs over the side of the bed, he finally brought himself out of a fog and got dressed.

Stepping into the kitchen, he was surprised his father wasn't up. *He's probably downstairs already*, he thought with a deep frown. That would be just like him. Peter slipped his head through his father's bedroom doorway just to check, but found him still in bed. His chest was still. Peter pushed the door open, rushing into the room.

"Father, Father!" He shook him gently. His father didn't move. Panic rising, he shook him harder, pleading for him to wake up. His father's body lay still, his eyes closed, his lips slightly apart as if he was about to snore.

Peter fell next to the bed, pleading for him to get up, yet knowing, his father was gone. He touched his father's hands and shook him again, but his hands were cold, and he didn't move.

Peter's body shook, tears spilling down his cheeks. He wanted to go back to bed and wake up, to find that it had all been a dream. An hour had passed when Peter finally got up, called the doctor, and waited by the front door. Last night's dough that he had made so his father wouldn't have to work so hard for the army, sat rising in the pans on the stove counters. He had to look away, his anger and grief boiling up inside.

A light knock on the door told Peter the doctor had arrived to make a formal pronouncement and sign a death certificate. Once Peter had it, he'd have to make arrangements for his father to be buried next to his mother and have a service.

"Thank you for coming, sir," mumbled Peter, shaking the doctor's hand.

"I'm sorry, Peter. I know you loved each other very much. I'm so sorry." The doctor headed up the stairs and confirmed what Peter already knew. He came back down with the signed death certificate and handed it to Peter, putting his other hand on his shoulder.

"Take some time," said the doctor. "Take time to grieve, Peter. I'll have the morgue pick him up within the hour."

The doctor saw himself out, telling Peter to keep the closed sign on, then shut the door.

Peter went to his father's room, pulling the chair up to the bed. The chair was his father's favorite. The wood was minus any varnish that had once polished its frame and the seat was well worn. Peter's mother had done the needlepoint on it, blue flowers intermingled with white daisies, although only half the flowers were still intact. His father had refused to get it repaired or replaced after his mother died. Peter understood why.

He reached over and wrapped his hands in his father's. Even though they were cold to the touch, Peter could imagine the strength in those hands, hands that had guided him his entire life. Leaning down, Peter kissed his father on the forehead, his eyes brimming with tears once again. "Goodbye, Father, I'll miss you."

Everything seemed so quiet, and as if it were going in slow motion. The mortuary came and took his father's body, leaving Peter the name of who he should contact to set up a service. Right now, he couldn't think straight and had no idea what to do as the next step. He felt numb.

The rising bread that he had no intentions of baking seemed to scream at him. *It was all that baking for the army that killed him,* thought Peter. Striding over to the counter, with one huge sweep, he let the pans fly, clattering to the floor, dough flying across the room. He didn't care. Peter kept the store closed all day with a sign noting a death in the family.

He shuffled up the stairs and lay in his father's bed, soaking in his smell. It would be the last of him, he thought as his body started to shake, his grief taking over. The sun had long set, and Peter's body finally gave in to mental exhaustion. He had fallen asleep on his Father's bed. Tomorrow, he would take care of burying him.

Dawn was just coming up when a loud knock sounded at the shop door. It kept getting louder before he realized someone was pounding on it. He rose and opened the door a crack. Two soldiers stood there, uniforms crisp, their guns hanging off their shoulders.

"Mr. Reinhold, we're here for the army's bread order. We apologize for knocking so loud, but no one came to the door, and it was locked." Peter just stared at them. "Sir? We're here to get the bread order for the army. Are you okay?"

Peter shook himself back to life. "I'm sorry, I, I don't have it," he stuttered. "My father died yesterday. I don't have it. I didn't think to call." The closed sign noting a death in the family no longer hung in the window, but lay at Peter's feet.

"I see," said the one in charge. "Perhaps you should call headquarters and let them know your predicament. We're deeply sorry for your loss. I don't mean to sound cold, but I have to answer to my superior. Should I expect the order tomorrow? The army still needs to eat, so I imagine they'll expect you to handle the orders soon."

"I, I don't know" he stammered, wishing they'd leave. "I still have arrangements to make." He could hear the anger rising in his voice. "I'll call your superior tomorrow morning. My apologies."

The soldiers clicked their heels together. "Heil Hitler!" they cried throwing their arms in a high salute, then turned and left. Peter did not salute back. He hung the sign back up, locked the door and started up the stairs, his legs heavy like lead. When he got upstairs, he would be alone. From now on, he would be alone.

The roaring got louder and louder. Peter rushed over to the front window. Neighbors were out, looking up to see planes covering the cloudless sky. For once, they weren't cheering. Peter wished his father was here to see it. The sadness seeped through his soul, as he realized his father was gone.

The planes kept coming, and soon the bombs started to drop, explosions echoing throughout the city, the ground shaking like an earthquake. Even though they were over thirty miles away, it was close enough to feel the effects. Peter's thoughts went to Anna. He was sure she was safe, but for how long?

The tremors from the bombing persisted for hours, Peter reveling in the thought of fellow Germans being destroyed. He didn't care what was happening miles away and how scared Germany was. It served them all right.

He slipped into his father's bedroom, staring at the place where he had taken his last breath. Peter's eyes stung from crying. He shut the door, and then went to his room, lying across the comforter and cried some more.

The sun shone through Peter's bedroom window, telling him it was past noon and yesterday was finally over. Peter sighed, rolled over onto his back, and stared up at the ceiling. He knew he had to move but he felt paralyzed. The phone rang, startling him. Slowly rising, he shuffled into the kitchen and yanked the receiver to his ear.

"Hello?" he mumbled.

"Mr. Reinhold, this is Lieutenant Braun, from headquarters. I understand your father passed away yesterday. The Führer and all of us are deeply sorry for your loss, but unfortunately, the war is still on. We must insist you fill the required orders. Our expectation is that once you've buried your father, you'll continue with helping the Fatherland. I've assigned two staff members to help in place of your father. I'm sure they can help with the load. They'll arrive tomorrow morning."

Peter stood frozen, his mind going wild. Now was the time. He knew what he had to do.

"I understand, sir, my comrades still have to eat. I'm making funeral arrangements for my father today, and will be ready to bake tomorrow. I have a neighbor that has stepped in to help, though," he lied, "so your staff won't be necessary. I would hate to think they'll be baking instead of helping where our Führer really needs them."

Peter's fists were clenched tight as he spoke the words. He couldn't care less about the Führer or his staff. "I'll have the order ready Monday."

"Your father would be proud of you, son," the officer spoke into the phone. Peter wanted to scream at him not to call him son. He wasn't his son.

"Yes, sir, thank you," Peter spoke evenly, with no emotion. "I'll expect the orders to be picked up on Monday. Good day." Peter hung the phone up. Before he could get the receiver down, enemy planes buzzed the sky again, and loud explosions rocked the ground, windows shaking, ready to break. That was close, thought Peter. Yes, now was the time.

Peter showered, brushed his teeth and shaved. Looking in the mirror, he saw the resemblance to his father that was clearly there. He had his father's mouth, nose, and prominent chin. He had his mothers' crystal blue eyes and dimples. Seeing his parents in the mirror, made him mourn them all the more.

Peter shook himself to reality. First, he had to take care of his father. Grabbing his father's favorite suit and his best tie, he headed to the funeral home. It was only ten blocks away, but it felt like miles. The earth shook from the bombs hitting their targets. He knew it wouldn't be long before they would decimate his home if the Führer didn't get busy defending Germany, but he didn't care because he wouldn't be there.

Peter stepped into the funeral home, the bell chiming his arrival. An impeccably dressed man entered the foyer.

"May I help you?" asked the man.

"Yes, I'm here to discuss arrangements for my father, Kurt Reinhold."

"I'm sorry for your loss, Mr. Reinhold. My name is Stephan and I'll be helping you with the service and burial." The man shook Peter's hand and then motioned him toward his office.

Peter looked around, then realized, *he* was now Mr. Reinhold.

"Thank you," he mumbled, nodding his head up and down, acknowledging the man.

He followed him to the office, accepting the green leather high-back chair. Peter couldn't get the smell of the place out of his mind. Why was it all funeral homes smelled the same and looked dreary?

"Shall we get on with the arrangements? I see you brought the clothes you wish us to use?"

Peter shook off his thoughts. "Yes, and I know what I'd like to do," he stated with authority. His father would understand. "I wish my father to be buried next to my mother in the Friedhof Stoffeln Cemetery. Here are the details you may need."

Peter pulled the papers from his jacket pocket and handed them to the man.

"I have orders from the army to complete the bakery orders, so I won't be able to have normal services. I can't expect to have special privileges for my loved ones when my comrades are fighting and dying at the front." Peter looked the man in the eyes, holding his gaze.

"Oh, I see." The man hesitated. This was very unfortunate, since he made extra money from holding funeral services. Burying the body gave little profit. It was all the extras, like beautiful caskets, flowers and programs they made money on.

Peter picked out a medium-priced casket and asked to see his father one last time. Normally, he would have paid for a casket with all the bells and whistles like his father had done for his mother, but times were different, and he knew his father would want him to save the money instead, considering his plans.

The funeral director showed Peter into the room where his father lay, a white sheet pulled up over him. Peter slid the sheet off his father's head, staring at his face. He was void of color and no longer resembled the vibrant, loving man Peter knew.

"I love you, Father," he whispered. "I know you'll understand." With those last words, Peter turned and left the room.

As he was paying the bill, the ground shuddered, and loud explosions filled the air. The funeral director looked scared, and Peter was glad. He had no sympathy for him. "I'll visit his grave to check, the headstone once you've completed the burial," said Peter, matter of fact. He wanted the man to know he wouldn't put up with any shortcuts burying his father, war or no war. He may not be coming back to check, but the funeral director didn't know that.

Peter exited the funeral home and headed to the bank. As he waited his turn for the cashier, Mr. Schneider, the manager came up to him, touching him lightly on the shoulder.

"I'm so sorry about your father, Peter. He was a good man. I greatly admired him." Peter nodded, and shook his hand, thanking him for his kind words.

"You don't need to wait in line, son. What can I do for you?"

Peter didn't really want the manager to know he was going to withdraw a lot of money. "Thank you, sir, but I don't mind waiting. I have a lot on my mind, so it gives me time to think, but thank you."

"Ah, I understand. Let me know if I can be of help, Peter." The manager patted him on the shoulder and excused himself. A few minutes later, the cashier waved him over to the window.

"I'd like to withdraw five thousand marks please," said Peter, looking the cashier in the eyes.

The cashier looked up at Peter, surprised at the large amount.

"So much, sir? I'll have to get Mr. Schneider's authorization." Peter wasn't pleased. He didn't need any questions, but he figured it was a long shot they wouldn't let the manager know. Peter waited while the cashier excused himself.

Mr. Schneider came up to the window, questioning Peter.

"That's a lot of money, Peter. I'm a little concerned, considering your father just died."

"Yes, I know, sir. I have a funeral to pay for, and my father had ordered new state-of-the-art ovens and equipment to handle the army's orders. I have to pay for all that equipment. The Reich expects me to continue helping my country."

"I see. That explains a lot. Perhaps we should transfer the money, it would be safer."

"It would be, but I have the ovens showing up tomorrow or the next day, and they won't set them up without payment first. My father had intended to wire the funds, but at this stage, it's too late."

Mr. Schneider's forehead wrinkled in concern, not happy about giving Peter cash. "Well, I don't recommend it, but it's your money, and if they're delivering tomorrow, it's too late to wire it."

Peter didn't say anything. He just nodded his head in agreement.

The manager nodded to the cashier, then turned and left. The cashier counted out the money and put it in a large envelope. Peter took it, thanked the cashier and left. Next, Peter headed to the hardware store. He had a list he needed to fill. Entering the store, the tiny bell over the door sounded his entrance.

"Hello, Peter." Mr. Gradwohl smiled. "I'm sorry to hear about your father. My deepest condolences. Please, let us know when the funeral is, we thought highly of your father and want to pay our respects."

"Thank you, sir," said Peter, "but there won't be a service."

"Oh!" Mr. Gradwohl's forehead furrowed in concern.

"The army expects me to fill their orders starting immediately, so I need to do my part," Peter explained. "My father would understand." Peter nodded his head up and down, waiting for the shop owner to agree with him.

"Yes, of course. He would be immensely proud of your dedication to the Führer," he said.

"I agree." Peter lied. His father hated the Führer but no one else needed to know that. It was the secret he and his father shared with each other but never said in public.

"What brings you in, then?"

"I need a few things. With the bombings and everything, I'd like to be more prepared, since I no longer have my father to rely on. He's the one who usually took care of everything. I need to be a grown-up now and think of what I might need."

"You're a smart young man. It's been hard for me to get resupplied, so you're smart to get what you can now. Here, let's see your list."

Pulling the items off the shelves, he stacked them in a neat pile. Batteries, matches, candles, rope and the other goods. "You're in luck. I still have these items, Peter, but I don't know how many batteries I can afford to sell you."

"Just what you can, would be really helpful." Peter waited patiently, while the owner wrapped the smaller items and then handed his packages off. He paid the man with cash and ration coupons and left, the bell declaring his exit.

Back home, Peter laid the items on the kitchen table. Looking over his pile, he made sure he added his hatchet, hunting knife, .22 pistol, ammunition, and then gathered up food that would last the longest. The icebox had been near empty, but there was a good amount of cheese and some deli meat. Emptying the cupboards, he piled the crackers, canned vegetables, and other items onto the center of the table.

Peter pulled his and his father's backpacks out. Stuffing them as full as he could get them, nothing was left behind. His pack held a sleeping bag, a few extra clothes, and all the food he could shove into it. His father's pack held the matches, candles, and other hardware items and the rest of the food.

With the packs filled, he took one last stroll through his parents' room. His father's watch lay on the dresser. Peter strapped it on, tucked his parents' wedding bands in his pant pockets, took a picture of him and his parents' when he was ten, right before his mother had died, as well as his parents' wedding photo, and left the room. He looked through each of the other rooms and sat to wait for nightfall, dozing as best he could. It would be a long wait, but he couldn't leave and be seen with backpacks on.

A loud knock at the door scared Peter. He wasn't expecting anyone, and he had made sure to put the closed sign back on the door. A nervous sweat ran down him as he made his way down the stairs. Opening the door, there stood officer Holtz. Peter just stared at him, no words escaping his lips.

"Peter." Holtz frowned. "I heard about your father. I came to give my condolences. Your father was a good man. He had to be to raise such a great son. May I?" Without waiting for a response, Holtz stepped into the bakery.

"I'm a little out of sorts," mumbled Peter, perspiration beading his forehead.

"Well, with your father gone, I understand. I know running the bakery will be hard." Holtz could see bread pans with old dough scattered over the floor, but didn't say anything. He chalked it up to Peter being distraught.

"I talked to the commandant, who has agreed you're welcome to join my staff. It will be a huge loss for the army to lose a baker, but he's agreed to my request."

"I'm so grateful you thought of me, sir. My father would be so appreciative." Peter almost vomited the words out. "I feel obligated not to leave the army shorthanded, so if you could give me a few days, it would be appreciated." There was no intention of joining Holtz, but he'd lead him on to give himself time to fulfill his plan.

"Of course, Peter. Finish up the next few days and then check in with me at headquarters." Holtz grabbed Peter and pulled him into a hug.

"I hope my son turns out as good as you" Holtz smiled.

Peter smiled back at him. "Thank you, sir."

Peter felt repulsed that this man thought of him so fondly. Just having him touch him made him feel dirty. Peter pulled away from him, trying not to be obvious he was annoyed.

"Thank you, sir, for thinking of me. Your praise means a lot. I'll come by in a few days then."

Holtz opened the door and stepped outside. Peter quickly said goodbye and closed the door. He was so nervous, he had sweated through his shirt.

Nightfall had finally come, the stars shining like tiny lanterns, ready to guide Peter to his destination. Slinging his pack onto his back and grabbing his fathers, he quietly slipped out the back door and headed into the woods. Before he disappeared into the trees, he turned around and looked at home one last time. He would never be back.

****

CHAPTER THIRTY TWO

Anna looked around her camp, amazed at how much had fit into such a tiny space. It had served her well. It would be hard to leave because it held so much of her parents, but the time was right. Somehow, she knew, even if Peter wasn't there to meet her, she'd have to move on. Bombs had been dropping close enough for her to realize that within the next few days the next explosion could be on top of her. Everything worthy of taking was laid out on her cot. If she wanted to move quick in the forest, she had to go light.

She picked carefully, taking only necessary items. She had no food left but she made sure her canteen was filled. Last, the photos of her parents and their letters, Mama's hair comb, and wedding ring she had insisted Anna take. Her pistol and money from her hut and under the tree were all gently tucked into her pack.

The explosions could be heard non-stop now. The farmer had packed up a couple of days ago and left. Anna thought of going inside the house to see if they had left any food but decided against it, not knowing if someone had stayed behind. She didn't think so, but it was better to be safe than sorry. She had made it this long, and she didn't need to do anything stupid now.

Tying her sleeping bag to the top of her pack, she crawled out the doorway. The sun was starting to rise as she slipped into the trees. Her next stop was Peter. Today was Saturday, and she hoped he would be there like he had promised.

Anna marched on, determined to get to the camping spot on time. The ground was muddy in places, leaving her footprints in plain sight. She'd have to take measures to walk over fallen leaves and on fallen tree trunks. She had no intentions of giving herself away. It was slowing her down, but safety was first Papa had said. She still let him enter her mind and give her tips on when and where to go.

A few hundred feet away, voices could be heard and lots of boots stopping together. As panic rose, Anna looked around and found a clump of bushes that had leaves on them. Pulling herself deep into the bushes, she lay on the dirt, covering herself and her pack as best she could. The marching was getting closer. Anna made a mental note to slow her breathing. Trying to camouflage herself, she strained to see what was coming. It didn't take long before a platoon of German soldiers marching in formation, two abreast, came into view. She shouldn't be looking but she needed information to decide where to go and when to leave. She needed to pass on all she could to Peter.

There were about twenty or more stopped near the river for a drink, and to fix their foot boils and adjust their socks. For well over an hour, Anna didn't move. Finally, the lieutenant barked out an order, and they all came to attention and started moving on. They couldn't have gotten more than a half mile away, when you could hear a whistling sound, and then all hell broke loose as a bomb hit the ground. She could hear screams, men calling for help, for their mothers. It was sheer chaos. Anna felt the jolt of the impact, and the force threw her from the bushes. Quickly, she got up and ran in the opposite direction of the soldiers.

More bombs fell, ripping trees off their roots, scattering limbs and debris everywhere. Anna just ran, hoping she was would be lucky enough not to get hit. She propelled herself forward, praying she and Peter would both still be in one piece.

****

CHAPTER THIRTY THREE

Joseph and Jacob woke early to an overwhelming eerie silence. Coughing racked Joseph's body, and he knew Jacob hadn't gotten much sleep because of him. Every breath Joseph took was hard. Pulling his legs over his cot, he pulled on his pants and shirt, and wrapped his bed blanket around his shoulders.

There were no sounds outside, which drew their curiosity toward the door. Joseph shuffled to the door and opened it. The coolness hit him in the face. The snow had melted weeks ago, the sun promising warmer days. Jacob joined him on the porch searching for movement in camp.

No soldiers could be seen, only prisoners forced to be in the concentration camp. Little by little, some of the camp prisoners came out of their long barracks. A few hours passed, as more prisoners filled the compound and stood by the prison gates. The gates were closed but unlocked, and still no one dared leave.

Prisoners walked around in a daze, not sure what to do. Some said they should leave, after all, the Germans were nowhere in sight. Others argued they could be waiting in the woods.

While prisoners flooded the kitchens, stuffing food into every pocket and place they could find, Joseph, Jacob, and Simon stayed in their quarters, unsure what to do and not trusting what looked like an escape.

No soldiers aimed guns from the watch towers, but where would they go, and how would they get there? If they were going to leave, they had to have a plan in place. It was one thing to make it past the gates, but what would meet them beyond that, and in their condition.

Joseph's cough came on hard, making him double over from the pain. He had been coughing up blood lately, which he knew wasn't a good sign, but there was no doctor to see or medicine to be had. The infirmary had been stripped clean by the soldiers before they left.

"Come, lay down, Joseph," said Jacob, pulling him by his sleeve toward his cot. "You need rest, and there's no one here to say what we can and can't do. Those bombers that have been flying overhead aren't ours. Germany is losing the war."

Jacob sounded sad, when he should be feeling joyful, but he was scared for his friend. The whisper of freedom was now a reality, but Jacob would not leave without Joseph, and he knew he wouldn't make it far unless he could get rid of his cough. No, he'd wait and try to help his friend. If it hadn't been for Joseph, he'd have been dead a long time ago. Jacob had silently promised himself that he'd help find Anna if they got out alive.

Simon and Jacob helped Joseph back to his cot. He lay there, coughing nonstop, his chest heaving, trying to draw a deep breath. All Joseph could think about was Miriam and Anna. Which one would he see first, the one in this life, or the one in the life after?

The gates of the camp were unlocked, and the Russian Red Army marched in. The stunned looks on their faces told prisoners they looked as bad as they felt. Everyone who was out of their barracks just stared at the Russians, their faces blank, their eyes and cheeks sunken into their skulls. Their thin striped pajamas hung like huge tattered sheets on their bodies.

The Russians had liberated the camp. They were free! The starving were being fed, filling the emptiness that had gnawed at their bellies.

Jacob had come out to see the commotion. A wave of elation swept over him. He grabbed some cheese and bread the Russians offered and ran back to the jewelry shop.

"Joseph! Joseph!" shouted Jacob as he rushed through the door. "It's over, we made it! The Russians are here, and they've saved us. I brought you some food."

Simon was kneeling beside Joseph's cot, wiping his forehead with a wet cloth. Simon looked up at Jacob, his eyes meeting his, and he shook his head slightly.

Jacob dropped next to the cot and held Joseph's hand. "Hold on, Joseph, you need to hold on for Anna.

We're free, and now we'll find her. I'll help you look for her."

Jacob opened his eyes, a smile lighting across his face. "Free, we're really free?"

"We are," whispered Jacob. "We'll find your daughter."

"Promise me, Jacob, you'll look for her. Tell her I tried."

"Just a little longer, please, that's all, Joseph. The doctors can help you. We'll find your Anna, me and you, together."

Joseph closed his eyes, a smile still on his lips. "Miriam's waiting," were his last words. His labored breathing slowed, and then he took one deep breath and was gone.

Simon and Jacob sat next to his body, numb, tears streaming from their eyes. It had been Joseph who had saved them both, yet he was the one who didn't make it.

Anger filled Jacob. Joseph would never know if his daughter was still alive, but he would. He would definitely find her.

The last piece of jewelry Joseph had made sat on the shelf under his work bench. It was beautiful. A two-carat blue sapphire pendant set in gold was surrounded by small diamonds that shone like a hundred chandelier crystals in the sun. Jacob put it in a small box and tucked it into his pocket, for Anna. He would have to find a place to hide it. He knew what the

Russians were like, and if they found it, they'd take it for their own. He was determined to give it to Anna as a keepsake of her father. The last thing his hands had created.

Jacob and Simon gathered all the gemstones into a bag. They were not going to leave anything for the Red Army to confiscate. The jewels belonged to the Jews who had been murdered. They could have the gold teeth if they had a stomach for it, but not the jewels.

Laying a blanket over Joseph, Jacob and Simon walked out of their building and mingled amongst fellow prisoners. Making their way to the fence line they sat down by a fence post on the cold ground. Jacob pulled out a large spoon and slowly stabbed at the dirt behind Simon's back. Jacob set the box and gems in the hole and shoved the dirt back over it. Pulling himself up, Jacob tapped the dirt firmly into place. Using the spoon handle, he carved a small "J," for Joseph, into the fence post. The only way to see it would be to get down on your hands and knees. When the time was right, they would come back for it, but for now, the bag's contents were safe.

Germany was coming to its knees. Finally, those who had mistreated Anna and her family, fellow Jews, and those who didn't conform or fit into Hitler's plan, were getting revenge.

****

CHAPTER THIRTY FOUR

Anna ran and ran until her sides hurt. She sat down against a tree trunk, gasping for air, her body shaking uncontrollably. She was so scared, she wasn't sure if she could move, but she had to meet Peter. She prayed he would be there.

Pulling herself upright, she ran on. She would run until she found him. Bombs were pounding the earth, trees blowing off at the stumps, limbs flying like arrows. It would be only luck if she made it out of there without getting maimed or killed.

Peter thought of Anna, as he crept through the edge of the forest until he was deep within the woods, and then he took off running. His pack was heavy on his back and the extra one weighed him down, but his mind and heart spurred him on as if he were light as a feather.

Planes flew overhead, dropping bombs nearby. The ground shuddered but it didn't faze Peter. He kept going. He was determined to get to Anna. Even over the thunderous exploding, Peter could hear the tremendous hum of planes in the air. Looking up, he counted ten, fifteen, but after twenty-five he stopped counting. The wing insignia, the round circle of red, white and blue said Britain. The only other insignia he wanted to see was the United States star.

The pounding made the earth quake and rumble, but Peter kept up his pace. He could hear the whistling of bombs spirally down, explosions decimating their targets. To Peter's relief, the pounding sounded farther and farther away. He was happy they were bombing the hell out of the German forces and his homeland, but he preferred to know Anna was safe first.

The bombing had subsided, and Anna felt relief that she may make it out alive. Soon she'd be with Peter, God willing. Another hour and she stepped into the clearing that used to be their favorite camping spot. The trip had been difficult, but now was the tough part, waiting for him. She prayed he had not been in the bombings.

Anna slid down against a huge tree and waited. Each minute seemed like an hour, but it gave her time to reminisce, going through a timeline of her life, remembering her parents. Deep down, she couldn't help but hope she'd be reunited with her father. He had worked hard to make sure she would live, and now she wanted to confirm his plan had worked.

The sun was high in the sky when a shadow fell across the clearing. Out stepped Peter. Anna rose and ran forward, wrapping her arms tightly around him. The emotions became overwhelming, and she broke down sobbing, tears running down her cheeks.

Peter hugged her back, burying his face in her hair. He also felt overwhelmed, and he could no longer hold back the tears. They held onto each other for some time. Finally, Peter pulled them apart.

"We need to leave here," he said. "It's way too dangerous. They're carpet bombing Dusseldorf and outlying areas, and it's only a matter of time if we stay here."

Anna nodded in agreement. "I ran into German troops some ways back. They stopped by the river for water and to fix wounds on their feet from their boots. I hid in the bushes until they left. About twenty minutes later, a bomb must have landed on them because they were screaming for help and for their mothers. I got up and ran as fast as I could get here!"

Peter pulled her into his chest and squeezed her tight, thankful she was still alive.

"That was too close. We need to head west. That's where the British and Americans are. I know you're tired, Anna, but we should leave now. Who knows when they could start the bombing again."

Anna was exhausted, but she agreed. She hoisted her pack on again and waited for Peter. Grabbing her hand, he made sure they were headed west, deeper into the forest. Slipping his free hand into his jacket pocket, Peter pulled out two rolls, handing one to Anna. Her mouth watered, her lips grinning from ear to ear.

"Oh, Peter, did your father make these for us? Is he meeting up with us?"

Peter stopped short, turning to Anna, the tears spilling from his eyes.

"What's wrong, Peter?" exclaimed Anna. She shook him hard. "Tell me, what's wrong!" Anna was now pleading to know about his father. "Please tell me, now!"

"My father had a heart attack two days ago. He died in his sleep, so I don't think he was in pain. I made arrangements to have him buried next to my mother. I couldn't have a service with all the bombings, but I did make burial arrangements." Peter spoke in barely a whisper, but Anna understood his pain.

Grabbing his hands, she looked deep into his eyes. "You did the right thing Peter. Your father would want you to be safe. He was always so proud of you. I would listen when our fathers would talk about us. He was tremendously proud of you."

They were both crying now. Peter pulled her up next to him and they started walking once more toward the west. Nothing more needed to be said.

Silence was their only company for most of the evening. They were bone tired, and Anna didn't think she could walk another ten feet. Tucking under a huge rock ledge, they both knew what needed to be done and began gathering large branches. Peter worked the branches over the ledge, while Anna attempted to find more. Old leaves and debris covered the branches, making it look like it was formed that way.

"I need to refill our canteens. I'll be back within twenty minutes, Anna. Here's my gun, just in case you need it." Anna refused, letting him know she had Papa's .22 pistol. Peter tucked his gun back into his belt.

He dropped his pack and went in search of water, while she crawled inside their camp and dug a small fire pit. Ten minutes later, small flames licked the tiny sticks laid across it.

Anna watched Peter as he came back from filling their canteens. She took in everything about him, his strength, his good looks, and the fact that he had grown into a man. She had left home watching a young teenager try to save her, but now she was watching a grown man. Her heart skipped a beat, and her body tingled all over. It was a feeling she had never experienced before.

Dusk would soon be upon them, and Anna's instinct kicked in. Pulling her sleeping bag off her pack, unzipping it, she laid it open under the ledge. Next, she pulled Peter's from his pack and zipped the two together. They had never slept this close before, but saving body heat was critical. Besides, she had Peter back, and she couldn't stand the thought of not being able to reach out and touch him.

Anna opened some canned beans she found in Peter's pack and let the fire lick the sides of the can until they bubbled. She pulled her coat sleeve down over her fingers and quickly pulled the can from the fire. Pulling out the one spoon she had thrown in her pack, she stirred the can and pulled a steaming spoonful out for her and Peter to share. If you could forget the bombings, they would have thought it was just another day camping.

Peter snuggled up next to Anna. He was silent, emotions running through him. Two days ago he had lost his father, and today, he was next to the young woman he had loved for years, and she finally loved him back. Those two things were certain. What worried him was the future. What would the future hold for them now?

Peter stoked the fire, the heat filling their hideout. Anna had succumbed to slumber, her head lying in Peter's lap. Peter stroked her hair, not wanting to disturb the moment. Despite all that had happened in the last few days, he was happy. He gently laid Anna down on the sleeping bag, pulled his bag over them, and lay watching her sleep until his eyes finally closed.

****

CHAPTER THIRTY FIVE

Jacob and Simon stood before the lieutenant who was recording each prisoner's name, information, and tattooed numbers the Nazis had given them. The information was to be used to relocate survivors with loved ones, and to confirm who had not survived.

The Russians were providing food and medical care to survivors, but had to limit the amount of food each person received. Prisoners were eating so much, so fast, it was making them sicker than they already were; some were dying from overfilling their bellies.

What to do now? There weren't many options for former prisoners. Most were afraid to go back home to a place that held bad memories and hatred. Both Jacob and Simon chose to go to one of the "Displaced Person" camps known as DP camps. They needed time to acclimate to freedom and the future. Many of the Jewish prisoners of war wanted to go to Palestine or America but the process for welcoming them was slow, if non-existent.

Jacob's goal was to find Anna, no matter how long it took. In a life that had been filled with lies and deceit, Jacob's word was gold to him. Joseph had saved his life, and he would pay him back. The DP camp had given detainees new clothes, and Jacob had sewn Joseph's sapphire pendant and half the gemstones that he and Simon had split into his clothes. He wanted to make sure he wouldn't lose them. The value wasn't in the money, but the emotional ties to Anna's father.

A list of survivors was constantly being updated and posted each day. Jacob and Simon checked it for the name Anna Feiner, and each day, disappointment greeted them. Jacob knew in his heart, he would always look for Anna. He'd never give up.

****

CHAPTER THIRTY SIX

P eter woke, lying next to the fire that had gone cold. He could see his breath in the air. Sometime during the night, he had turned on his back, and Anna had snuggled up, her body tight against his, her arm hanging over his chest. He reveled in the moment. This is what he had always wanted.

Finally, Anna stirred, and Peter pulled the bag up tight around her as he slid out. He wouldn't make a fire. They needed to get up and get moving. The bombing had subsided, but they didn't know which forces were roaming in their area, or what the allied forces planned.

"Anna, Anna." Peter gently shook her awake. She opened her eyes, trying to get her bearings. The sleeping bag was warm, but she knew she had to get up.

Pushing the bag off, she sat up, smiling at him. Last night, she had felt safe for the first time in years.

Peter smiled back, his familiar dimples greeting her. "We need to get moving. We have a long and hard road in front of us."

Anna nodded and pulled herself out from under the ledge. They rolled up their sleeping bags and covered their now cold fire with dirt out of habit. Peter pulled some cheese and a loaf of bread from his pack, pulling half the loaf off and tucking the other half back in for later. He cut two chunks of cheese, one for each of them, handing Anna one and a huge piece of bread. Anna didn't miss the fact that he had given her the biggest of both.

They were both famished and ate with intensity. Finishing up with a few gulps from their canteen, they pulled on their backpacks and headed out. Unsure which way the British or Americans were, Peter elected to lead them in the direction the planes came from. Sooner or later they'd see more signs to go by.

They traveled at a fast pace, and finally, at midday, they stopped to rest. They could hear a booming in the distance, but they had been lucky not to be in its midst. They had eaten the other half of the bread and then moved on.

Dusk was setting when they finally stopped. There wasn't much for shelter, but they were both resourceful.

"Here." Peter nodded, pointing to a small area at the base of some trees. "We'll have to make this do."

Looking around, Anna acknowledged him with a nod and dropped her pack. It felt good to get rid of the weight that had pulled on her shoulders all day. In unison, they both started picking fir branches for under their sleeping bags, to hold in heat. Peter had managed to string some rope between two trunks and laid his tarp over it, making a low tent. Anna brought over more fir branches and laid them gently up against the tarp, camouflaging their camp.

"I don't think we should start a fire," said Peter. "Will you be okay?" He knew she would, after all this time living on her own, but concern for her was habit to him.

Anna cocked her head and couldn't help but laugh. "Yes, I think I'll be okay," she said. She pulled up next to him, then leaned in and kissed him gently on the lips. It felt so natural to her now.

Peter didn't want to abuse his feelings for her, but he pulled her in again, and kissed her long and deep, wrapping his muscled arms around her. His feelings ran deeper than a kiss; he'd have to keep his body in check.

Same as last night, Peter slept on his back, Anna curled up next to him, her arm over his chest. It took him awhile to close his eyes, enjoying the moment.

The days were still cold, but the morning broke to sun greeting them through the trees. Peter shook Anna awake, and they quickly rolled their bags and packed up. Pulling the last of the cheese from his pack, they split it, eating as they hiked. They had been hiking for over a week now, and they were hungry and tired. Occasionally, planes flew overhead, and Peter and Anna would get excited. The American star was emblazoned on their wings. If they were seeing Allied planes, then they had to be getting closer to safe territory.

"Listen," said Peter. Anna stopped next to him, standing still, listening carefully. Then they both heard it, a low rumbling. It was coming from behind them and heading in their direction. "It sounds like tanks," whispered Peter. He grabbed Anna's hand, telling her they needed to move faster. Even though they were moving faster, the rumbling was getting louder.

"We need to hide!" said Peter. Anna could hear the fear in his voice. Scoping out the surroundings, they opted for a grouping of trees with dense brush around the trunks. Peter pushed their packs into the brush, making sure they were totally covered.

"Hide in here," he told her as he gently pushed her back toward the brush. She crouched in the brush and Peter made sure she couldn't be seen.

"Wait! What about you?" she asked, popping her head up. "What are you doing?"

"I'm going to look and see what's going on. We need to know where they are and where they're going, or we'll walk right into them. We don't know if they're Nazis or Allied forces. I promise, I'll be back."

Peter made himself sound positive, but, in his mind, he prayed he'd make it back. "Listen, Anna, if morning comes, head for the Swiss border, but be careful. I'll catch up with you if I'm not back tonight. Take the food out of my pack, in case I can't pick it up and have to detour."

"I'm going with you!" she exclaimed. "We're safer together."

"No, we're not, and if it's the Nazis, you know they'll kill me, but you, well, you know what will happen to you. Please, for me, stay here." Anna knew what he meant. She wasn't happy letting him go without her, but she trusted him. Peter leaned down, quickly kissed her, and she scrunched back into the brush. Peter made sure she couldn't be seen, and then headed off in the direction of the tanks.

Peter's legs were tired, as he had been moving at a high speed to find their location and confirm who it was. It had been almost two hours when the rumbling came up loud, behind him.

Peter felt panic rise through him. There wasn't much to hide in where he could see what was going on. Peter jumped up and grabbed a tree limb of a huge fir tree, working himself high into the limbs. The best surveillance would be from the trees, and the fir branches could give him some cover, at least he hoped. He climbed until he was almost to the top, sure he wouldn't be seen.

The rumbling continued and drew even closer. They had to be almost on top of him, but so far, he couldn't see anything. Peter waited and drew up his binoculars.

Off in the distance were at least twenty German tanks, along with over a hundred infantrymen. They were heading the same direction Peter and Anna were, but if they kept at the same course, they'd miss them by under a mile. Peter breathed a sigh of relief, knowing they'd miss Anna. The tanks were now almost right under Peter, and he could see the faces of the soldiers as they marched through the brush. He didn't dare leave now or he'd be caught.

Out of nowhere, multiple blasts landed in the middle of the tank formation, sending men and tank parts flying into the air. The infantrymen ran for cover, and Peter was thankful it was not in his direction. The blasting continued, exploding craters of dirt skyward. The explosions were so intense that dirt and rocks and body parts flew up toward Peter. He was holding on for his life.

Where the bombing was coming from was unclear, but it had to be from the Allied Forces. The tanks started to scatter, but most were unlucky and sat idle, burning in place. Soldiers inside the tanks were burned alive.

The bombing continued as Nazi soldiers retreated, leaving the injured behind. The tanks that were still functional also retreated, but less than half were left.

Dogs! Thought Peter. *Leaving the wounded behind.*

Finally, the bombing stopped, but he still couldn't tell where it had come from. Peter scurried down the tree in a rush to get back to Anna.

He hadn't run more than fifty yards when, out of the brush, staggered a young soldier, reaching for Peter. He was covered in blood from head to toe, his uniform hanging in tattered shreds.

"Help me, please," he gasped. Blood gurgled from his mouth, making a steady stream onto his uniform.

Peter grabbed him as the man slumped to the ground. He lay there looking into Peter's eyes. Peter hated the Nazis, but he was still a human being with a family, and Peter knew the soldier was minutes from dying. Gripping the soldier's hand, Peter smiled down at him.

"What's your name?"

"Hans," the soldier whispered. He was choking on his own blood. Peter propped him up against a tree to keep the blood from pooling in his throat.

"My wife, please, my wife's picture." He raised the bloody stump that was once his hand to reach into his uniform, unaware his hand was missing. He was in shock, and Peter actually felt sorry for him.

"Let me help you," said Peter, gently pulling what was left of his uniform open.

Reaching into the inside pocket, he pulled out a few photos. One was of a man and woman who were older, probably his parents, thought Peter. The second one was of a young woman, in a beautiful dress trimmed in lace, wearing a huge smile. No matter their differences, in some ways, he and Peter were a lot alike. They both had women they loved and would die for. Peter held the picture up so the man could see his wife, and a smile spread across the soldier's face.

"Liesl," he whispered. "You're so beautiful Liesl. I didn't want to do this. I'm so sorry." His eyes stared at the picture, tears slipping down the corners of his eyes.

"My son?" he asked. Where's my son?" There was one photo left, and Peter held it up in front of the soldier. A young boy of about two was sitting on a blanket, obviously at a picnic, probably the last one the man's family had together.

"Wilhelm, my sweet boy." Tears continued to stream from the young soldier's eyes. Peter held up all three pictures together, so the dying man could see his family.

"Thank you," the soldier whispered. His last words were, thank you, to a man who hated the Nazis.

Tears filled Peter's eyes. He knew what it was like to love someone and know you'd never see them again. Peter knew many soldiers had no choice in joining the army. He set the pictures back into the soldier's inner breast pocket for safekeeping.

"God be with you, Hans," said Peter as he got up and headed back toward Anna.

Blood soaked his jacket, but there was nothing he could do about it now. Peter would have to find a creek to wash his jacket off before they tried to meet up with the Americans or British. A bloody coat wouldn't look good.

The humming got louder and louder as Peter made his way back to Anna. The planes came in so low you could see the faces of the pilots. They dropped bomb after bomb at the tanks that were retreating. Machine gun fire blasted continually, making Peter shudder at the thought of all that coming at those soldiers at once. He hoped Anna and he were close to the Allies.

It had been a couple hours when Peter softly called out Anna's name. Popping out of the brush, Anna stumbled forward, grabbing him, crying. "I heard the bombings. I was afraid you wouldn't come back!" Anna was sobbing uncontrollably now, her hands over her face.

"Anna, I'm here. I'm here now. Everything is okay." Peter hugged her tight, pulling her hands away from her tear stained face. Her eyes were swollen from crying, and Peter wiped her tears with his thumbs. He held her tight until her sobbing finally subsided.

"We're okay," he whispered into her ear, "but we need to go. Okay?" Anna just nodded.

Peter pulled their packs from the bushes, helping Anna with hers. He took her hand, pulling her next to him, and they headed in the direction he thought they would most likely find the friendlies.

****

CHAPTER THIRTY SEVEN

It had been three days, and Peter thought they would have run into the Americans or British by now. He wasn't sure how they'd treat him, probably as a prisoner of war, but at least Anna would be safe. They had kept close to the bushes, in case they needed to hide quickly, but out of nowhere, a bullet whizzed through the air, and Peter's body suddenly fell backwards. Shock registered on his face.

"Peter! Peter!" screamed Anna. "No! Peter!" Peter lay on the ground, groaning. Anna dropped to the ground and pulled Peter's head up. "Look at me! Peter!"

Anna was hysterical, screaming for help. She pulled his jacket back to see a hole spurting blood. Quickly, she pulled off her scarf and pressed it into his wound, but it was soaked in minutes.

"Anna, Anna," mumbled Peter. His body went limp, his clothes soaked with blood. Anna shrieked his name over and over again.

Out of nowhere, a half dozen American soldiers appeared, guns drawn.

"Get your hands up! Now!" yelled the sergeant. "Now!"

"You killed him!" shrieked Anna as she got up and ran at the soldier. One of the others grabbed her, accidentally pulling off her hat, her long hair tumbling down over her shoulders.

"Sir! She's a girl!" The soldier spun around and slowly lowered his weapon.

"You killed him! He's not a Nazi! He saved me from them! You murderer!"

The soldier kept holding onto Anna, not sure what she was saying, or capable of. He didn't speak German, and neither did anyone else. The others knelt beside Peter, the sergeant examining the wound. Pulling sulfur packs and bandages from his kit, he tried to fix Peter as best he could. He knew there was no hope, but he'd try. Soldiers grabbed him by his coat and legs, lifting him off the ground.

"We'll take him back to headquarters," said the sergeant. "The doctors will take it from there, if it's possible."

The soldier holding on to Anna gripped her arm and led her behind those carrying Peter. She already knew he was gone. She didn't want to live anymore. Was anyone she loved still alive? Peter had tried to save her, and it had cost him his life, and it wasn't even Hitler who did it. Anna sobbed, putting one foot in front of the other. She had nowhere to go, and no choice but to follow the Americans.

A mile and a half later, the soldiers arrived at camp, green tents everywhere. The place was swarming with American soldiers, and some she thought were British. Some insignias she didn't recognize. She hated them all. They were supposed to be the heroes, not murderers.

The four soldiers carrying Peter delivered him to the hospital tent, expecting the worst outcome. A doctor came over, looked him over, took his pulse, and slowly shook his head.

"Bring him in," he said. "There's little hope, but we'll give it a try."

The medical staff cut off Peter's clothes, leaving him naked on the table. Peter's vitals said he was dead, but the doctor started to pump his chest. A nurse started an IV, hanging a bag of blood for transfusion alongside a saline bag. His heartbeat was erratic, but it was there. The doctor gave Peter a shot of adrenaline and kept talking to him.

"Come on, boy, come on, you can do this! It's not your time!"

Peter was still bleeding profusely, but his heart started beating, catching a regular rhythm. *Beat, beat, beat, beat.* The doctor opened Peter's wound and dug the bullet out, stopped the bleeding, and then sewed his wound closed. Peter lay on the table, unconscious, but at least his heart was beating.

Anna sat at a table in the mess tent, a Red Cross nurse offering her coffee and a sandwich. Anna just stared into space; she felt numb. She had no realization that the nurse was even there. Anna sat there for hours as guards stood close by, but she didn't see them. She no longer cared. Night was falling, a million stars lighting the sky, and still, Anna hadn't moved.

"Excuse me, miss," a young soldier said and touched her shoulder lightly. Anna looked up but didn't say anything. "Are you the young lady that came in with the young man who was shot?"

"Yes." Anna nodded. He spoke broken German, but she understood what he was trying to say.

"He's awake and keeps calling for Anna. He's very weak, but he's awake." The young soldier was using his hands, hoping Anna would understand him, despite how little German he knew.

"What? I, I thought he was dead!" Anna's head was spinning. Was this just a bad dream and she'd wake up and he'd still be dead?

"Well, he tried to die, but the doctor wouldn't give up. Brought him back, actually. He's one lucky guy." He was fairly sure she hadn't comprehended what he said but he motioned to the hospital tent to help Anna understand.

All Anna could do was nod. She followed the soldier into a huge green tent full of cots. The injured lay row upon row, nurses scurrying back and forth between patients. At the very end, there lay Peter. His eyes were closed, and he looked ashen, but his chest was rising and falling, telling Anna he was alive. A soldier stood just feet away from his bed, guarding him.

The soldier pulled a chair up for Anna, and she sat down and gently touched Peter's hand. He opened his eyes and smiled, his eyes slowly closing again.

Anna cried, gently rubbing the back of Peter's hand with her thumb.

"Peter, I thought you were gone," she sobbed uncontrollably. Don't ever do that to me again!" Her voice became angry, as she started sobbing again.

"I'm sorry," he whispered. Anna looked up at him, tears spilling down her cheeks.

"I'm sorry," he said again, and he smiled a weak smile.

"Miss, we need to let him sleep. It's going to be a long recovery, and he's still not out of the woods," the soldier said, gently putting his hand on her shoulder. "You can see him tomorrow. We need to fill out some papers on what happened, so if you could follow me to command, I'd appreciate it."

The young soldier was doing his best with the little German he knew, but Anna just looked at him confused. He finally pointed at Peter, and then folded his hands together, laying his head on his hands for a sleeping motion. Anna realized what he was trying to say, nodded, and got up from the chair. Her legs were like rubber, and the soldier grabbed her under her arm, giving her some support.

"Danke," said Anna. The soldier just nodded.

Anna now sat in a chair with what had to be an official who was of much higher rank than the gentleman who brought her in. She sat there, waiting for him to speak. He had an interpreter, which made it easier to communicate, but Anna was still hesitant of the Americans, considering what happened to Peter.

The interpreter introduced her to Major Dixon, letting her know he would be requesting information and he would be their go-between in regard to language only.

"My apologies, miss, on your," the lieutenant hesitated, "your husband?"

Anna sat stoic, not saying a word. He could think what he wanted.

"We had intel that German soldiers were throughout that area, and your husband was mistaken for one before we noticed he wasn't wearing a uniform. The doctor thinks he has a good chance of making it. I need to fill out records, though, so why don't we start with your names?"

Anna began to panic. When would things get easy?

"Peter and Anna Reinhold," she blurted out.

"Okay, then. He nodded, taking the information from the interpreter. "And children?"

Anna, looked down, fidgeting with her hands. Red crept up her cheeks, thinking of her and Peter in that way.

"No," she finally said.

"Nationality, miss?'

"Jewish."

"Oh!" Surprise registered on Major Dixon's face. Anna didn't say a word. He'd have to dig if he wanted information. "I have to say, neither of you look Jewish. Do you have papers?"

"No," replied Anna. "I'm Jewish, and my husband is German, but he helped the Jews. He hates the Nazis. We had to run, and papers were the last thing we cared about."

"I see. Was he in the Army?"

"No!" Anna shouted. "He'd never join Hitler! He hates them! He saved my life. He and his father helped feed me and my family when everyone wanted us dead!"

"I don't mean to anger you, Mrs. Reinhold, but I'm required to ask these questions. I mean no disrespect."

Anna nodded but stayed silent. She was no longer sure if they should be considered friendly or the enemy.

"Occupation?" asked the lieutenant.

"My husband is a baker. He and his father owned a bakery, until his father died, and he wouldn't work with the German Army. I'm a homemaker." Anna didn't consider herself a homemaker, a survivalist was more like it, but she would try and give them the answer they wanted so she could keep herself and Peter safe.

"Your parents are Jewish? Do you know where they are, what's happened to them? Again, I'm sorry I have to ask, but we want to try to unite loved ones as much as possible. I understand this can be an emotional question." The lieutenant showed genuine concern, and you could tell he didn't enjoy this part of his job.

Anna folded her hands in her lap, staring at them. She felt hollow, drained of emotions that she wished she still had, but she had nothing left to give.

"I don't know," she said. "My father, Joseph Feiner, was a jeweler, and my mother helped him in the store. Her name was Miriam Feiner. I think my mother passed away after I escaped from the ghetto, and I don't know about my father. I have no one left but my husband."

Anna hoped they didn't find out that Peter and she weren't married, but she didn't want to be pulled apart again. She couldn't bear to be without him, he was all she had left. Besides, it was none of their business.

"We're compiling information on all internment prisoners, and those who have been liberated from the camps. We're overtaking the German army and finding more camps every day. We try to provide updated information promptly, so families can be reunited quickly. We post the revised list daily on a post outside the hospital area. Perhaps you should check it out tomorrow." The lieutenant cleared his throat, and you could tell he was uncomfortable. He knew most looking for their loved ones would find them under the deceased listing.

"You must be tired. I'll have one of the nurses find you a suitable place to sleep, and you can see your husband in the morning. I have more paperwork, but I think you've had enough for one day."

Major Dixon smiled at Anna, got up from his chair, and had his aide request a nurse to help her with sleeping quarters. Anna got up and turned to the officer, quietly thanking him. The aide held the tent flap back for her and introduced her to one of the nurses who was taking over. Anna was glad. She was spent. The nurse took Anna to a tent with a cot and two wool blankets on it, and best of all, a nice soft pillow. A small table held a hot cup of tea and a sandwich.

In perfect German, the nurse addressed Anna. "I thought you may be a bit hungry, so I had an orderly bring you something. I took the liberty of tea instead of coffee, but we can always change it."

The nurse was probably in her mid-twenties, and Anna could tell she cared what happened to her by the warm smile and tone she used when she spoke to her.

Anna smiled back. "Danke, a cup of tea sounds wonderful." Anna sat down on the cot and lifted the teacup to her lips. Closing her eyes, she could almost imagine Mama was there with her, having tea in the afternoon, just like they had done so many times.

Anna must have fallen asleep because the nurse that had been so kind last night was gently shaking her awake. Someone had pulled the covers over her during the night. Anna shook her head, trying to come out of the daze she was in. She sat up and focused. It was morning and she was in the American camp.

"Peter!" exclaimed Anna. "I need to see Peter!"

The nurse who spoke perfect German, had slept in the one chair that was in the tent. She must have been there all night.

"Peter!" exclaimed Anna again.

It's okay, miss. He's doing pretty well this morning. He's in and out of consciousness, but that's to be expected."

"I want to see him, now!" pleaded Anna. "Please, take me to him."

"Of course, but why don't you freshen up a bit, and then we can head over. I brought you in a few things you might find useful. You have a beautiful face but I'm sure you want to wash up a bit and look your best for him."

The teacup and plate had been replaced with a pitcher of water, a brush, a mirror, and a toothbrush. Anna's surprise showed on her face, and a slight smile spread across her lips. She turned to the nurse, and without thinking, hugged her.

"Danke, danke!" she exclaimed and smiled.

The nurse laughed, saying, "It doesn't take much to make us women happy, especially out here."

Taking both of Anna's hands in her own, she smiled. "Take your time. Peter will be waiting. He can't go anywhere."

The clean water and washcloth felt good on Anna's face. She scrubbed it a couple times, until her cheeks were a rosy pink. Her hair needed a good wash, but just getting to brush it out felt luxurious.

The final act was brushing her teeth. Somewhere along the way, she had lost her toothbrush. For weeks she had been using water and her finger. She scrubbed her teeth, squeezing on a generous amount of toothpaste. She felt refreshed and anxious to see Peter.

The hospital was filled with injured soldiers, some with missing legs or arms, bandaged heads, and other bloody injuries. Anna slowly made her way to Peter's cot. He lay there, asleep, a blanket pulled up over him. She found a chair and sat next to him, hoping he would wake up and know she was there.

She was told he hadn't talked to anyone except the few words he said to her last night, and Anna was relieved. She needed to tell Peter she had become his wife, even though he hadn't popped the question yet. She knew it was presumptuous, but she had her reasons.

Peter lay on the cot, his eyes closed. He looked peaceful. Anna pulled up a chair next to his bed and slipped her hand into his. He had more color in his face today, and Anna felt relief. It had to be a good sign.

More than three hours had gone by, and still, Anna sat. She planned on sitting there all day until he woke up. Thankfully, Peter soon opened his eyes, and the first person he saw was the woman he loved. Anna smiled, bent over, and kissed him on the forehead.

Peter's heart surged. Anna's lips were soft and warm, just like he remembered. "I love you," whispered Peter. His throat was sore, and he sounded gruff, but to Anna, it was the sweetest sound she'd ever heard.

"I love you, too," she murmured. "I love you, so much."

Peter's eyes became heavy, and Anna knew she better fess up now, and hopefully he'd remember everything she was going to tell him.

"Peter, I need to tell you something." Peter focused on Anna, but he was fighting to stay awake, as the doctor was keeping him heavily sedated. "We're married, Peter." There, it was out. "The lieutenant thought we were married, and I let him believe it. I didn't say anything because I don't want them to separate us." Despite the chill in the air, she was sweating profusely. "I can correct the lieutenant, but I was afraid of what they'd do if they didn't think we were together. I'm, I'm so…"

Peter interrupted her before she could finish. "I love you, Mrs. Reinhold. "He smiled big, his dimples sinking into his cheeks. His eyes were getting so heavy, but before he drifted off, Anna heard him ask, "When's the honeymoon?" Peter was now deep in sleep and he couldn't see that Anna was blushing. She wanted a honeymoon, she wanted to be his wife.

"Mrs. Reinhold?" The nurse who had been so kind to Anna was talking to her. "Would you like to get some breakfast, Mrs. Reinhold? Also, the lieutenant told me you may want to check the, um, the concentration camp list," she said with hesitation. "He mentioned you may be looking for your parents." You could see the concern in the nurse's eyes, and Anna felt she was someone who could be a friend.

"Please, call me Anna. I suppose I should check the list, but I don't think I'm ready for that."

"I understand, and you can call me Helen, Helen Schamber. Why don't we just start off with breakfast?"

"That sounds good," Anna agreed.

Helen took Anna over to the mess tent and they both got some breakfast. Anna picked at her plate, even though she was starving.

"Can I ask you a question, Helen? Do you know what will happen to me and Peter now?"

Helen couldn't help but feel sorry for her. Seeing Anna's uncertainty and pain in her face, made her feel even worse.

"I don't know, Anna. The best person to ask would be Major Dixon." Helen reached over, placing her hands on Anna's in sympathy, wishing she had answers for her. "Ask the major. I'm sure he can answer your questions."

"Danke. I'm just curious, how is it you know German?"

Helen laughed. "My grandmother was born in Germany, but came to the United States when she was a young girl. They spoke German in their house, and their town consisted of mainly Germans who had migrated. They all like to stick with their own kind. My mother always spoke German to her, and I guess through osmosis, and if I wanted to communicate with my grandmother, I had to speak her language. And, here I am in Germany, speaking to you. Tell me about you, Anna. What's your story?"

Anna folded her hands in her lap, studying them. Finally, she told Helen about how she and her parents made a hiding place, how she had escaped the ghetto by pretending she was dead, and how Peter had saved her life. When she finished, Helen got up and wrapped her arms around her.

"I'm sorry, Anna."

Anna looked up at her and shrugged. "Life doesn't always turn out the way you think it will. Can you tell me, is English hard to learn?"

"Well, I guess it depends on the person and how bad you want to learn it. Do you want me to teach you some?"

"Yes." She nodded enthusiastically. "I would really appreciate it. I think someday, Peter and I would like to go to America. I know it may take a long time and be more difficult for Peter, but he hated the Nazis, and he saved me and tried to save others."

Helen patted her arm, "God works it all out, Anna. You've made it this far, so I'm sure he has plans for you and Peter. Now, for your first English lesson: the word 'Danke' is 'thank you' in English. Now you say it."

Anna smiled. "Thank you, Helen"

"Very good! I think you'll be a fast learner! How about ten new words a day? Try 'guten morgen' which, in English, is 'good morning'. It's very similar."

Anna sat up tall in the chair as if she were attending grade school and decisively pronounced, "Good morning."

"Excellent," Helen smiled. "Here's another one: 'hallo' is 'hello'. Try 'guten abend,' which is 'good evening.' And the last one for now, Anna, is 'liebe' which is 'love' in English. Try that one on Peter," she chuckled. "If you want to tell him you love him, you say, 'I love you.'"

Anna smiled a huge smile. Just thinking of Peter made her happy. She had a hard time believing she had ever thought of him as a brother.

A week had passed with Anna constantly at Peter's side. Helen continued to check in on both of them and make sure Anna was taking care of herself. They had quickly become good friends. It was common for Helen to have some of her meals with

Anna, and during them, she would teach her new English words and phrases. When they were together, Helen would point at objects, say their English name, and make Anna repeat it.

During their second week in the American camp, Anna finally found the courage to check the list of surviving and dead prisoners from the concentration camps. The list was long, and it took some time, but the last name revealed nothing. She wasn't sure how she felt about it.

Peter was getting better and was sitting up in bed for parts of the day. His favorite part of the day was when Anna came to visit. She was teaching him the English that Helen was teaching her. They both realized they needed to acclimate to the Americans. Peter always tried to say 'please' and 'thank you' in English, which pleased the medical staff.

Sergeant, Robert Mares, who had shot him, came in to check on him frequently. He had been given the details how Anna had escaped the ghetto and survived living in a wood berm and how Peter had saved her from being shot by a Nazi officer. He felt bad he had shot Peter, but he couldn't undo it. He was just trying to be helpful now. He knew Peter wanted to learn English, so he would drop in when he was off duty and play cards, which seemed to be universal, and teach him some English.

Anna was getting bored with the same routine, except for seeing Peter. Helen advised her that they needed help in the hospital and if Major Dixon authorized it, she could volunteer.

"Can you go with me to ask?" she pleaded with Helen. "If you're with me, I have a better chance of him saying yes."

Tucking her arm around Anna's shoulders, she gave her a squeeze, "Of course I will. Let's go!"

The major's aide knocked on Major Dixon's door and entered. "Sir, nurse Schamber and Mrs. Reinhold would like a moment with you." Dixon looked up, wondering why they would want to meet with him. The aide shrugged, indicating he didn't know.

"See them in," Dixon said, gesturing to let them enter his office.

Anna was a nervous wreck, but Helen was completely calm and collected.

"What can I do for you, ladies?" questioned Dixon, leaning back in his chair.

Helen couldn't help but notice how smokey his office was. A lit cigarette resting in an ashtray lay burning, the ashes a good inch long, but it hadn't been smoked. All the men smoked, and a lot of the women nurses. Helen hated the smell but elected to keep her thoughts to herself for the moment. It was not the time, and he was her superior.

"Sir, we're short-handed in the hospital, and Mrs. Reinhold has selflessly volunteered. She'd like to be useful while Mr. Reinhold is recovering. With your permission, I'd like to put her to work, sir."

Both the women stood very solemn, waiting for the major to respond. He mulled it over and finally nodded his head.

"That would be fine for the time being, but I can't guarantee things won't change. We could be ordered to pull up and move at any time."

"I understand, sir. I'll definitely make sure that she understands the situation. Thank you."

Recognizing the word thank you, Anna nodded, smiling at Major Dixon and quickly said "Thank you."

"I have a lot of work, ladies. Is there anything else?"

"No, thank you, sir." Helen nodded and touched Anna's arm, letting her know they were leaving. Once they were outside, Helen broke out into German, letting her know she was authorized to volunteer.

"I have to tell you, though," she said seriously, "he said the regiment could be ordered to pick up and move, and he couldn't say what would happen then."

Anna tried not to let the anxiety she felt show at hearing they could pick up and move. What would happen to her and Peter? At least for now, though, she had something to do, and it allowed her to see more of Peter and endear her to the Americans. If the Americans uprooted, maybe being in their good graces would help her and Peter.

Anna was worried, but excited, and rushed to tell Peter. She found him sitting on the edge of his cot playing cards with the soldier who had shot him, Sergeant Robert Mares. Peter had told her to forgive him as Robert and he were now friends. He also told her to look at it as a Godsend that they had been found and were now being taken care of. She was working on it, but she was still a bit cool toward this particular soldier.

Seeing her come in, Robert excused himself, giving Peter a warm smile and a pat on the shoulder. He didn't blame Anna for being cold toward him, and he tried to be respectful of her feelings.

"Anna, my beautiful wife." He chuckled. Anna still blushed whenever he said that. Peter grabbed her arm, pulling her down onto his cot. Gently, he leaned over and kissed her. She wasn't used to public affection, and she blushed scarlet red.

"I have some good news," she said. "I've been authorized to help out here in the hospital. I can be useful, and they'll see they need us!"

"Wonderful." Peter smiled. Anna pulled back and looked at him. She had no idea what he had just said. It was obvious Robert was teaching him English too. Peter laughed, telling her in German what it meant.

Anna wasn't sure if she was jealous of Robert teaching him more English, or that Peter knew more new words than she did. *I need to let it go,* she thought.

She chuckled lightly with him, not wanting him to see her jealousy.

"So, what other new words have you learned?" she asked, leaning into him.

****

CHAPTER THIRTY EIGHT

It had been a couple of months, and both Peter and Anna had become part of the American Army's community. A few of the soldiers didn't like how well Peter was treated, but most did, realizing he felt like they did toward Hitler. Not every German was a bad one, and some had been trying to survive under Hitler's control.

Peter was healing well and would join Anna in the mess tent for meals most of the time. He was going nuts living in the hospital tent. You could only play so much poker.

Anna and Peter sat next to each other, eating lunch, when a huge commotion came from the cooks' area. You could hear metal pans hitting the floor and profanity coming from the kitchen.

Peter recognized that sound and along with everyone else, got up and went to see what was happening.

A cook stood in the middle of a pile of pans, dough and food cluttering the floor. He was covered in flour and looked like he was going to go berserk. Most everyone started laughing, but not Peter.

"It's okay," he said in English. "I've been there." Then he started picking up the pans, throwing the unbaked rolls and bread into the garbage. Anna pushed through the crowd and started to help. The rest of the crowd, embarrassed for cheering at the young cook's misfortune, stepped in to help, and some, red faced, quickly took their exit.

Peter smiled at the cook the whole time, patting him on the back, and just kept cleaning up. When everything was finally picked up, the cook held out his hand to Peter. Peter took it and shook the man's hand, smiling his understanding of what it was like to be so frustrated.

"It won't do you good to strain yourself," said Anna. "You need to lay down and rest." Reluctantly Peter agreed, but he was tired of his boring routine. It didn't take him long to succumb to slumber once his head hit his pillow.

The next morning, Anna came to get Peter for breakfast, but his bed was empty. She felt the panic rise in her chest. Where was he? Did they ship Peter off somewhere or worse, did he die? Surely, they would have said something to her!

Robert passed Anna standing outside the hospital tent, fear written on her face.

"Mrs. Reinhold, are you okay?" He knew Anna didn't like him, but he felt responsible for both her and Peter.

"No!" exclaimed Anna. "Peter's gone!" Robert was relieved she spoke in English. Otherwise he didn't know what he'd do, since he still did not understand a word of German.

"No, no," said Robert, touching Anna's arm. "Come." He was smiling, leading her off to the mess tent.

Once inside, Robert took her back to the kitchen, where she could see Peter, in a white apron covered in flour, making rolls. Peter turned to see Anna standing there, as she burst into tears. She broke into a tirade of German, giving Peter a not-so-nice piece of her mind in between sobs.

Peter tried to only speak English when he was around the Americans, but this was not the moment. He wrapped his flour covered arms around her, gently whispering in her ear that everything was okay.

"I was bored and decided to help the cooks since I know how to bake. I need to give back, and I can't keep sitting in bed. I'm sorry, Anna," he said, lifting her chin up to look into her eyes. "I'm sorry. I should have told you, but I thought I'd be back before you came to get me. I won't let it happen again. I'm sorry." He hugged her hard, leaving a dusting of flour over her clothes and her chin.

She understood his need to give back. Their circumstances were rare, and they needed the American Army to know they appreciated letting them be there. Still, she made it clear that he should say something to her next time, instead of scaring her to death.

Anna no longer picked Peter up for breakfast, but would meet him at the mess tent, where he'd take a break from baking. He still had to take it easy, but working was giving him his strength and confidence back. None of the cooks were actual bakers, so the increase in the quality of rolls and bread could be tasted by all. It was now common for those coming in for breakfast to find Danish waiting for them. At dinnertime, everyone grabbed the rolls first, before they were gone.

****

CHAPTER THIRTY NINE

Peter and Anna knew they would always remember this day. They were sitting in the mess tent having lunch together, when a soldier burst into the tent and excitedly announced that Hitler was dead! He was talking so fast in English it took them a minute to digest the information, but once realization hit, Peter picked Anna up, swirling her around in his excitement. Stopping, he looked at Anna, and they both started crying and laughing with joy that Hitler was finally dead, where he belonged.

Hitler had committed suicide after realizing that Germany was losing the war and it was only a matter of days before he would be captured.

Two weeks later, May 8th, 1945, the war in Europe ended. Celebrations could be heard all over the camp for days. Peter and Anna were unsure what would happen to them now, but at least they knew Hitler had lost and they no longer needed to run. Most everyone considered them friends now, and they could only hope they'd be allowed to stay with the Americans. They were determined to only speak English unless it was just the two of them. They were getting rather good at it.

A few days later, Peter was given the good news he'd be officially taken off the wounded list and dismissed from the hospital. Colonel Williams should be sending Peter to an internment camp, but he couldn't do it. Peter was relieved when he was told he could stay and help in the mess tent. Everyone would have missed his baking.

He knew he would be discharged, but now what? Everyone expected him and Anna to be together. Peter wanted that too, but they weren't actually married, and he knew it would be hard to keep his desire in check if they shared Anna's sleeping quarters. No, they needed to be married. Peter started hatching a plan.

"Excuse me, sir," said Peter. The chaplain turned around from cleaning his makeshift altar to see Peter standing there.

"Peter, our wonderful roll and sweets maker." He chuckled. "What can I do for you?"

In broken English, Peter proceeded to tell the chaplain what he wanted to do. "I feel like Anna and I are starting a new life, and I'd like to renew our vows with all our friends here. I'll be moving into her tent tomorrow, and I'd like it to be special. We've been through a lot, not that all of you haven't too, being away from loved ones and losing family and friends." He hesitated, knowing his situation was no needier than anyone else. "I'd like to have what you Americans say, a redo?"

The chaplain laughed at the "redo," but nodded his head in understanding. "You mean you want to renew your vows. I think I can accommodate that, Peter. In fact, I think this camp could use another reason to celebrate. Let's have a "*redo* wedding!" He slapped Peter on the back.

Peter could feel relief slip over him. He hated deceiving the chaplain, but he couldn't take the chance in telling the truth. He wanted to be officially married before he joined Anna in "their" tent.

"Let's get planning," said the chaplain. A camp wedding would take place tomorrow. Of course, no one knew that this was a real wedding, Peter would keep that to himself. He knew that to make it official, he'd have to have permission from Colonel Williams, and he'd say it was outside the official rules for the U.S. Army.

Peter didn't care about official rules, and he hoped Anna didn't either. What mattered was in the eyes of God and what was in their hearts.

Peter and the chaplain let a few people in on their secret, Helen, Robert, Major Dixon, Colonel Williams, and of course, his fellow cooks.

****

CHAPTER FORTY

J acob searched for Anna, determined to follow through with the promise he had made to Joseph. He was going to find her, and give her the last piece of jewelry Joseph's hands had made. It belonged to Anna and no one else.

The allied forces were busy compiling lists of the survivors, and the dead, but many of those they searched for, lay in ash. It was going to take months, if not years, for the missing to be identified. Over six million Jews had been exterminated, piled like logs, in mass graves. The only consolation Joseph and Simon had was, Joseph had not ended up in a nameless grave.

Prisoners who had managed to save themselves from the gas chambers, died in their bunks, the skeletal living, still sleeping beside them. The lists of the dead and living failed to acknowledge everyone. Jacob moved from one DP camp to another, praying he'd see Anna listed with the living.

For weeks, Jacob felt discouraged. His fingers slowly moved down the new list, focusing on each name, one after another. The list was long, but there it was, Anna Feiner. He blinked over and over, clearing his eyes, to make sure her name was really there, listed as alive, at an American Army hospital. His mind reeled. Hospital? Did it mean she was wounded?

Filled with urgency, Jacob packed what little he had in a small canvas bag and headed on foot to find her. Jacobs adrenaline spurred his frail body forward. Hitch hiking across Germany, he was lucky enough to get multiple rides from American and British G.I.'s. A week later, Jacob walked into the hospital camp.

"Excuse me," said Jacob.

The soldier eyed Jacob, taking in his thin frame, clothes hanging on his bones.

"Mess tent?" asked the soldier, motioning his hands as if eating. He didn't speak German. But figured from the look of the man, he must be hungry.

"Nein, no," said Jacob, shaking his head. Jacob felt frustrated, realizing the soldier didn't speak German.

The soldier was frustrated as well, not knowing what the man wanted.

"Anna Feiner," said Jacob.

The soldier raised his eyes brows in surprise.

"Anna Feiner?" Jacob questioned again.

Everyone in camp was protective of Anna and Peter. The soldier nodded, still leery of Jacob's intentions. Motioning him to follow, the young soldier led him to Sergeant Robert Mares.

"Sir, this man is asking for, Anna Feiner."

Robert looked Jacob up and down, wondering what he could want with Anna.

"Father?" asked Robert.

Jacob didn't know English, but some German words were familiar.

"Nein."

"Soldier, get me someone who speaks German," ordered Robert.

The young man ran off to find someone to interpret. It was only a few minutes later when Helen approached.

Helen stared Jacob up and down, doubtful she'd let this man near Anna. "What do you want with Anna?" asked Helen, in German.

Jacob exclaimed he was a good friend of Anna's father, and of his promise to find Joseph's daughter.

Helen's shoulders drooped in disappointment. Anna's father was dead. She didn't want her to find out from this stranger. Excusing herself, yet assuring Jacob she'd be back, Helen went in search of Anna.

Stepping into the hospital tent, Helen found Anna caring for a wounded soldier. From the look on Helen's face, Anna knew something was wrong.

"Peter?" questioned Anna.

Motioning for her to sit down next to her, Helen pulled Anna's hands into hers. "A man showed up asking for you, he says he's a friend of your father's."

"Is my father with him?" she asked hesitantly. Her eyes met Helen's. She knew what the answer was going to be, from the sorrow in Helen's eyes.

"No," Helen hesitated. "I'm sorry, but your father died in one of the concentration camps."

"No!" she screamed. Anna burst into tears, her body shaking with convulsions. Helen wrapped her arms around her shoulders, knowing no words could make Anna feel better.

A good fifteen minutes later, Anna wiped her tears and sat up straight. "I want to see this man," she said.

"Of course, I'll take you to him."

Making their way to the mess tent, Anna stepped inside, to find a man with sunken eyes, drowning in his oversized clothes.

Jacob stood up, bowing slightly, not knowing how to greet her.

"You knew my father?"

"Yes, said Jacob, almost in a whisper.

Anna motioned for him to please sit, pulling a chair up beside him. "My father?"

Jacob told Anna everything, answering all the questions that brought nothing, but sadness. Finally, pulling a piece of fabric from his pants pocket, he unfolded it, to reveal the blue sapphire pendant, that Joseph had made.

"Your father saved me and Simon from sure death. I'd give anything for him to be here instead of me. I promised him, I'd find you."

Anna's eyes filled with tears, spilling onto the beautiful sapphire and diamond pendant, making it glisten even more. A piece of her father. The last piece of work that his loving hands had touched. She hugged it to her chest, her other hand grasping Jacobs hand.

"Danke. You're a good man. Bless you for keeping your promise to find me."

Jacob's eyes filled with tears. "His last words were of you and your mother," Jacob choked out.

Anna smiled at him, tears still spilling down her cheeks. Somewhere from deep inside, she had known her father wouldn't make it, still, he had managed to bless her with his friend finding her.

Anna excused herself, letting Jacob know that he'd be well taken care of and she'd see him later.

Despite the news from Jacob, Peter insisted the wedding plans continue. Helen and Robert had been given permission to drive to the closest town to find a suitable dress and flowers. Since the war was over, and they were in recovery mode, it was now safe to drive outside of their unit.

The cooks were concocting a small feast, while Peter was in charge of his own wedding cake. Anna had no idea what was going on behind her back. Tonight, she would officially be Mrs. Reinhold.

It was lunch time, and Anna headed to join Peter for a bite, like she did every day. Two of the nurses, Francis and Betty, were responsible for making sure Anna stayed in the hospital ward, and they grabbed her before she could leave. "A couple of us are feeling rather ill and need some extra help. Would you mind skipping lunch and helping out?" They feigned a bad stomach and even though Anna hesitated, she made sure they knew she was more than happy to stay and help.

"Just let me go tell Peter not to expect me for lunch," she said.

"Oh, we took the liberty of sending Sergeant Mares over to let him know, and to bring you back a bite to eat. We figured you'd be kind enough to stay." The two nurses exchanged glances, and relief covered their faces when Anna agreed to their plan.

Anna was sad she wouldn't be joining Peter, but she needed to help her friends who were always there for her. The staff kept her busy, but they hoped it wouldn't go beyond the planned time.

It was three o'clock. Helen and Robert had returned with not only a beautiful knee-length cream lace dress and a simple bouquet of flowers, but a pair of light brown dress shoes to top it off.

Seeing all that his friends had done for him, Peter choked up. He'd never had friends like them before. He was truly blessed. Before Peter could totally break down, Robert grabbed him and told him he was off to the showers.

In the meantime, Helen went off to find Anna and head her off to the showers too. When Helen walked into the hospital ward, the nurses sighed with relief they were no longer in charge of keeping her from Peter. Anna was happy to see Helen. Learning her father was dead had devastated her. She felt emotionally spent. Now, maybe she could be off duty and be able to see the one person she was dying to see. She thought Helen was there to take over.

"Oh, no!" exclaimed Helen. "I have orders from the major to handle a special project. Here, let me help you before I leave, though." Anna frowned but nodded okay. She couldn't blame Helen.

Determined to follow through with Peter's plan, Helen picked up a bedpan that had recently been the recipient of a patient's liquids, faked a trip, and landed the pan on Anna's legs. Anna was horrified and so were the other nurses. They had to applaud how far Helen would take getting Anna in for a fresh shower before her "wedding," but they couldn't have done it.

"Oh my gosh!" exclaimed Helen, pretending to be upset with herself. "Oh my! Off to the shower, Anna. I'm so sorry."

Still mortified with the thought of urine running down her legs, Anna headed off to the women's showers.

Helen turned to the other nurses as she escorted Anna out the door, shrugging her shoulders and saying, "You do what you have to do."

Freshly showered, Anna stepped out, wrapped in a towel. Helen was standing there, holding the beautiful dress, perfume, and flowers.

"What's going on?" Anna asked. "What's all this?"

Helen cocked her head, smiling. "Anna, you have the sweetest husband. With all you two have been through, he wants to renew your vows before he moves in with you. He spoke to the chaplain and he even made all the arrangements!"

Anna was shocked, and just stood there with her mouth open. Her mind reeled. Today was her wedding day, and she had just found out! She was really getting married! Now she was flustered and didn't know how to react or what to do.

"Here," said Helen, "let's get your hair done, and yes, I know all about your mother's hair clip. Here it is." Helen held up the clip that was adorned with rubies and diamonds. Pulling Anna over to the wood stove, she brushed Anna's hair out, drying it, and then twisting it up before setting the clip in place.

Next, she had Anna pull a slip up over her legs, setting the shoulder straps in place, then, she unbuttoned the back of the lace dress and Anna stepped into it.

"You're beautiful," Anna, you're just so beautiful." Helen added a tiny bit of blush on Anna's cheeks and a light lipstick. Then she grabbed Anna's hand and pulled her over to the long mirror in the women's bathroom.

Anna sucked in her breath. She couldn't believe that was her own image staring back at her. It had been years since she had dressed as a girl, except when she had gone to buy on the black market and had run into the German soldier, Franz.

She couldn't help but turn and look at every aspect of her body. Time had turned her from a teenager to a young woman. Her hand went to her hair, seeing Mama's comb gleaming from where it was nestled within the strands. Anna smiled, her eyes glistening with tears. What would Peter think? Helen dabbed perfume behind Anna's ears. Last, Helen pulled the pendant from her dress pocket, and fastened the chain around Anna's neck.

"Finished!" Proclaimed Helen

Peter had showered and was surprised to find a crisp white shirt and a chestnut brown suit ready for him to put on. Would his friends ever stop surprising him? He fastened his belt, but was too nervous to finish his tie.

Robert laughed. "Here, let me do that, Mr. Groom. You'd think you were getting married for the first time!"

Peter just laughed, thinking, *if you only knew*.

Finally, Robert and Peter went into the mess hall that had been transformed into a wedding hall. Some tables had disappeared, and the others were draped in white sheets. Two draped tables were set to the side, set with the silver metal food holders, waiting to be heaped for guests to eat. A small table set with a large bouquet of pink roses on it and a guest book for people to sign was arranged toward the front. White cutout paper stars hung back and forth across the ceiling, throughout the hall.

Peter was touched and surprised. On a draped table, off to the right, sat the three-tiered wedding cake he had made for his bride. He hoped she would like it. It had white cream frosting set with tiny pink variegated roses around the bottom of each tier, and light green leaves expanded from the roses. The top of the cake had various sizes of roses, in pink. Even though he didn't have his cake tools, he had managed.

The guests started arriving at six o'clock, many in their dress uniforms, congratulating Peter. Soon the hall was filled to the brim with those who had now become friends. Peter was becoming a mental wreck. Today he was going to marry Anna, the day he had only dreamed about, never imagining it would become his reality.

He was standing by the chaplain when a violin started playing softly. It was unexpected, and it touched Peter's soul. The crowd parted, and there, standing at the end of the hall, her hand wrapped on Colonel William's arm, stood Anna, making her way toward him. She was beautiful! Peter had never seen her so beautiful! She took his breath away.

Anna smiled up at him. She felt almost shy now. She was about to make a promise to be with Peter for the rest of her life, officially Mrs. Reinhold. Peter looked so handsome. She had only seen Peter in a suit one other time, and that was when he was a young boy at his mother's funeral.

A rush came over her, thinking today was the happiest day of her life. The thought that her parents weren't here to see this moment in her life made her momentarily sad, but she knew they would not want her to focus on that, only on the wonderful man in front of her. They had loved Peter. The colonel and Anna stood by Peter now, and the music stopped. Anna stood next to Peter, ready to cry, but this time out of joy.

The chaplain stepped up and started the ceremony. He couldn't help but think this was the best moment he had experienced during his stint in the army.

"We are gathered here today," the chaplain began, "to celebrate a love between two people that even war has not been able to pull apart. If anything, it has strengthened their resolve and love toward each other." He asked who gives this woman to marry, and Colonel Williams spoke up.

"I do, along with this whole army unit," he said, smiling. A huge cheer went up in the room.

Peter had snuck into Anna's tent earlier and retrieved her mother's wedding ring. He hoped it fit her. He had his father's ring. Peter had made the excuse to his friends that he hadn't been able to buy rings when they first married, but he felt compelled that they should honor their parents by wearing the one thing they had left of them, their rings.

Robert, his best man, held out the rings to the chaplain, who blessed them, and then handed Miriam's ring to Peter. Anna gasped, recognizing her mother's ring. It had been cleaned. and the huge diamond now sparkled.

The chaplain continued, and with the words "with this ring," Peter slipped it on her finger, seeking Anna's eyes, knowing what this ring meant to her. He hoped it meant even more to her now.

Anna slipped the gold band that had been his father's onto Peter's finger. The words, "I now pronounce you man and wife," hung in the air as Peter and Anna stared at each other, not believing they were actually married.

The chaplain reached over and touched Peter on the shoulder.

"I said, you may now kiss the bride." Everyone was laughing and started chanting, "Kiss the bride!"

Peter pulled Anna toward him, leaned in, and kissed her softly on the lips. Then he gently hugged her, whispering in her ear, "There'll be more of that tonight."

Anna blushed and whispered back "I'll be looking forward to it."

The crowd broke into cheers, and everyone came up to congratulate them. Food was brought out, and the real celebrating began. Someone had brought a record player, and music filled the room. They all made Peter and Anna have the first dance, and then Colonel Williams insisted he have one with Anna.

Some of the service men were Jewish and made sure some of Anna's Jewish traditions were included. They had enlisted others to help. Peter and Anna's chairs were hoisted into the air while they sat in them, while those who knew the words sang the traditional Jewish wedding song, "Hava Nagila," and everyone danced around them. Peter hadn't expected it, but he was happy that Anna's heritage had not been left out. Peter and Anna's wineglasses were wrapped in a napkin, which Peter placed on the floor, stomping on them, and shouted "Mazeltov!"

Finally, Peter guided Anna over to the wedding cake. She was in awe.

"It's beautiful!" she exclaimed. "It's just beautiful. Thank you. You made this, didn't you?" Peter nodded, a huge smile spreading across his face.

Someone had a camera and took pictures of the bride and groom throughout the night, during and after the ceremony, the first dance, cutting the cake and finally, when Anna and Peter felt it was time to make their exit. Everyone threw rice. As they left, Anna stopped to hug Jacob.

"Thank you, Jacob. You brought me answers to my questions. I can be happy, knowing my father had a good friend with him, before he died. Thank you."

The party continued, but Peter and Anna slipped off to their tent. Peter pulled the tent flaps back, picked

Anna up, and walked her across the threshold. Her arms clung around his neck, her head resting on his chest.

"I love you, Mr. Reinhold," said Anna. Peter's face beamed.

"I love you, Mrs. Reinhold, I always have."

Peter set Anna on her feet and they both looked in awe at the transformation that had taken place in their tent. A makeshift double bed had been made from wood with a heart shaped headboard from woven branches adorning it. A real mattress with crisp white sheets covered the bed, and magically, a real comforter was folded on the end of the bed.

A gas lantern hung from the middle of the tent and a cream heart homemade paper garland was draped from the middle of the tent to each corner. A small table sat next to the bed, set with a vase of flowers and white candles flickering their soft flame. A tin bucket sat next to the table filled with more water than ice, with a bottle of champagne to celebrate their honeymoon.

All Anna could say was, "Magical, it's magical." Peter ran his hand through his hair, not believing all this was for them.

Anna sat on the bed; Peter next to her as he popped the champagne. Neither had tasted it before. They had tasted wine, but never bubbly.

"To today, Mrs. Reinhold, and many more wonderful tomorrows together. I'm the happiest man there is right now, Anna," Peter toasted.

Their glasses clinked, and they toasted their future together, the fizzing tickling Anna's nose, making her laugh. Peter got up, blew out the lantern, and all of the candles but one. Anna reached up, pulling him down onto their bed.

"I don't care what the future brings, Peter, as long as it's with you."

"Me either," he whispered. "As long as it's with you." Peter blew out the last candle.

****

------The Jeweler's Daughter------

------The Jeweler's Daughter------

------The Jeweler's Daughter------

------The Jeweler's Daughter------

Made in the USA
Middletown, DE
29 June 2021